9150

Berkley Books by Martin Gross

THE RED PRESIDENT
THE RED DEFECTOR
THE RED SWASTIKA
THE FOURTH HOUSE

THE
FOURTH
HOUSE

MARTIN GROSS

BERKLEY BOOKS, NEW YORK

THE FOURTH HOUSE

A Berkley Book/published by arrangement with
the author

PRINTING HISTORY
Berkley edition/December 1993

ISBN: 0-425-14005-9

BERKLEY®
Berkley Books are published by
The Berkley Publishing Group, 200 Madison Avenue,
New York, New York 10016.
BERKLEY and the "B" design are trademarks of
Berkley Publishing Corporation.

PRINTED IN THE UNITED STATES OF AMERICA

10 9 8 7 6 5 4 3 2 1

1

THE DESERT SUN had begun its descent behind the arid landscape of Nevada, but the retained heat still pushed the thermometer to 110 degrees Fahrenheit.

Josh Semmelweiss tried to wipe away the humid stain on his face as he left the office and moved his lean frame across the parking lot, obsessively avoiding the sticky tarred cracks between the concrete.

He popped another salt tablet, hoping that dehydration, not total exhaustion, explained his fatigue. The day had begun at 6:45 that morning, and it was now almost 8 P.M.—a stretch of thirteen hours spent exhorting his subordinates. As he opened the door of his Mercury Grand Marquis, the heat of the baked interior wafted toward him. He slid over onto a pad covering the hot leather and started the engine.

The dour Nevada landscape, with its exhilarating sunsets and its absence of true winter, usually held a magnetic attraction for a man raised in the six-month chill of New York. But summer was one season in the desert he could do without. Quickly he turned on the air-conditioning, consoling himself that all would soon be right in a world in which the outdoors was only a pit stop between refrigerated relief.

At the gate of Consortium, Inc., a subcontractor on the Air Force-NASA X-30—sometimes called the NASP or National Aerospace Plane—he pressed his ID against the window. After a friendly wave from the guard, he turned onto the highway spur especially constructed for the desert facility cut out of nowhere.

Pressure from the Pentagon was a gnawing fact of life in what Semmelweiss smilingly called "the military not-so-industrial complex." But Air Force Brigadier General Larry Mulhaney in Washington was a more personal pain. The reigning brass on the hypersonic (over Mach 6) X-30, Mulhaney reminded him—daily, it seemed—that the President wanted the prototype ready for a joint Allied flight no later than summer.

As materials project manager, Semmelweiss was in charge of refining the titanium and carbon–carbon matrix body so that it could withstand the 5,000-degree heat of the initial move into space and the reentry back. It also had to handle the −450-degree cold needed to keep its liquid hydrogen fuel from vaporizing.

The White House cutbacks had demoralized the defense industry, but the Pentagon was promoting technology that had solid peacetime applications. The X-30 was at the top of that list. The hypersonic plane could travel in the atmosphere at the abnormally high speed of 17,500 mph, half circling the globe, from New York to Tokyo, in an hour.

But it could just as easily break into space, moving about and orbiting at will. With a simple rocket command, it could then return to earth, and behave like any conventional plane. Not only would it replace the cumbersome space shuttle on many missions, but it would revolutionize aerospace technology, Semmelweiss was sure.

The Pentagon also saw it as the fighter plane of the future. Invincibility was its middle name. At speeds of 17,500 mph and a cruise altitude of up to 200,000 feet, the X-30 would achieve superiority in both air and space. It would become, the Pentagon was sure, the most valuable weapon since the A-bomb, which had kept the peace for fifty years.

Already 5,000 people were at work in 150 locations, busily producing the two-seater space plane the size of a Boeing 727. Since 1990, half the supercomputers in the nation had been pressed into service to design the unusual plane, with its wing-body configuration.

No wonder all eyes were now focused on Semmel-weiss, who was straining to get his materials ready for the X-30 to fly at the air show in Britain in August.

Sometimes the heat—from Washington and the summer desert—was too much even for his tempered Bronx soul. Like tonight, when he felt the pangs of loneliness, sorry that his wife, Laurie, would be at her back-room job at the Desert Shade Casino in Vegas until eleven. That left three hours to fill with TV dinners and bad television. Not a very exciting prospect.

As the Grand Marquis moved down the road toward his condo in Sands Crossing—a spread of fifty units with golf course, tennis, pool, and hot tubs, built on the edge of Vegas, not far off Highway 66—Josh indulged himself in an innocent fantasy.

In the comfort of the cooled air, his mind's eye could see the X-30 take off from the dried lake bed at Edwards Air Force Base in the western Mohave and fly smoothly through the sonic boom, approaching Mach 8, or over 5,000 mph, in minutes. The nation oohed and aahed as the air-space ship pushed its liquid hydrogen engine, reaching an altitude of 300,000 feet before roaring at Mach 25, into space, where it would orbit, then move freely about under its own rocket power.

He gleefully imagined its return into the atmosphere, landing like any plane of its size. It was the culmination of decades of aviation and space research. The Buck Rogers cartoon had come to life in an all-purpose vehicle that could do virtually anything in air and space, in peace or war.

Now Josh's daydream switched, like a Hollywood cutaway, to the White House. The President was pinning the

Medal of Freedom on ingenious citizen Semmelweiss, who had been shaped into a refined scientific instrument at high-academic Stuyvesant High School in lower Manhattan, then CCNY in upper Manhattan, and finally in the near-sacred halls of Cal Tech. Now it would all meld into recognition from the nation.

The consortium of five firms commissioned to build the NASP would surely reward him with a raise and a bonus. But honed by the ethos of 1950s scholarship and patriotism, money had little meaning to him, as long as he could pay his bills and make a yearly pilgrimage to Europe.

The next trip, he had promised Laurie, would be to the Orient. He was curious to see Red China, the last stronghold of Communism, with its mass of 1.3 billion people, almost a quarter of all the souls on planet Earth. From friends, he had heard rumors of extraordinary Chinese progress in military technology, including the production of advanced former-Soviet fighters and the frightening underground explosion of a thousand-kiloton H-bomb, the most destructive weapon ever built by man. To the extent he could, he would check up on China's new technologies on his trip.

He wondered whether the West was beginning a new conflict with a Communist state that was more populous, perhaps eventually more powerful and more threatening, than the Soviet Union itself.

"Don't turn your head. It could mean your life."

What was that? Josh moved rapidly out of his reverie. Was it a hallucination conjured up by exhaustion? The comforting explanation evaporated with the frosty feel of a pistol barrel against the small of his neck.

"Say nothing." The voice came from the rear of the Mercury. "Keep driving with your eyes glued to the road."

Josh was too frightened to speak and too embarrassed to laugh. Had he escaped the criminal rhythms of New

York only to become the victim of the Western pick-up truck mentality? Who was it? A simple thief or a junkie? Shouldn't the thug have had the sense to pick on a Mercedes, or a Lexus? His wife had warned him about his absentminded habit of not locking his parked car. Now a human vulture had crawled into the backseat and was threatening to pick his pocket, if not his bones.

"You're not hip, man," Josh laughed self-consciously. "I've got maybe sixty dollars in my pocket, and this car's too old to be chopped for more than a few hundred dollars. Do you really know your business?"

The silence was punishing.

"I don't want your money or your car," the intruder finally said. "Just keep driving." The pistol pressed centimeters deeper into his neck.

Josh stretched to catch a glimpse of the intruder in the rearview mirror. But even the arm holding the pistol was hidden by his own head. The voice? It was somewhat high-pitched, but hardly feminine. At first he thought it belonged to a gruff New York "wise guy." But as Semmelweiss listened closely, he detected a trace of refinement underneath. What was it? A touch of British? The thought frightened him. Maybe he wasn't dealing with an ordinary thief, probably not even a junkie.

"If not my money, what do you want?" The strain in Josh's voice betrayed his anxiety.

"None of your business."

The intruder again turned silent. The gun barrel felt colder against Josh's flesh.

"There's your place on the other side of the highway—Sands Crossing. Make a left across the double line and head toward the condo garage. If you've forgotten, it's the first right off the communal road."

Semmelweiss was astonished. He drove down the road as directed and turned into a cul-de-sac of garages. "Yours is the third one in," the man said authoritatively. The Mafia street tones were now fading. Yes, Josh could hear the British diction coming to the surface. "Raise the garage door with your gadget and bring the Mercury in."

"That doesn't take us anywhere," Josh complained, stalling for a break in the frightening scenario. "The garage is not connected to my condo."

"I know all about it. Just do as you're told."

Josh's response was Pavlovian. He pressed the remote button and the garage door swung open. The Marquis entered its stable, coming to an abrupt stop near the far wall.

As the garage door closed in on them, a thought seered Semmelweiss's brain. Was this connected to the X-30? But if the intruder was an agent, what could he steal from him? Or—his imagination leapt—was it like a scene from a bad television movie? Was he about to be kidnapped and sent eastbound, chained in the bowels of a North Korean freighter?

"Sit just where you are and don't move." The intruder had now virtually dropped his tough-guy disguise. "I'll come around and open the front door of the car."

Josh waited rigidly. When he looked, the sight was as upsetting as the abduction, if that's what this was. The man, or perhaps the apparition, was standing alongside the car, pistol in hand, wearing a black turtleneck, black slacks, and—this he could hardly believe—what looked like a World War I gas mask. It hid most of the gunman's face. On his chest was a tank, like that of a scuba diver, only considerably smaller. Tall and wiry in build, the intruder stood impatiently, waving the gun—Josh thought a 9-mm Beretta—like an baton master.

"All right, Semmelweiss." He had addressed Josh by name for the first time. "Do as I ask and I'll make it all painless." The voice was muffled by the mask, but the words were understandable. "Take off your shoes and lie down across the front seat of your car, faceup, head against the driver's side door."

Josh couldn't move. The exhaustion of thirteen hours at Consortium, Inc., combined with this bizarre misadventure, had brought on a temporary paralysis. He stared blankly at the strange intruder.

"I told you to get down on that seat," the man half shouted, leaning into the car. With his knees on the front seat, he pressed the Beretta firmly against Josh's right temple. "You must understand how serious this is, Mr. Semmelweiss. Do as I say or your brains will soon cover these dreary walls. The gun has a silencer, so no one will hear us."

Josh's senses woke instantly. He removed his shoes as ordered and placed them one at a time on the front floor of the car. His mind raced for solutions, as if survival were a scientific problem. Eyes never leaving the black-garbed man, Josh lowered himself onto the buttery leather. His head was pressed firmly against the left door. His long legs extended out over the passenger side.

"Like this?"

"Exactly. Stay as you are. I'm coming around."

Semmelweiss waited only seconds. The driver's side door was soon opened. He could see the man's black-sweatered arm over his head, the keys to the Mercury in his fingers. The intruder inserted one into the ignition slot and turned it. The car purred, then raced as the man pressed down on the accelerator. After holding it in one place for a minute, he opened the electric windows and closed the car door.

"I want to be sure the engine's going well, and you get all its benefits," the intruder said. "We'll just sit here and listen to the music of internal combustion."

The intention was clear, if not the motive. The man intended to kill him in his own garage with carbon monoxide fumes. It took less than his Ph.D. to realize that death would come in thirty minutes, or less. The mad Englishman—if that's what he was—was protected by the gas mask, vintage or otherwise, and sustained by the small tank of what apparently was oxygen.

Disrupt. Break the killer's methodical pace, Josh told himself. Whatever followed couldn't be more ominous.

He could already smell the noxious gases filling the garage. Lying on his back, Josh surveyed the situation. The line of sight between himself, the killer, and the car's ignition key was partially blocked. Slowly, he inched his left hand away from direct view, then moved it in the direction of the ignition. In a rapid, almost reflexive, sweep, he hit the key blindly with his fingers. The engine stopped as efficiently as it had started.

"What-in-the-hell are you doing?" the intruder shouted. Swiftly opening the car door, he kept one hand on the gun and used the other to turn the engine back on.

Semmelweiss countered in desperation. He leapt off the leather seat. In an improvised karate stroke, he crashed the edge of his palm down on the killer's gun hand. The pistol dropped onto the car rug.

"Damn bastard!" Josh screamed, scrambling for the gun. Spotting it half-hidden under the passenger seat, he had stretched his arm toward it when he felt the sharp pain of a fist on his neck. The light weakened in his brain. He staggered and fell off the driver's seat, his head glancing off the edge of the car frame just before he hit the concrete.

Josh could feel the warm blood on his forehead, but he was now immune to pain. From the corner of his eye, he instantly took in the chaotic scene. The black-sweatered man had found the gun and was raising it to take aim. Josh sprang off the garage floor and raced toward the closed door in a flight of desperation.

"Stop or you're dead!"

Like a cardboard caricature, Semmelweiss froze in place.

"Now, come back and we'll start all over again. This time, I'll watch you more carefully."

Josh walked back to the car, his gait a limp of resignation. As he lay down on the car seat as ordered, his mind was already foggy from the monoxide fumes. Like a patient entering surgery, he sensed the coming of incomprehension.

He lay silently on his back, thinking of Laurie, of the X-30 and the President, of the trip to the Orient that would never be, until two strange thoughts entered his fading consciousness.

He thought he saw the intruder place a sprig of white flowers on his chest. The very last words he heard were alien, coming to him as if in a dream.

"Sleep well, Mr. Semmelweiss. Mary sends her love."

LONDON, THE FOLLOWING WEEK

"DAMN INCONSIDERATE OF him," Sir Malcolm Asprey muttered to no one in particular. "Nick knows I hate three-handed pinochle."

Seated with two colleagues at an ancient, pitted table in London's Brigadier pub, Asprey rose and stretched his long arms skyward. It was, he sensed, a bit unseemly for a man of his stature—both physically and in the unwritten rules of the British upper class. But Asprey was feeling the pangs of impatience.

The three men had already waited a half hour for Nick Thorne. He was not exactly a colleague, more of a client, one of a tribe of casual scientists assigned by the Home

Secretary to Sir Malcolm's custody. Thorne was their
pinochle ace, the sharpest mind of the quartet.

The telly noise in the Brigadier was discreet, as were
the military appointments that gave the pub its special elan, more of a clubby than a commercial atmosphere. Red-striped wallpaper provided a backdrop for the
framed souvenirs of the British Empire wars, from etch-
ings of Nelson, Wellington, and Kitchener, to mounted
dress swords, scarlet sashes, and woven gold epaulets.

"Any idea where the hell Nick is, Sir Malcolm?"

The question came from Chris Steiner, the second man
at the table. The mathematician of the scientific intelligence group, Steiner looked more the accountant than the
theoretician. He was pink-faced and portly, his blue blazer
and flannels bourgeois by Daks, his shoulders padded in
seventies fashion, his manner deadening middle-middle
class, fashioned in Golders Green, a crammed London
suburb.

Asprey still stood, his eyes traveling across the pub.
He fitted neatly into the Brigadier, a haunt for types
like himself, a former Army colonel who had moved
into security, specifically MI5 counterintelligence. His
assignment: overseeing a handful of less-than-predictable
research talents serving the Crown.

The Brigadier had once been the watering hole of the
Duke of Wellington, who was fond of regaling admirers
with stories of the Napoleonic wars. As it happened,
the pub was now nestled smack in the center of the
cream-painted town houses of Eaton Place and Belgrave
Square. The setting for the *Masterpiece Theatre* classic
"Upstairs, Downstairs," these real-life flats brought a
million pounds apiece, for an ephemeral ninety-nine-
year lease, to their landlord, the ultra-wealthy Earl of
Cadogan.

The fashionable polished-faced youths of the area,
basically Chelsea and Belgravia, now frequented the
place. But at his rear table, Asprey tried not to notice. He

strained to drown out the banal chatter with free-flowing ale, cards, and more mature conversation.

As always, he was impeccably garbed. Sir Malcolm's six-foot-three frame was covered in the subtlest of Savile Row sharkskins. The dappled silver-gray tie was knotted in a perfect wide Windsor knot over a yellow-and-white striped shirt. His granite features, topped by gracefully swept graying hair, seemed surprisingly mobile for such a resolute face.

"I don't have a ghost of an idea where Thorne could be," Asprey finally answered Steiner, signaling the waiter for another round of stout. "I lost track of him early this afternoon."

Steiner peered at his steel Seiko through thick tortoise-rimmed glasses. "It's already past eight and Nick's still out of it," he sighed. "How does he expect us to keep a game going?"

"Only Jehovah knows, and he's not talking." Asprey curbed a sudden flash of temper. "Nick's always been a laissez-faire type, which probably accounts for his genius at pinochle."

Though Asprey had worked with Thorne for four years, he still found him unpredictable. The most talented of his charges, Nick had an extraordinary mind. But monitoring his sexual partners had proven to be too much. Thorne had led the whole MI5 unit a merry chase, cohabitating with as large a selection of female security risks as Asprey had seen since the end of the Cold War. Still, he liked Nick. And more, he loved his skill and what it had provided the Crown and its American cousins.

Asprey retook his seat at the table and turned toward the third man. "Remember, Guy, there's a 250-point minimum bid."

Guy Lauder cast a wistful eye at the pinochle "widow," the three discarded cards in the center of the table. Only one—an enticing ace of clubs—was faceup. "What do you hear about Nick and the X-30?" he casually asked the others.

The contrast between Lauder and Sir Malcolm, his mentor, was almost startling. Besides the quarter-century gap in age, the younger man's reddish hair was long, and his guardsman mustache untrimmed. His casual tweeds and checked shirt announced more the West End theater director he was rather than the incognito agent he doubled as for Asprey. But his cover, or his full-time occupation—however one looked at it—was convenient. His theater, the Irving, near the Strand, was a stone's throw from their innocuous-looking counterintelligence office behind a rehearsal loft.

"Nick's kept me a little too much in the dark," Asprey confessed. "I only know that he's been making good progress at British Aerospace on that U.S. Air Force X-30 contract. This afternoon he was supposed to meet with an agency guy from Grosvenor Square, a shoot-'em-up Montanan. Nick told me he'd fill us in on everything tonight."

Lauder nodded, then glanced intently at his fifteen cards, his unscientific mind grasping for pinochle melds. "I can do 340 points. Surely somebody can beat that."

He turned to Asprey, whose hands were now clasped at the back of his neck, his fingers pressing in and out at the hollow.

"What about you, Sir Malcolm?" Guy asked.

"No, I'm afraid I was dealt a poor hand."

"Not by life," Lauder offered.

Asprey smiled and glanced at Steiner. "Chris, you're the mathematician of the group. What do you make of Guy's bid?"

"He's operating by blind intuition," Steiner said. "I think Lauder's been smitten by the ace-up in the widow. But I pass. You, Malcolm?"

Asprey discarded his hand onto the table with a flourish. "Chris, what are the chances that the X-30 will actually fly? The Prime Minister expects it to be ready for the Allied air show here in August."

Steiner seemed to ponder, but before he could speak, he halted in mid-breath. The noise from the telly was no longer discreet. The newsreader seemed to be shouting.

"The body was found on Victoria Embankment, mangled in a fall from the Clock Tower, over three hundred feet above the Thames," Asprey could hear the announcer say. The voice suddenly hushed as the camera panned to Big Ben, across to the blackened Houses of Parliament, then down to the Embankment, the scene of the death.

For a moment, Asprey and Steiner were diverted by Lauder, who had just slapped two key cards, a jack of diamonds and a queen of spades, on the table. "Pinochle!" he shouted.

But his cry was quickly drowned out by the animated BBC announcer.

"The dead man has been identified as Nicholas Thorne, an aerospace engineer working on a secret government contract. The police believe he committed suicide by jumping from the roof of Big Ben, which has been closed to the public for some time. A scrap of paper was found in his pocket, with the simple message 'Love, Mary.'"

Ashen-faced, all three men stared wordlessly at the colored box.

"Police are somewhat puzzled by the note," the BBC newsreader continued, "but they believe that a thwarted love affair with Thorne's secretary, Mary Cochran, may be the cause of the suicide."

For a few seconds, they stayed with the screen, paralyzed. Then they rose as one. Sir Malcolm placed a five-pound note on the etched wood table as they moved to exit the Brigadier.

"Are we doomed forever to a three-handed game?" Asprey asked, tears gathering at the corner of his pinched eyes.

3

JOHN DAVIDSON FORCED his head back against the leather wing chair in the second-floor library of the Cosmos Club in Washington, D.C., and closed his eyes.

He had just finished reading the New York and Los Angeles papers and had turned to the *London Times*, scanning the pages nearly at random, as was his habit, for substance and trivia to add to his mental encyclopedia. Suddenly, as he focused on a two-paragraph item on an inside page, he blinked involuntarily.

"BRITISH SCIENTIST DIES IN FALL FROM BIG BEN TOWER; SUICIDE SUSPECTED"

Davidson opened his eyes and reread the item, then braced as he considered the juxtaposition of the London clip and a seemingly independent story in the *Los Angeles Times*. Together they set off a nervous connection in his head.

"Someone to see you, Mr. Davidson."

"Oh, thank you. Who is it?"

The retainer had broken his thought rhythm, but Davidson's response was still courtly. Davidson seemed an integral part of the traditional setting, the very portrait of a relaxed nineteenth-century gentleman at home in his well-appointed world. His face was thin, almost gaunt, with oversize black eyebrows, a full head of undulating silver hair, deep-set chocolate-brown eyes that announced his intelligence, and a strong nose that started straight near the brow and bent only slightly on its route downward.

In all, he gave off a near-hypnotic aura—not that of the CIA counterintelligence chief he had been, but that of a professional Shakespearean actor of an earlier time. Surely unlike any other persona in his trade.

"It's Sir Malcolm Asprey, Mr. Davidson. He left his card."

"Asprey?" Pure serendipity, Davidson thought. "Surely. Tell him to come right up."

Early that morning, Davidson had left his gentleman's dairy farm outside Leesburg, Virginia, and, in his near-antique 1976 Volvo station wagon, driven to the gray stone Cosmos Club at Massachusetts and Twenty-third. Once the French-style mansion of Sumner Welles, patrician assistant secretary of state under Roosevelt, the club was now the prestigious haunt of the Washington powerful—which in the case of the Cosmos meant brains rather than money, which was more the badge of the rival Metropolitan Club.

At least once a week, Davidson held court in the Cosmos library, receiving an irregular stream of visitors from the Hill, the press, foreign diplomats, academics, ex-Agency and military personnel. All came to pick the mind and memory of the retired seer who had frustrated the Soviets in the old Cold War, and who now chose his friends and adversaries in the chaos of the so-called New World Order with the expertise of an appraiser of old Masters.

John "The Baptist" Davidson—the name had stuck after he had smuggled a family of Christian Baptists to freedom in Finland from the U.S. Consulate in Leningrad in the 1960s—had been the Agency's CIC, chief of counterintelligence, for a quarter century. In his head were catalogued untold and untellable tales, a shelf of potential best-sellers if he were to write his memoirs. But Davidson had stubbornly refused the pleas of hungry, if generous, New York publishers and intended to stonewall them for life.

Despite his heralded victories overseas, he had been outmaneuvered at home. In the wake of Watergate, eight hundred agents had been purged in the "reform." Sights were then set on Davidson, who had been labeled a "paranoid" for his suspicions of men high up in the seventh-floor hierarchy at Langley. In a strange perversion of the Cold War politics, the man who had passionately blocked the KGB for a generation was privately accused of being a "Soviet mole," and pushed toward early retirement without formal charges.

History had since reversed that judgment. He had been shown to be a victim of those he suspected of being "disloyals." Davidson had been rehabilitated by time and the Oval Office, but despite pleas by several presidents, he had turned down requests to head the Agency. Now sixty-five, he found the role of an unpaid independent to be more stimulating, and less taxing.

"Asprey? The aristocratic Brit?" Davidson flexed the calling card in his tapered fingers. "Sir Malcolm Edward Asprey, Ministry of Defense."

It was, and it wasn't, a cover. Asprey, a brilliant chemist at Oxford, later an army colonel, was now in the government, where his open responsibility was new weapons technology. His secondary—or true—job was MI5 coordinator of counterintelligence in the British defense industry, once heavily infiltrated by Soviet spies. Now, rumor had it, it was the target of an assorted phalanx of Third World and Red Chinese espionage agents, a shift that reflected the changing power structure of the modern world.

Over the years, the two men had become fast associates.

"Why, Malcolm, it is you!" Davidson called in mock surprise. He rose respectfully from the wing chair. "What in the world are you doing so far from the Thames?"

The Englishman grasped Davidson's shoulder as the two men moved back to the quiet library corner.

"Baptist! Good to see you. I just arrived for a NATO conference at Dumbarton Oaks. Thought I'd come by and say hello. What are you up to?"

The Englishman topped Davidson by half a head. There were strong similarities, especially in demeanor, but each veteran of tradecraft gave off his own special aura. Davidson was lithe, medium-size, professorial, and tweedy. Dressed always—in winter or suffociating Washington summer—in a three-piece gray herringbone, he enjoyed rumors that it was either his only suit, or one of several clones rotated to fool Davidson watchers. He was a man clearly out of his century.

Asprey was tall, muscular, elegant, and punctilious in dress, a replica, some said, of former Foreign Secretary and Prime Minister Sir Anthony Eden, if considerably more nimble mentally. Though Sir Malcolm was a decade younger than Davidson, they viewed each other as contemporaries, sharing a cynical view of their respective organizations. Personal contact between long-trusted friends such as themselves, the Baptist had long decided, was the safest form of transaction in their duplicitous profession. Fortunately, at Langley, Davidson had several such unofficial associates—the *nashi*, Russian for "ours" or "real"—who could be trusted with anything, even his modest Agency pension.

"What's up with me?" Davidson asked rhetorically. "Very little. I'm between assignments. And you? I notice that Nick Thorne is gone." The Baptist pointed to the short article in the *London Times*. "The paper says suicide. Anything to it? Wasn't he working on the X-30 for the U.S. Air Force?"

Asprey's smile was almost painful. "I should have known you'd learn about it, John. Yes, it was horrible. Thorne was a client, but we had become good friends. Pinochle partners, in fact. But that never was your game. You preferred—what was it?—bridge."

Davidson nodded. "But why suicide? Isn't that too pat an answer? Why not consider the more sinister possibility—murder?"

Asprey shook his head. "It might seem that way, but I knew Thorne well. He was overworked and depressed. Had been for months. Refused to see a doctor or even to take a week off to go to Malta, or even your beastly Caribbean."

Sir Malcolm's mouth dropped as he spoke. "And, John, he was obsessed with the X-30. Had been working on the wing configuration for a year, fifteen hours a day. Hogged every damn supercomputer in southern England. Nick was a real genius, you know. Now I suppose the whole project will be set back. But murder? No, John, I think he just lost control."

Davidson didn't respond. He returned to his wing chair and began rummaging through the newspapers on the Chippendale table.

"Thankfully, things are looking good in the materials area," Asprey continued. "Semmelweiss is doing a hell of a job in Nevada."

Davidson looked up from his newspaper work.

"Was, Malcolm."

"Was?"

"Yes. Take a look at this clip from yesterday's *L.A. Times*." Davidson folded the paper in quarters and handed it to Asprey. The short item was circled in green marker.

"AMERICAN AEROSPACE SCIENTIST DIES IN HIS GARAGE; SUICIDE SUSPECTED."

"I'm probably as paranoid as they say," Davidson continued, "but two X-30 scientists dying within a week, both by supposed suicide, strikes me as too much of a coincidence."

Asprey grasped the paper, his face gray. "My God, that is bad news."

"Malcolm, was there anything unusual connected with

Nick Thorne's supposed suicide?" Davidson asked. "Maybe a note left behind?"

Davidson could see Asprey staring blankly at the bookshelves, as if returning to the grisly scene at Victoria Embankment.

"Just one thing."

"Yes?"

"The police did find a note in his pocket. A small scrap of torn paper, really. It just said: 'Love, Mary.' "

"Who in the hell is Mary?"

"At first, we thought it was Mary Cochran, Thorne's secretary. He was a wild ladies' man, and the two were having an affair. Some thought maybe a break-up had pushed his depression deeper. But . . ."

"But what?"

"Mary Cochran told the police that they were never happier. In fact, they were planning to get married. At least, she says so." Asprey stared down into the bright Heriz rug. "But don't let that feed your paranoid imagination, John. There's still no reason why it couldn't all be a coincidence. Two overworked, obsessive men, acting irrationally in sudden breakdowns. Any evidence to the contrary?"

It was now Davidson's turn. "Well, I spoke to the coroner in Las Vegas. He says Semmelweiss fell to the floor at one point and cut his head. That doesn't sound consistent with suicide."

"Why not? If Semmelweiss was dizzy from the monoxide and got up for any reason, he could have fallen." Asprey was countering in this chess match of intelligence masters. "I don't see that as proof, John."

"No, you're right. It's not proof. But my smeller is working overtime. Malcolm, if you're playing roulette and the black comes up fifteen times in a row, it could be a statistical aberration."

"So?"

"So, over the years I've found that instead of probability at play, it's usually a case of the croupier having his finger on a hidden magnet."

"You win, John." Asprey laughed in his mellow Mayfair tones. "When I get back to London, I'll put my two best men—Steiner and Lauder—on it. We'll find out if it's chicanery or just the Baptist's paranoia working overtime."

IN HIS PRIVATE sanctum on the fourth floor of the embassy of the People's Republic of China on Portland Place near Marylebone Road in London, Dr. Li Chen sat cross-legged on an upholstered red-and-black lacquer bench.

In front of him was his portable desk, a plain birch table barely eighteen inches square and only a foot off the ground. The walls were covered with ancient hand-painted Chinese wallpaper, a three-hundred year-old pastoral scene of gnarled winter trees, with birds perched defiantly on their branches.

Li was dressed in a traditional Chinese robe of green silk, a costume abandoned after the successful revolution of 1949, when the 8th Route Red Army left Manchuria and swept through the mainland, bringing Communism and severe Mao jackets to the population.

Like others in China, Li had been forced to wear the baggy clothes of Communism for years. But now that he had a choice, he had turned his back on Western attire, at least in private. He also deplored what he believed were other Western seducers of the mind and spirit—greed, fashion, mob rule, debased mass culture, lax education, disrespect for elders, and a failure of discipline.

Dr. Li considered himself a modern Mandarin, in the tradition of scholars who had ruled the Chinese Empire for over a thousand years. Scholarship, not egalitarianism, had been their hallmark. As a philosopher-technocrat, he was determined to return China to that mold. Ever since the Sun Yat-sen revolution of 1912 broke the grip of weak emperors and foreign exploiters, his country had gone through three unsatisfactory upheavals: after Sun, there was the warrior-leader Chiang Kai-shek, followed by the Leninist-faithful Mao Tse-tung, whose Cultural Revolution had been the insane thrashings of a poorly schooled leader, Li was convinced.

Then only a college youth, Li had been denounced and banished to a farm, but he didn't regret the experience. In the last dozen years, Deng Xiaoping had brought some reason back to Chinese affairs, but still . . .

Dr. Li dipped his brush into the pot of ink, gleaned from octopus residue, and swept his hand into the graceful motion of calligraphy, practicing as one would the martial arts. His hand lifted then lowered, sweeping from side to side, painting one after another of the thousands of ideograms that made up the written Chinese language.

Just as his ancestors, going back 4,200 years, had brought not only discipline, but wisdom, to government, so he—Li Chen, deputy chief of the feared TEWU Secret Police—would be in the vanguard of a new nation based on scholarship and pragmatism. Yes, he was a Communist, but his true beliefs were in the philosophies of Confucianism, Taoism, and Buddhism. But perhaps the most important was worship of one's ancestors. If that were properly plumbed for the truth, China would know the way of the future, Li was sure. If one understood the story of one's nation and the nature of man, then all things were possible. If not, there would be only chaos.

To Li, the failure of philosophy among the leaders of the former U.S.S.R. was a case in point. Claiming faith in Marx and Lenin, they had instead created a corrupt society, complete with an underground capitalist economy, extreme privilege, and a secret admiration for the West. They had not been defeated in the anticipated military battle, preparation for which had cost them their national treasure. Instead, they had expired with barely a whimper because of their lack of sound philosophy. They had not been true Communists, or pragmatists, or democrats. They had withered away through the poverty of soul. That, he swore, would never happen to the People's Republic of China—*Zhonghua Renmin Gonghe Guo* in his own language.

Dating back to the Xia Dynasty, which ruled two thousand years before Christ, Chinese culture had reached its zenith during the Song Dynasty (A.D. 960 to 1279), which had developed movable type, gunpowder, astronomy, and mathematics, and produced great art, poetry, and cuisine at a time when many Europeans were illiterate and some were still painting their bodies blue and foraging the forests for berries. Chinese greatness, Li consoled himself, had stayed intact through the Ming period, which ended in 1644. But it was that era's contacts with the technically superior West that had undone his people. They had lost faith in the idea of the "Middle Kingdom"—that China was truly the center of the planet.

Now, with easy access to technology and a supposed détente with the Americans (yet still wary of Westerners, whose body odors could be unbearable), Li saw China's future not in the wave of democracy sweeping the world, but evolving from a correct, workable national philosophy. To hesitate was to die. That had been the fate of both the Chinese emperors and the Russian Marxists.

Both had been seduced by the untrustworthy, inscrutable West. That would not happen again, Li had promised his ancestors.

The U.S.S.R. was surely an example to avoid. The anti-West conspirators had lost their resolve at the last minute, failing to assassinate Gorbachev and Yeltsin. But he, Li, had not wavered in Beijing. The crackdown in Tiananmen Square was proof of that resolve. Like the discipline of calligraphy, it had shown results: thousands were imprisoned and hundreds executed. The next attempt to disrupt China's path to power would result in even greater punishment, he swore.

He had to laugh at the foolish West, in private, of course. They took pleasure in China's experiments in capitalism, believing them to be a sign of capitulation. Nothing could be further from the truth. China would use some of the techniques of Western capitalism, but would never allow it to poison their moral system. Ugly capitalism, now flourishing in south China, was bringing in billions in hard currency and sharpening the people's skills. Technology would provide China with work, power, arms, and strength for the ultimate clash of the two cultures—China of the East and the United States of the West.

This was no short-term battle. It would not be measured in years, but in decades, even perhaps a century. It would be a confrontation in which the superior philosophy, discipline, and patience would win out. It had taken the West seventy years to defeat Soviet Communism. China would accomplish its task in perhaps even less time.

Eventually, Li had concluded, the West would disintegrate through greed, shallowness, poor education, and moral degeneracy. Meanwhile, he had two immediate goals. Glancing down at his calligraphy board, he placed the last ideogram on the paper, the red and black brushes moving in magnificent concert.

"Chui!" he called out. Within seconds, his assistant, a young man with an ascetic face, dressed in an impeccable gray worsted Western suit, appeared before him, bowing humbly.

"Yes, General Li. What can I do?"

"Please make sure all our operatives are alerted. I want our program to be accelerated—with no obstacles or excuses. Do you understand?"

"Yes, General," his aide responded eagerly.

"Use our foreign exchange accounts in New York, London, and Switzerland. Pay whatever is necessary in dollars or sterling, but get it done. Make sure Mary is alerted."

Li bent his head and resumed his calligraphy, his agile wrist now working more rapidly than ever.

"That is all, Chui. Can't you see I'm busy?"

"PLACE YOUR BETS, ladies and gentlemen."

Staring into Davidson's chocolate-brown eyes, the flirtatious female croupier said: "*Faites vos jeux.*"

Davidson laughed, but realized how much he stood out from the crowd. His usual gray herringbone, blue oxford shirt, and Princeton rep tie set him apart from the tourist gamblers, who were casually dressed in lurid sports shirts and luminescent sweat suits.

Las Vegas was hardly Monte Carlo or Evian-les-Bains. The Baptist had come to Nevada, America's fantasyland, an oasis of architectural bombast in the desert. Arriving on the Strip earlier that day—his first adventure into this gaudy centerpiece of Americana—he couldn't help but smile at the raucous display of neon signs and the brightly painted stucco shapes meant to shock rather than house.

Friends had always put down the crudity of the town, but Davidson found it humorous, even intriguing—vulgar, surely, but as authentic as the car tail fins of the 1950s, or the blatant fakery of a Disneyworld. The Baptist saw them all as authentic expressions of America's native restlessness, even its courage and directness. Perhaps that's what the country was losing—confidence in its uniqueness. Maybe it had bought too many Mercedes and Italian designer gowns for its own good.

Well, here in the windowless, clockless betting caverns of the Desert Shade Casino, one felt at home in America. The room, almost the size of a football stadium, was filled with hundreds of slot machines, roulette and crap tables. It was crammed with over a thousand happy tourists intent on giving away their money to the multibillion-dollar gaming firms whose stock had been among the best performers on Wall Street. That alone should have told customers something about the loaded odds, especially at the roulette table, where Davidson was now betting five-dollar chips in an attempt to waste time and even up the gambling statistics.

But Davidson hadn't come to Vegas to gamble. He was at the Desert Shade at ten in the evening, waiting to speak with Mrs. Laurie Semmelweiss, widow of the materials scientist on the X-30. Mrs. S. worked in the casino's busy back room, which handled mountains of cash, silver dollars and chips, giving it the feel of a banking institution gone half-mad.

The widow would be off work at 11 P.M. Davidson concentrated on the roulette table and the attractive young croupier, to whom he smilingly threw two chips as a tip. In the few moments he had, Davidson decided to play the red, a compliment to his former Cold War enemies. He took out a small spiral notebook to mark his system. Three-fourths of serious roulette players lived, and usually died, using two systems, neither of which had any mathematical value. Davidson had discovered the truth the easy way, through simple probability equations.

In the famous D'Alembert system, a player stays with one color, either red or black—or low or high numbers. Every time he loses, he adds a chip or more, until he wins. After each win, he reduces the bet by an equal amount. The theory is based on the Law of Equilibrium, or the Maturity of Chance, which accurately states that in the *long run*, each of the colors will come up 50 percent of the time. The variance in bets will supposedly provide a profit.

The problem, of course, is that in the long run, all players will be broke and dead. Roulette bettors operate in the *short run*, and there, *luck*, more than probability, is at work. The Martingale System, and the Great Martingale, are similar, except that each time a player loses, he doubles his bets, pushing himself that much quicker to financial extinction.

Because of the zero and double zero, the house has a 6 percent advantage. Davidson knew of only one mathematical concept that advanced the player's odds: Fouquet's Theorem, a method of changing bets more irregularly than either of the other two, and according to a formula. It did increase the odds for the player somewhat, but it took rapid scribbling and figuring. Davidson stayed with Fouquet, and with a little luck, walked away thirty-five dollars ahead. He threw another five-dollar chip to the young lady, who broke house rules and blew the old spy a kiss.

As arranged, he waited at the $5 million jackpot machine for Mrs. Semmelweiss. Look for the eccentrically dressed man, she had been told. He'll be in winter herringbones.

"Mr. Davidson."

He turned to the right, where a woman, probably in her late forties, was standing facing him. She smiled wanly. A bit overdone and bleached, he thought, but overall an attractive matron of the frontier. Though a few pounds overweight, she was more voluptuous than heavy.

"You weren't hard to find," she added, her voice soft and southwestern.

"Pleasure, ma'am," Davidson said. "Why don't we sit down in the coffee shop and talk?"

They spent a few minutes getting acquainted. Davidson learned that she was a native Las Vegan, a rarity. She had met Josh when he came west to work on the X-30. They had no children, and in every inflection and word, she seemed to sorely miss her husband.

"You're from the government, I understand."

"In a manner of speaking. I'm the retired chief of counterintelligence of the CIA, and I'm out here to find out what really happened to your husband. The police report says it was suicide, by car exhaust. Is there any reason why your husband would want to kill himself?"

Mrs. S. sobbed in a slow, tragic tempo, then dabbed her eyes.

"I know I have to get over it. That's why I go to work every night, and take tranquilizers. But sometimes it's too much for me, Mr. Davidson. No, he had no reason to kill himself. He loved his work, and from what I knew, he was having great success."

"Would you say he was depressed?" Davidson remembered Asprey's comment about Thorne.

"Josh was tired and overworked. But depressed? No, I wouldn't say so. Our backgrounds were different, but we were as happy as two lovebirds. The city boy got to love the desert, and I developed a taste for kosher pickles. No, Mr. Davidson, there was absolutely no reason why he'd kill himself. Do you think it could have been . . . you know, foul play?"

She started to shake. Davidson had an impulse to hold the woman, but it was inappropriate, especially in a hotel coffee shop.

"All right if we continue?"

She nodded. "Yes, Mr. Davidson. I want to do anything to get at the truth."

"Can you think of anything—no matter how small—that was unusual. Something that didn't seem important at the time?"

Laurie lowered her head as she resurrected that night for Davidson. From work, she had come back to the apartment at eleven-thirty and found that Josh was out, which surprised her. She waited until midnight, then walked over to the garage to see if the car was there. He might have gone out to visit a friend or neighbor. When she opened the garage door, she quickly pressed back from the rancid odor of exhaust fumes. After the air cleared, she went in and discovered her husband's body.

"I've gone over and over it with the local police, just as I'm doing with you. But no, I can't think of a thing that would help."

Davidson waited for her to calm. "Mrs. Semmelweiss—when you found his body, how was it lying?"

"Just stretched out on the seat. His hands were at his sides, like he was sleeping. And on his chest, he had some flowers. I suppose he'd brought them home for me. But he wasn't sleeping. He was dead."

"Flowers?" Davidson reacted instantly. "What kind of flowers? A bouquet from the florist?"

"Oh no, Mr. Davidson. Just a single stem with a few small white flowers. Sort of sentimental, I suppose."

"Do you still have them?"

"Oh yes, I pressed them in a book. The very last thing from my husband. Would you like to see them?"

6

THE SUN WAS still relatively high in the sky at 7 P.M. The desert heat made the scrub surrounding the installation seem to waver in the haze of heat pulses.

Except for the massive wind-tunnel facility poking out of the horizon, the Arizona landscape was unbroken by civilization as far as the eye could see. By design, this X-30 testing ground was the only habitable area for some twenty miles in all directions.

The perimeter was surrounded by an electrified wire fence, and constantly patrolled by Air Force jeeps, their rears shrouded in tarpaulin covering their machine-gun ports. Security was heavy. Within the enormous shed was the only completed prototype of the X-30, going through static test runs which would determine not only how the short-winged titanium/carbon–carbon matrix body would behave while flying, but how well the enormous scramjet engine would function at speeds of Mach 25, at heights of 300,000 feet, then later in space.

The scramjet (for "supersonic combustion ramjet"), fueled by liquid hydrogen, was capable of pushing the space plane to a speed of 17,500 mph. The X-30 had successfully gone through wind-tunnel trials at Mach 8, or 6,000 mph, at NASA Langley in Hampton, Virginia, but that was not enough. Scientists had to test its body and scramjets above Mach 8—in fact, all the way up to Mach 25—to learn if the oxygen and liquid hydrogen would safely mix in the engines at these enormous speeds.

Before building the "real time" Arizona facility, engineers had had to rely on simulation worked out on supercomputers capable of a billion calculations per second. The computers had "taken" the plane and its engines up to Mach 25. The readouts were gratifying, but no one—with good reason—fully trusted silicon chips to predict whether men would live or die in that rarified atmosphere at seemingly impossible speeds.

The Arizona desert had been carved up. Man had brought technology to raw nature, and the scars included septic tanks, plumbing, smokestacks for heating, garbage disposal, and the ugliest accoutrements of civilization. In the center of it all was the world's largest wind tunnel, a city block long and nine stories tall, a duplication of the forces that would affect the plane once the X-30 became airborne.

Project Manager Jack Langer had looked forward to this day for four years, the time it had taken to complete this facility at a cost of $350 million. The X-30 prototype had traveled to Arizona in two pieces on a specially constructed twenty-four–wheeler truck. Covered with a squared-off canvas to hide its shape, it gave the appearance of a large mobile home on the move. Not that its configuration was a secret: that had already been publicized worldwide by the Air Force. But the plane had been disguised to thwart possible saboteurs.

Langer now stood in the control booth, whose closed-circuit television would relay all the visual information he needed. Receptors on the prototype would send signals to the mainframe computer to record the effect of the heat and speed on the airframe and engines. He stared into the monitor at the awesome sight of the full-size billion-dollar prototype in the center of the enormous chamber, waiting for its travail.

The test facilities were in two parts. The body configuration was being tested with compressed air in what was known as a "blowdown tunnel." Air was pushed by fans at one end, and then pulled at the other end by large vacumn spheres outside the building. The double effect created the simulated speed. With a small model at Langley, helium had been used instead of air, which gave engineers a three-to-one advantage. Measuring helium at Mach 8 was as effective as measuring the wind effects of air at Mach 20.

But NASA and the Pentagon were now demanding a "real time" test. Besides, helium was of no value in evaluating the scramjets. Air and oxygen were needed to put a working scramjet engine through the true environment—outside heat of up to 20,000 degrees created by friction with air molecules. To test these temperatures in a thin-oxygen environment, NASA had to construct an enormous arc jet.

It was at those enormous temperatures that the heated air would mix with the liquid hydrogen fuel—which would turn gaseous at the point of ignition.

Surprisingly, the heat surrounding the X-30 would not be at its highest at the reentry point from space to atmosphere, as in the case of the space shuttle. Actually, it would reach its maximum during its *ascendancy* into space, something man and his machines had never experienced. Since the NASP wouldn't make its upward journey in a vertical line like a rocket, it had to travel through the atmosphere less slowly and at an angle— about forty degrees—to reach the 300,000-foot "escape" point. Fighting air molecules, it would create heat all the way up. The Arizona facility would try to duplicate that environment on earth.

At Langley, portions of the engine had been tested at up to Mach 12, and full-scale engines at Mach 7. But this was the first attempt to put a full-size scramjet through its paces at Mach 25. The largest arc jet in the world was capable of a hundred-megawatt production, only enough to test a small model. But to test a full-size scramjet, which stood almost four feet high,

an arc jet that generated four-hundred megawatts was
needed. Langer's group had finally built the giant arc,
and it was ready for the tests.

In an arc jet, air was blown through a tube in which
a manmade lightning bolt had been created. Inside, temperatures could reach as high as 30,000 degrees for
a split second. But to handle this, the four-hundred-
megawatt arc has to be almost twenty feet long, with
a nozzle almost two feet in diameter. Nothing like this,
in size or complexity, had ever been built before.

"All right," Langer called to his operator, "we're going
all the way. Take her up from zero altitude to 300,000
feet, then push it into space. Let her rip!"

The arc jet fired. Its bluish-white lightning seared
the air in the tube, which fed from the nozzle into
the engine. The engine first took in the air mix at sea
level, then continued to roar while the oxygen became
leaner and the plane rose in simulation. Fed with the
now-gasified liquid hydrogen, the engine performed like
the clock on a Rolls-Royce. Heat started to accumulate
around the engine parts, but the scramjet handled it
like central air-conditioning in an exclusive Phoenix
restaurant.

As the plane "rose," the engine continued its roar. Fifty thousand, one hundred thousand. As the X-30 "lifted,"
its speed increased, from Mach 2 to Mach 4, then Mach
10 at 100,000 feet, the practical ceiling for conventional
aircraft.

"All right. Now let's try for Mach 20 at 300,000 feet!"
Langer called into his microphone. "Nine, eight, seven,
six, five, four, three, two, one. Go."

The arc jet fired up its lightning bolt. The X-30's
scramjet screamed as it roared through the simulated
heavens—Mach 12 at 150,000 feet; Mach 14 at 200,000
feet; then straining toward Mach 20 at 300,000.

Then it happened. The engine first spurted its usual flam-
ing exhaust, then sputtered, the fire coming in irregular

rhythms. Like a dying firecracker, it simmered to a stop.

"Cut the arc jet! Cut the engine! Close everything down!" Langer shouted from his command post.

He turned to his assistant, his face drained. "Goddamn it. Get Larry Burns on the horn in England. Tell him to go back to his computer. We need a new design—and quick!"

7

IN RURAL EAST Anglia, some sixty miles northeast of London, Michael Cavendish lovingly tended his plants.

Ample rain and surprisingly mild weather from March through October had made this part of England a quilt of gardens. Not far from Cambridge University, it was also the home of the English who first settled New England in the seventeenth century.

In 1628, in the Cambridge rooms of sophomore John Harvard, the Puritan squires of this region— men of considerable wealth and education, including John Winthrop, attorney for King Charles's estates— met and pledged their names, their honor and fortunes to leave England and colonize America. The small Plymouth Colony had already been founded by English religious outcasts living in Holland, but these powerful squires planned a massive resettlement in Massachusetts.

By 1630, they had left England with two-thousand middle- and upper-class men and women, including 138 graduates of Oxford and Cambridge—the most educated group of people in the world. Included were scores of noblemen who had renounced their titles, and hundreds of skilled carpenters, millwrights, and tradesmen, all aboard an armada of a hundred ships laden down with furniture, gold, silver, tools, muskets, and all that was needed to shape a great city. Named after a neighboring town in East Anglia, where Richard Mather was minister, the new world city of Boston was to flourish almost overnight. By 1636, it had built Harvard University, honoring the prematurely deceased scholar, John Harvard, who had left a few pounds to found the new college.

Cavendish knew his Anglo-American history. He had been a student at Cambridge himself, but botany, not history, was his love. He had spent five futile years trying to breed a "true blue" rose, but had given that up to concentrate on more practical work. A large green-and-gold sign—"Horticultural Specialist"—hung at the side of his cottage. Both locals and experts from throughout Britain in search of counsel kept the small bell ringing from daybreak on.

A tall, painfully thin man, with craggy features and a head of full, flowing gray hair, Cavendish had just returned from a symposium on hybrids in Southern California. He still had his tan, a rarity in this cool summer clime. As he stooped over a hybrid gladiolus about half the normal size, the phone rang at the end of his greenhouse.

Cavendish moved slowly down the aisle, not altering his usual calm pace to accommodate the sound. He lifted the phone after the fifth ring.

"How did the American trip go?" a masculine British voice asked, opening the conversation.

Cavendish smiled, after which his expression turned to one of self-satisfaction.

"Oh, very well, thank you. From California, I went into the Nevada desert to pick some wildflowers. I plucked a particularly important one, just as you suggested. Great deal of fun. Any more ideas?"

The other end was silent for a moment. "Yes, as a matter of fact I have," the voice finally continued. "There's some wonderful spring color up at Cambridge, right on the banks of the Cam. Why not try a field trip to the university? Check it out with Mary."

Cavendish brightened. He glanced across at his extraordinary collection of plants, then returned his attention to the phone. Once again, he'd be enlarging his horizon, and his income.

"Why, that's wonderful." Cavendish's tone was enthusiastic. "Good. Tomorrow is open. I'll motor up and look around for the day. Sort of get my horticultural bearings, if you know what I mean. I like working for Mary— always such variety. And . . ." Cavendish paused. "And the pay is good. I'll give Mary your love."

The botanist hung up. With much the same deliberate gait, he returned to his gladioli, warmed by the thought of the coming expedition to Cambridge.

PROFESSOR LARRY BURNS stood alongside the River Cam and looked out over its tranquil banks, a sight that always lowered his natural anxiety.

On this peculiarly chilly June day, the water was almost empty of boats and the air was freshened by a breeze. Strolling along the "Backs," the graceful greens between the colleges of Cambridge University and the river's edge, Burns—dressed in his usual chino slacks and red cashmere pullover—was pleased.

The hurried call from Jack Langer, the wind-tunnel manager in Arizona, had interrupted his sabbatical. It had forced him back to the university supercomputer, which had been made available by the Ministry of Defense after Whitehall learned about the design crisis on the X-30.

With *Perspective*, the three-dimensional stress software, Burns reran his calculations on the X-30 scramjet engine, work that had already taken a year under an Air Force contract.

News that his original calculations were flawed—that the X-30 scramjet had misfired at Mach 20 at 300,000 feet altitude—had pushed Burns into a depression. His ego suffered a punishing deflation, one that had worsened until he had made his breakthrough. After two weeks of sixteen-hour days at the terminal of Cambridge's Super, he had seen his error and corrected it. By morning, embedded on two hard discs, the new calculations would be on their way to Wright-Patterson AFB in Ohio by diplomatic pouch. A courier had been arranged to come to Cambridge from the American Embassy on Grosvenor Square to pick them up. Now, Burns's spirits had soared past depression into elation.

Just before 9 P.M., the late summer sun at the fifty-one–degree northern latitude of Cambridge was just beginning its descent. Only a few courageous punts were still in the water. Most were now tied up, giving the river back to its drowned trees.

"Dr. Burns." A voice rose from the water.

He turned and saw a shallow-draft punt moving closer to the bank.

"Who's there?" Burns strained to see into the declining light, then recognized the source of the voice. "Tony, what the hell are you doing in such a tame boat?" he called out.

Burns could make out one of his senior physics students, Tony Alcott, a twenty-five-year-old American, sculling champion on a Cambridge "eight," and the college's leading 220-meter swimmer.

"Just a busman's holiday, sir."

Alcott was dressed in a blazer with an embroidered Cambridge seal, gray flannels, and a college tie—a rather formal outfit for punting, Burns thought. Like so many Americans, Alcott was infatuated with the traditions of Cambridge. Burns admitted to the same Anglophilic disease, but checked it short of dressing like a cardboard fool. Unlike himself—lanky, almost emaciated, with graying skin, thin dark hair, and a stooped walk—Alcott was tall, muscular, unabashedly blond. Burns had a sudden, uncharitable thought. Alcott looked the caricature of an American jock, not the scholar he had proven to be.

The young man was pleasant enough, but he seemed to be pressing himself on Burns lately. Alcott had even hinted he knew that Burns was working on the aerospace plane, which was highly classified and open to very few eyes.

Burns watched as the young athlete pushed himself toward shore with the pole, extending his hand so that he could be tugged in.

"Professor, I'd like to talk to you about something— real confidential. This is an awkward place. Could we chat out on the river, in my punt?"

Burns eyed Alcott more carefully. Why would the grad student want to meet in such an unconventional place and time? Was it something as superficial as his grade? Alcott should have known he had won easy honors in physics. The whole thing made little sense, and besides, Burns had a mortal fear of water and drowning. Periodically, he dreamt of the uncontrollable liquid engulfing, then suffocating him.

"It's getting too late, Tony. Besides, I can't swim a stroke. I'd rather not. Maybe some other time."

"Don't worry, Professor. I can swim for both of us. And what I have to say is really important."

Burns stared out at the near-desolate Cam, now empty of all except this one punt. The sun was a wan ball casting blackish shadows over the water. He moved one step back, as if to leave the scene, then suddenly reversed himself, realizing he was hooked on his own insatiable curiosity.

"OK, but let's make it quick. We don't have much daylight left."

As the professor silently took his place in the front of the punt, Alcott heaved the pole into the river and started the boat upstream toward Grantchester.

"So what's so important, Tony, that we have to go punting by moonlight?" Burns asked. His tone was purposely professorial.

Alcott was quiet for a moment. When he answered, he seemed embarrassed.

"I hate to admit it, Professor, but I've been super-interested in your project. It seems so damn exciting. So I did a little hacking at the terminal the other day, playing around with passwords they use on the super. Well, by luck—I suppose—I got entry to your work. I know it's about the X-30 aerospace plane, and I've got to tell you, it was sheer brilliance."

Burns was shocked. He had security clearance in both Washington and Whitehall, but now some damn nosy grad student had hacked his way into the system. Surely, Alcott now knew everything about the X-30's crucial wing-body design and its revolutionary liquid-hydrogen scramjet engine. What in the hell was he supposed to say about such a major breach? Especially sitting here in the middle of a river? Did they have these problems on the Manhattan Project? The wild thought suddenly flashed through his mind.

The less said the better, Burns decided.

"So, Alcott, what do you intend to do with the infor-

mation?" he asked. Burns's voice was muted, disguising
his anxiety.

"Do? Nothing, sir. I'm not so stupid that I don't know
it's top secret. I made sure not to take any notes and
didn't touch the printer. By this time, I've forgotten
much of the detail."

"So why this watery rendezvous?" Burns asked.

"Because I think you should get everything off the
super disc. Make a hard printout, then erase it. If I
could get entry, then it's not very secure. There are
better hackers than me at Cambridge, and some might
want to sell that kind of information. If you know what
I mean."

Burns knew exactly what he meant. He felt somewhat
relieved. He even admitted to himself that Alcott's suggestion made good sense. But now that he had learned
the reason for the strange rendezvous, he was eager to
return to shore. His eyes instinctively searched through
the declining light. The landscape was barren except for
the riverbank and the drooping willows.

"Tony, I appreciate the suggestion. In fact, I'm going
to take care of it tonight, as soon as we get back." Burns
surveyed the scene again. "We'd better hurry. It'll be
pitch dark soon."

Alcott nodded. He stood and dug in his pole to begin
the abrupt turn. The punt was completing the counter-
clockwise movement when the air was shattered by a
loud call.

"*Ahhhhh!*"

Burns leapt up at the crude sound, then realized the
shriek was coming from the young American.

"What's wrong?" he shouted at Tony.

His answer came swiftly from the boat itself. The
punt began to wobble crazily from side to side in the
suddenly turbulent water—which was unknown on the
Cam. Burns stared at Alcott, who was lurching with the
undulations, trying desperately to stabilize the punt.

"What's doing it?" Burns called out anxiously.

"I don't know, Professor. But sit down!"

As Burns bent to retake his seat, he could see the young American maneuvering more frantically. Then the sound—"*Ahhhhh!*"—again filled the air. The punt lurched violently. One side dipped, its edge splashing against the water line. Burns looked up just in time to see Alcott shifting futilely to retain his balance.

In an instant, the young man fell into the black water with a resounding splash.

"*Tony!*" Burns shouted into the night. He felt himself sliding, forced down on his knees at one side of the punt. He grasped the pole, which was still embedded in the mud of the river bottom, and pulled it back into the punt. Then he grabbed the side to keep from joining Alcott in the water, but the punt rocked more violently, as if in the grasp of some mythical river monster. His elbows hit first one side of the boat, then the other. He held on prayerfully, eyes closed, his hands clamped to the boat's edge.

Burns sat quietly, waiting. For what he had no idea. The punt was adrift in the river darkness, and he was alone and unable to swim a foot. Now on his knees, he stayed immobile for more than a minute. The punt first rocked and rocked, then abruptly stopped its gyrations. It settled softly, regaining normal balance with Burns still on his knees.

"Alcott!" he screamed. His eyes scanned the dark. Surely, Burns consoled himself, Tony could save himself easily in any depth of water. It was he who could have been—still could be—claimed by the Cam.

His eyes narrowed, hoping to penetrate the night. But there was no sign of Tony. Petrified, he picked up the discarded pole. Though he had never navigated a punt, or any boat, he stood up and punted violently back toward Cambridge. After a few minutes, he had gained some confidence. He decided it would be safer to bring the boat to the bank and walk back the rest of the way.

The punt was turning when it happened.

"Oh, my God!" Burns screamed as the rocking motion started again. Quickly, he was thrown onto the bottom of the boat, followed by a second, more massive whirl. His head was forced against the side of the punt, cutting a gash in his forehead. Still conscious, he touched the blood, but there was little time to contemplate the injury.

In one powerful flip, the punt was suddenly upside down. His body was thrown into the river. His face was now under the Cam, the water pressing against him like an amorphous mask, covering his nose and mouth. Just as in his recurring dream, he was surely about to drown.

In a desperation move, Burns shot his feet toward the river bottom, hoping to propel himself upward for a second chance. Could he hang onto the upturned punt and drift to shore? With his loose moccasins off, his feet touched bottom almost instantly. As he stretched upward, his head popped out of the water.

He was standing on the river bottom! He didn't have to swim anywhere. He was safe!

Burns touched his bloody forehead and grinned with satisfaction as he moved with an ungainly shuffle through the mud toward the bank. He had advanced three steps when he suddenly felt his progress impeded. Something—was it a river snake?—was grasping at him.

My God! It was a man's powerful hand, which had encircled his waist and was pulling him backward and down. He fought to ward it off, but another hand stretched to the top of his bent head and—he could feel an extraordinary human force—pressed him downward into the water.

Again the river enveloped his face. The water crushed into his open mouth, filling the nose cavity, blocking the air. With the remaining adrenaline in his system, Burns pushed himself loose, then up and above the water line. But only for a second. Exhausted, he immediately fell back into the river. The powerful hand grasped him once more, pushing him ever downward. The air bubbles of his life ebbed out before his eyes as he sank lower into the muck of the Cam.

His last thoughts ripped at him as powerfully as the pain. Was it young Alcott's brutal hand that was forcing the life out of him? Then, with an excruciating sense of frustration, Burns realized that he had solved the dilemma of the X-30. But for him it was already too late.

"MR. DAVIDSON, COULD I see that sprig once more? I'm pretty sure I know what it is, but I want to be certain."

The Baptist had rushed back from Las Vegas, and was now at the U.S. Botanic Gardens on Maryland and First Street in Washington, just blocks from the capitol. He was in earnest discussion with Lucian Carver III, a resident botanist, whose manner, dress, and expression gave away the fact (Davidson had heard) that this career was pursued mainly to establish Puritan work credentials in a family with a $300 million inheritance from early traffic in the slave trade and cotton, then in textile mills.

"I've never before seen the flower, but it does have a beautiful snow-white, bell-shaped blossom," Davidson said, offering up the blooms given to him by Mrs.

Semmelweiss, which were now preserved in a transparent plastic envelope.

Carver III stared at the sprig, then turned it over in his hand. He seemed to caress the petals, ever so softly.

"Yes, I see now that I don't need a reference check," the slight, effete botanist said in a pronounced Southern drawl. "These are definitely the blossoms of the *halesia*, a flowering ornamental tree that grows to about thirty-five feet in height." He smiled at Davidson. "It's native to the Carolinas and grows as far north as Ohio and Illinois and south to northern Florida. I've even heard that the English have transplanted some. A beautiful flower."

Davidson listened carefully to Carver's tone.

"Are you from South Carolina—Charleston, to be exact?" Davidson asked.

"Why, yes. How would you know?"

Davidson thought it less than politic to explain. The unique accent was among the thickest of Southern speech porridges. Born in the back plantation country of South Carolina as early as the seventeenth century, it had borrowed heavily from the inflections of black slaves.

"Just a hobby of mine," Davidson shrugged. "Is there anything else you can tell me about the flower?"

Carver's face suddenly lit up.

"Why, yes. We used to call the flower . . . what was it? Oh, yes, *silver bells*. Yes, that's it, Mr. Davidson. Silver bells."

Davidson retrieved the sprig and enthusiastically shook the hand of the surprised botanist.

"You've been a great help, Mr. Carver. A great help."

"Sir Malcolm, this is Davidson calling from the States. Just wanted to fill you in on the latest symptoms of my paranoia."

He could hear Asprey's laugh at the other end. Davidson had reached the MI5 specialist at his London

home, a town-house duplex with private elevator, part
of a sixty-year lease in Mayfair. The Baptist had waited
until 2 A.M. at his own colonial farmhouse (circa 1783)
in Leesburg, Virginia, to catch Asprey at 7 A.M., London
time, just as the British aristocrat was having eggs-over
with toast in bed.

"This is Davidson calling from the States," he repeated.

"Oh, yes, Baptist, what I can do for you?"

"Malcolm, at the Cosmos Club you mentioned that
the note found on Thorne's body said, 'Love, Mary.'
Well, I've just gotten back from Las Vegas—"

"You in Babylon?" Asprey laughed. "Did you win?"

"Matter of fact, I took in thirty-five dollars. But I was
really there to see the widow of Semmelweiss, the X-30
materials man."

"Did you learn anything?"

"I'm not sure. It depends on you, Malcolm."

"On me? Why is that?"

"I'll tell you in a moment. Meanwhile, could you
call the medical examiner at the Metropolitan Police
and find out if anything else was found on the body
besides the note."

"Such as?"

"That's my question, Malcolm. Please get on the horn,
then call me back."

"At two in the morning your time?"

"That's fine. I sleep little these days. Too much to
do and too few years to do it in. I have a real dead-
line."

"OK, John. Be right back to you."

Davidson sat up in bed and opened a biography of
Churchill. He turned to the early years in Parliament,
when as a liberal, the young grandson of the Duke
of Marlborough shocked his friends by associating
with "radicals." Like Churchill, Davidson had gone
through several political reincarnations—from liberal to

conservative, then back toward the middle. Conditions change; so do philosophies.

He read for about twenty minutes before the phone rang.

"Baptist? This is Asprey. As I thought, you're having another paranoid attack. I checked with Scotland Yard. There was nothing else on Thorne's person except some keys and a wallet with two five-pound notes."

"Absolutely nothing?"

"As I said, just his personal effects and the note from 'Mary' with a small sprig of flowers attached."

"Flowers? Why didn't you say so before?" Davidson was jolted out of his chair. "Are they white, in the shape of small bells, and about an inch in size?"

"Why yes. How did you know that?"

"It's the same flower that was left on Semmelweiss's chest in the garage. My God, Asprey, they're silver-bells, and they were sent by Mary. Don't you know what that means?"

Davidson listened to the transatlantic silence.

"Oh, John, I see," Asprey finally said. " 'Mary, Mary, quite contrary, how does your garden grow? With silver bells and cockleshells and . . . ' Yes, I see. Then it wasn't just your paranoia."

"Malcolm, it seldom is. The world accommodates my personality by being perpetually conspiratorial. Please send me a sample of the flowers by express mail, soonest. I'll return it. OK?"

He heard a silent cough, then a faint "All right," followed by a short laugh and a click of the receiver.

10

"WHERE ARE PROFESSOR Burns's living quarters?" asked Sir Malcolm Asprey, pressing his credentials into the face of the porter at Burns's Cambridge college.

The call had come in to the Irving Theater's backroom office from the Cambridge police. They had found the body washed up on the banks of the Cam. The punt itself had floated downstream and was picked up as well.

"Don't touch anything until I get there, Sergeant," Asprey had instructed the police. "Burns was an American scientist whose security was in our hands. I suppose we haven't done the greatest of jobs. In any case, I'll be there posthaste."

The helicopter, a special bird with civilian markings, at MI5's disposal, lifted Asprey from the landing pad near Tower Bridge right onto one of the grassy Backs of the University. Sir Malcolm had walked just a few steps to the college unit when he met Constable Barney.

"Come with us, sir," Barney muttered, his working-class accent anvil-like on Asprey's ear.

"Professor Burns's rooms are on the third floor," said the porter. "But I don't think you'll find him there. I haven't seen him the whole day."

"Thank you. We'll just go up and look around. Do you have the key?"

The two men mounted the stairs and moved to flat 3B. Asprey had barely touched the knob when the door opened. The rooms were chaos incarnate. Nothing was in its original place. The computer was thrown over, the disc files ransacked, the bed mattress and pillows slit open, as were the backs of the pictures.

"Hello, what have we here?" the constable asked.

"We have intelligence gone amok, Constable, and probable proof that Dr. Burns's demise was murder. We have to find what they came for, first here, then at the university supercomputer. I asked my mathematician, Chris Steiner, to meet us there."

Steiner, assisted by a Cambridge lecturer in computer science, had already taken the supercomputer through its paces by the time Asprey arrived, having conducted a futile search of Burns's quarters.

"There are two hard discs missing, Sir Malcolm," Steiner reported. "Mr. Jensen here tells me Burns had been married to the super for two weeks. He believes he was working on an X-30 scramjet engine problem before he walked out—they say smiling brightly—just before 9 P.M."

Steiner explained the scramjet failure in the arc jet test in Arizona. Burns may have come up with the solution, but if so, it had vanished. Or more likely, it had been stolen.

"All his work is missing," Steiner added. "Jensen tells me one of the grad students, an American named Tony Alcott, had been hacking through Burns's material, but Alcott's missing too. Someone saw them in a punt together just at 9 P.M. I suppose that means both our leads are dead."

"What do we do now, Chris?" Sir Malcolm asked, his voice tinged with desperation.

"Pray that some other genius can replicate the work. Or that Tony Alcott somehow shows up."

Asprey turned toward the door, motioning for Steiner to follow.

"The bird is waiting to take us back to London, Chris. I'll have to call Davidson. It seems the paranoid old spy was right after all."

"MY NAME IS John Davidson. The President is expecting me," he told the policeman at the northwest gate of the White House, on Pennsylvania Avenue.

The guard checked his driver's ID perfunctorily. Recognizing both Davidson's sharp profile and his dented 1976 forest-green Volvo wagon, he waved him through. The Baptist parked in the visitors' section, then moved toward the West Wing, where he showed his pass to the Secret Service guard in the anteroom of the Presidential office quarters.

Built in 1905 by Teddy Roosevelt to get his staff out of the crowded mansion, the Wing suffered from a strange architectural oversight, Davidson noted. No provision was made for a tunnel or closed walkway. To this day, American presidents—even in winter blizzards—had to walk from the mansion to the Oval Office across a roofed but open portico, the one often seen as a television news backdrop.

Davidson sat in the small anteroom, smiling at the Secret Service agent, whose radio plug stuck prominently out of his ear. A regulation .38 Smith & Wesson revolver peeked out of his shoulder holster. The two waited like patients in a busy doctor's office.

"Mr. Davidson, such a pleasure to see you again."

Les Fanning, assistant to President Hawley Briggs, greeted him, brightening the early morning rendezvous. A chalk-skinned brunette with jet black hair, Les was Davidson's ideal of feminine beauty—softshell on the outside, but with a keen mind and unlimited resilience inside. Surely, the ingredients for a Presidential aide.

"It's been a while, hasn't it, Baptist?" Fanning asked. "I believe the crisis in North Africa. Am I right?"

"Yes, that's true. And Les, I must tell you that I greet each new assignment as avidly as a schoolboy in September—or at least what I remember as a grand time of year."

"And why has the President called you in this time, Mr. Davidson?"

Davidson almost balked at the question as they walked the corridor toward the Oval Office.

"To be frank, Les, the President hasn't asked me a thing. I'm troubled by some events, and I wanted to get his opinion."

Les laughed. "That's a pleasant reversal. Well, here we are. Pleasure, again."

Davidson watched her retreating shapely body. At times like these, the waning of his libido struck him as punishing. The handsomeness and warmth of Les Fanning evoked aching memories of another era, perhaps another man.

"John, welcome to the White House."

President Briggs waved him toward one of the twin wing chairs flanking the marble Adams fireplace. "I understand you have something on your mind."

As Davidson sat facing the President, the contrast between the two men came into sharp relief. The Baptist was Eastern America incarnate. Groton- and Princeton-bred, his diction—despite his birth in Boise, Idaho—was aristocratic New York and precise, a tone almost extinct in America. His omnipresent tweeds were impeccably fitted, his hair and heavy black eyebrows neatly trimmed. He seemed of the present, yet of the past, and unchanging.

President Briggs was a Southern "good 'ol boy," and everything about him spelled rural America. A tall, somewhat overweight man with thin, sandy, generally uncombed hair, Briggs looked as if his clothes had been tailored for someone else. His shirt hung a bit twisted; his tie dangled at less than the perpendicular. His whole demeanor was inexact.

He had once been described as a small-town hardware store owner, which is exactly what his father had been. Hawley had later trained in the law, but his formative boyhood years were spent in the stockroom of the family store.

To their later chagrin, some politicians were taken in by his folksy manner. Those who underestimated his razor-sharp mind later regretted playing that game.

"Yes, I do, Mr. President," Davidson finally answered. "It involves the X-30 and I think it's important."

"Important?" the President asked as he partially rose from his chair. "John, anything to do with that plane is vital. We've drastically scaled back our defenses, which has given us a peace dividend. But there's been a bad fallout as well. We're losing part of our industrial base and some of our best technical programs. We've got to switch from war to peace yet somehow hold on to the old skills and facilities. That's where the X-30 comes in. Imagine going to a space station or a satellite, or even to a moon colony, just by hopping on a plane and taking off. It's the kind of technology that will be a replacement for the Cold War. Discovery is the route of any great nation, and I'm expecting the X-30 will lead us into the twenty-first century."

Briggs started to pace, his mind now fully invested in the future. He turned toward Davidson.

"That's to say nothing of the promise of hypersonic travel here on Earth. We let the supersonic plane pass us by, but now we'll leapfrog generations ahead. And, John, the X-30 will also make our air force impregnable in war. Look what air superiority meant in Iraq. Yes, overall—in science, space, defense, travel, materials research—the X-30 is the future."

Davidson smiled at the President's presentation.

"I don't suppose you've practiced much law, Mr. President, but you'd do great in a courtroom."

"Don't kid yourself, John. My first three years out of school, I was the best ambulance chaser in Dixie. I had the ladies in the jury crying." Briggs paused. "But I'm sorry I got carried away. Now, what's your info on the X-30?"

Davidson marshaled the evidence in his mind, then told the President about the two supposed "suicides" of X-30 scientists within a week.

"And just this morning, MI5 in London told me that another X-30 researcher, an American working at Cambridge University, was found drowned. I've already checked out the first two deaths, and I've concluded that the so-called suicides were no coincidence. Both men were actually murdered, probably by someone trying to slow down our X-30 program."

Briggs's eyes widened in surprise. "Murder? What's your evidence, John?"

"Just two sprigs of white flowers, and love notes from someone called Mary."

The President leaned back and laughed. "John you've made my day. Now, what in the hell does that mean?"

"It means that many killers, being pathological, have obsessions that defy understanding. This one leaves small white flowers on his victims, and some mention of 'Mary, with love.' When I was out in Vegas, no one had noticed the flowers except the victim's wife, who thought it was a sentimental gift from her husband. I took a sample of the blossoms just in case. Then I learned that the same thing happened in London. After I alerted them, MI5 sent me a sample of the flowers. Yesterday, I took them out to the Botanic Gardens and showed them to a botanist."

Davidson had now captured the President's attention. He stared at the old spy.

"And what did he tell you?"

"That they're both from a tree called *halesia*. It has a snow-white bell-shaped flower that's usually called silver bells."

"So?"

"So, do you remember your nursery rhymes, Mr. President? The one about Mary?"

The President's eyes lit up, then he started to hum.

"Of course, John. 'Mary, Mary, quite contrary.' Sure— silver bells!" He looked up at Davidson. "Is that it?"

"Exactly. The killer is a braggart, leaving his little messages in code. I have no idea who Mary is, but I'm sure it's part of the puzzle. In any case, someone is systematically trying to kill off our X-30 scientists in order to slow down, even destroy, the program."

"But who and why?" The President paced, then suddenly halted directly over the federal eagle woven into the Oval Office rug.

"At this juncture, I haven't the slightest idea."

"So what do you want me to do?" the President asked.

"Well, on this one I'd like to be a little less on my own. Without tipping the Congressional oversight people to the full details, I'd like you to issue a finding to give my operation some legitimacy. That way I can work quietly, but still be able to tap into the Agency or other government bureau if I need help. Normally, it's warmer out there than it is inside—where it's real cold. But this time I may need help."

The President extended his hand to Davidson, a sign that the meeting was over.

"I'll do that, John. I'm getting tired of the world's

largest intelligence agency being supported by an unemployed intelligence man. I won't pay you a salary, or even per diem, because then you'd be one of us—and maybe just as hopeless. But give me your chits for expenses, and I'll get them paid. Is it a deal?"

"Deal, Mr. President. Meanwhile, could you have the FBI and Defense Intelligence beef up surveillance on the X-30 scientists and installations? Our nursery rhymer may have other deadly intentions."

"Shall do, John. And good hunting. This is an important one," Briggs said, leading his compatriot-in-intrigue toward the door of the Oval Office.

THE SECURITY BARRIER to the small private street was raised for the night's festivities. A half-dozen London bobbies stood outside the embassy of the Russian Republic, screening the guest invitations for security.

Located at 13 Kensington Palace Gardens, one of London's smartest enclaves, the embassy was one of a score of mainly Victorian mansions that lined the unusual thoroughfare. More than a half mile long, it began at Kensington High Street and ended at Kensington Palace, the home of Princess Diana and other British royals. Over the years, the street had housed innumerable outstanding members of British society, including novelist William Makepeace Thackeray, earning it a status it still enjoyed.

With the white, blue, and red flag of the Russian Republic perched over its portico—put there in 1992 to

replace the obsolete red hammer and sickle—the embassy
was tonight the site of a great gala. The diplomatic world
of London had turned out to celebrate the second anniver-
sary of the release of Russia from Communism's iron
grip.

One invitation had been arranged by the President of
the United States himself, through the American ambassador, Sy Belkin, the head of a giant clothing discount
chain and a major contributor to the party. That guest
was John Davidson, ex-of-the-CIA, who was coming as
an aide to the American embassy's cultural attaché, a
hoary cover that gave him not only diplomatic immunity,
but use of the embassy facilities on Grosvenor Square.
Davidson had already been put up in a former storage
closet, perhaps eight by nine, cleaned out for his arrival.

Davidson wasn't distressed. In truth, he suffered the
reverse of claustrophobia. He preferred small, tight enclo-
sures to large open areas. He had speedily settled in,
placing his reference books on a portable shelf. His prized
Roladex, with forty years of accumulated contacts, was
perched on a four-foot-long French provincial desk he
had picked up on Portobello Road, a London flea market.

London and Davidson were old friends. He had first
arrived in the city near the end of World War II, as an
eighteen-year-old volunteer in the OSS, the forerunner
of the Agency. Davidson had dropped out of Princeton
and enlisted to help win the war for the Allied cause. On
his second day in England, he had fallen asleep in the
second-class compartment of the train from Paddington
Station to Oxford and had the sweetest dream of his
life. When he awoke and walked the grounds of the
venerable university, he realized that he had arrived
home—a journey that had taken three hundred years,
the long way around, via his family's emigration to
Virginia in the seventeenth century.

Jung would have called it the "racial unconscious." To

Davidson, it was more the re-creation of English novels, films, and biographies, all come to life in their authentic setting.

Over the years, as an Agency operative, then as chief of counterintelligence, Davidson had used any excuse to wend his way to the U.K. This time he needed no such subterfuge. He was in the city that Samuel Johnson had equated with life itself, and he was at this splendiferous embassy reception, only because the death of three X-30 scientists had made the visit imperative. Of the three, two had died, or more likely been murdered, in England. Simple logic had brought him here.

"Baptist! A sight for Cold War eyes!"

The man advancing toward him across the marble foyer was none other than Sergei Makrov, once chief KGB *rezident* in Washington, and a formidable adversary in the chess match of counterespionage. Makrov was now the new Russian *rezident* at the London Embassy. The chessboard might have changed, but the pieces were still the same, Davidson was sure.

"I've just heard from my people in your embassy— yes, Baptist, we still have them there—that you're now an aide to the cultural attaché," Makrov half shouted, turning heads. He shook Davidson's hands, then gave him a Russian bear hug. "How very wonderful. Not only are we working on the same side, but we have the very same job! You are looking at the cultural attaché for the great free democratic Russian Republic!"

Davidson shook his head in friendly recognition. "When was the last time we squared off, Sergei?" Davidson asked.

"Just four years ago in Washington. Remember? The little incident of the Midgetman missile plans. I really did a magnificent job, if I say so. But of what use? Now we are both spending billions *destroying* what you and I tried to steal from each other. But the game goes on. No?" Makrov laughed uproariously, obviously pleased to see a fellow warrior from the old days.

"So whom do you report to now?" the Baptist asked. "The military, or the MVD, or what's left of the KGB?"

Makrov couldn't resist. He gave Davidson another bear hug.

"Oh, no, John. We've gone totally respectable—more or less. I am now in the Intelligence Division of the Foreign Ministry. KGB? Heaven forbid. Same job, but new name. Most of the old KGB hardliners have been folded into the Interior Ministry, the MVD, along with the KGB border guards and the KGB police. But we remnants have been recast as true diplomats—completely separate from the KGB. At least that's what they tell us."

Makrov looked around and placed a finger to his lips. "But, John, please say nothing of this to the ambassador. He is sure I am *solely* his cultural attaché in charge of ballet and Dostoyevsky."

Makrov, a bowling ball–shaped man, laughed again.

Davidson surveyed his one-time foe. Makrov had amorphous, somewhat sprawling Slavic features and a physique that was not unlike Khruschev's. But his clothes, manner, and voice were of a different world, a reasonable Moscow imitation of the Mayfair British gentleman. His suits were Savile Row's best flannel pinstripes, his shirts from Turnbull and Asser at $110 each, his ties an exiled king's ransom, from Hermes.

Makrov's English diction was a unique blend of Russian sing-song and Cambridge clipped, as if Prince Charles had spent a misguided youth in the Young Communist League in Pinsk. Overall, Makrov might be taken for an entertaining lightweight, which would be a grave error in perception. Davidson had long ago learned that the Russian was a potent adversary. After all these years, he was pleased that they were finally on the same side.

The twosome wandered through the reception area, Makrov balancing a vodka glass, Davidson nursing an iced tea. Acting as one of the hosts, Makrov introduced Davidson to representatives of various governments, adding an occasional private aside.

"That's Count Telnitz—he's with the BND, the German intelligence," Makrov commented as they moved on. "John, if I were to really do CVs on all these diplomats, I'd probably find that half of them are in our business." Makrov suddenly stopped and swiveled. "Oh, you *must* meet someone."

Makrov walked briskly over to a tall, slender man with tight, high cheekbones, dressed impeccably in a somber dark gray suit, with a white shirt and navy tie, an outfit that had been unfashionable for at least a generation. The man was obviously Oriental, but his expression, even his only slightly slanted eyes, were incongruously reminiscent of the West. The Russian tapped him on the shoulder.

The man winced at the unexpected familiarity.

"Professor, I'd like you to meet an old comrade-in-arms, John Davidson of the U.S., formerly of the CIA—now retired. That's right, isn't it, Baptist?" Makrov paused. "Excuse 'the Baptist,' Dr. Li. It has no religious connotation. Just a professional nickname for Mr. Davidson—though John does remind me of a minister, always subtly preaching the case for democracy."

He turned toward Davidson. "And this is Dr. Li Chen, mainland China's foremost authority on Oriental religions. He's now working out of the Chinese Embassy on Portland Place. What is your title, Doctor—chargé d'affaires?"

"Yes, Comrade Makrov," Li responded, his voice thin. His English was studied and perfect, with only a subtle trace of the Orient. "I hope you don't mind if I use the proper title of my country—the People's Republic of China. We are, after all, the last of the great Marxist-Leninist nations. Am I right, Mr. Davidson, that you in the West are surprised that we haven't yet crumbled, and taken our billion people into the welcoming arms of democracy?"

Dr. Li's silken voice was lined with condescension.

Davidson nodded from the neck, respectfully.

"No, not quite, Dr. Li. I've always made a distinction between the U.S.S.R. and China. Russia was too close to the West, geographically and spiritually, not to be seduced by our gods—both the good and bad ones—from our freedom to our supermarkets to our raucous popular culture. But, yes, I recognize that your nation is different. It has the patience of the Orient, and a different attitude toward religion. Am I right?"

Dr. Chen smiled broadly, perhaps recognizing a kindred soul.

"Yes, Mr. Davidson, history is all a matter of religion in the long run, isn't it? The Soviet Union had a Marxist shell, but it and its satellites were really supressed Christian civilizations only waiting to be redeemed. And now it's happened. But we've never been Christian, Mr. Davidson, and never will be. Thus we cannot be seduced, either by your gods or your goods. That is the failure of the West's perception of us. It's not so much that Marx is eternal but that our beliefs are. Remember, we have no image of an anthropomorphic god-man like your Jewish Jehovah, or your Christian Jesus, both of whom you are always trying to please. Sometimes in very confusing ways."

"But you have Confucius," Davidson interjected.

"Yes, but no real gods, only teachers. We value the goodness of Buddha, the wisdom of Confucius, and the mysteries of Taoism. We seek a balance, a harmony in life, an inner enlightenment that you Westerners know nothing about. You are always anxious, always greedy, always restive. We do not concern ourselves with what you call 'human rights,' which in excess we believe can lead to great inhumanity."

Davidson could feel the intense stare of Dr. Li.

"No, we in the East require only that our rulers be just, that they rule by a Mandate of Heaven. That is why Mao fell. He forgot the ancient wisdom. We shall not make that mistake again, but neither shall we imitate you, Mr. Davidson. If we do that, then we shall also fall like the U.S.S.R. But don't hold your breath."

"But aren't you already?" Makrov asked. "Look at your capitalist enclaves in South China. And all the new millionaires."

Li smiled knowingly. "Comrade Makrov—and please excuse my salutation—that policy is mere expediency. We must build a modern socialist state. What better way then to have enclaves of capital that bring in billions to strengthen our technology and our military? Mr. Davidson, you know we already have a $15 billion trade surplus with the United States, and it is growing. But seduction, no. Just a bit of clever, targeted imitation, which we open and close at will. You know, Mr. Davidson, the world might be considerably safer, even happier, if it had more than one superpower to contemplate—and fear."

Li's smile was enigmatic. Makrov and Davidson bid him farewell with polite smiles of their own. The two Westerners then moved on, searching out more candidates for Davidson's initiation into the London scene.

"Clever man, no, Davidson?" Makrov said.

"Clever? More than that, Sergei. It's plain to see that Li is of the old Mandarin school, the philosophers who ruled China when it was truly the Middle Kingdom, the center of the civilized earth. We should never underestimate them. But what is such a man doing in London, in their Foreign Corps?"

Makrov laughed. "Oh, Baptist, sometimes you can be so American—so naive. Li knows us well. His maternal grandfather was English, from the old Victorian British enclave in Shanghai. So his mind spans both cultures. And not only is he the London chief of TEWU, the

Chinese secret police, but he's in charge of clandestine work for Red China in the entire West. You may even be looking at the future leader of Red China's billion people—which will soon include Hong Kong."

Davidson pursed his lips in surprise. "Really?"

"And he might even be valuable in your own search," Makrov added.

Davidson's interest sharpened. "And what do you know of that?"

"Come now, Baptist, when didn't I know about your activities? I might also be of some help."

"In what way?"

Makrov swiveled his head in a quick survey of anyone who might overhear.

"Moscow has instructed me to work with you to find the killers of the X-30 scientists. That's why you're here, isn't it? We Russians want no part of such 'shenanigans.' Isn't that what you call it in the States? And the X-30 is too expensive for us. And for what use in our impoverished nation?"

"Well, that's kind of you, Sergei. But where do we start?"

"Perhaps right here in London, even right in my own organization. We must talk."

13

HE WOKE FITFULLY and stared around at the nearly empty off-white room. He was in a bed—not his own—and the place looked like a hospital.

What in the world was he doing here? He pulled his body up against the pillow, the pain shooting through his side. Had he been beaten up or was it a muscle spasm from lying in bed? Whatever it was, and wherever he was, his mind was disoriented.

"I see you've finally come to. Good boy." He could hear the voice before he saw the form. An attractive middle-aged woman wearing a nurse's cap was approaching. "Young man, you gave us quite a scare. Thank God you're up."

It was a pleasant beginning to the day—if this were the beginning of the day.

"Where am I, Nurse? What's happened?" His voice was working better than his head.

"You're in the Newnham Hospital, and you've been in a coma for four days."

"Coma? What happened to me?" he blurted out.

Then, as the last word left his mouth, he was struck with a flood of memory, as if it all had happened just a minute ago. He could feel the punt undulating, then the sense of his falling into the river. The cold water was again suddenly up around his neck. He sensed himself going under, being pushed by someone—down and down.

"I remember now," he said. "Our punt turned over and I fell into the river." He decided to withhold his suspicions. "What happened to Professor Burns? Is he all right?"

"No, young man. I'm afraid he drowned. They've recovered his body. But you were lucky. A boy found you on the banks and called the police. They brought you here. We pumped your lungs, but for a long time it was touch and go. We've been feeding and treating you intravenously. You're lucky you're young and strong."

The woman came around and plumped up his pillows.

"What's your name and where are you from? We found no ID on you. Your wallet must have fallen to the bottom of the river."

"I'm Tony Alcott, an American. I was one of Professor Burns's graduate students at Cambridge, and we were out on the river talking shop when it happened." His eyes blinked as the nurse opened the blinds onto the bright sun. "How long do you think I'll be here?"

"Well, I'll get the doctor in to examine you. But my guess is only a few days. You're a very lucky young man."

Once on his feet, Alcott returned to where he hoped he could clarify events. Surely someone, or something, was responsible for Burns's death and his own near demise. At Cambridge, he visited the local police, who told him about the theft of Professor Burns's hard discs. It corroborated his theory of foul play.

"Try giving a call to Sir Malcolm Asprey at MI5 in London," the sergeant advised. "I'm sure he'd like to hear from you. You might also try the American Embassy. There's a man there named John Davidson who's taken an interest in Professor Burns's case," the constable explained.

His phone calls to both men proved futile. It was Friday afternoon. Their offices explained that Asprey and Davidson were away. The English country weekend, you know.

"But where can I reach either one of them?" Alcott asked Davidson's pool secretary at the American Embassy. His voice was plaintive, but his anger at whoever had tried to kill him was rising. He had little experience with violence, outside of college boxing. But his life had almost ended prematurely, and his curiosity was growing. Who in the hell was behind this?

Alcott explained his situation, including his near miss with death to the secretary, who seemed intrigued with this young American from Cambridge.

"I probably shouldn't tell you this, Mr. Alcott, but they're both in the same place—at Hollow Oaks, Sir Malcolm's country place near Cambridge. Please don't tell Mr. Davidson that I let you know."

14

NOW ARCH COULD see it all plainly.

Kevin Arch, a small, gnarled man, bent uncomfortably as he focused through the telescope at the Chinese Embassy, on the other side of Portland Place. Not far from Oxford Street in Central London, Arch and his Russian colleague, Andrei Voshkov, were in a small third-floor office suite reserved by MI5 solely so they could keep the Chinese enclave under surveillance.

The telescope was attached to a parabolic mirror, part

of a sound reproduction system that bounced off any window in the embassy it was aimed at, gathering sound waves from conversations inside. As in the receiver of a telephone, the impact of the voices on the window set up sound frequencies that could be reinterpreted into words by the sophisticated equipment in the room.

Arch—who had been assigned by Sir Malcolm Asprey—had a fluent knowledge of Chinese, picked up in Hong Kong, where he had been an MI5 man. He sighed in near-torment whenever he thought about 1997, the year the exotic British Crown Colony was being turned over, lock, stock, and capitalism, to Red China.

His partner, Voshkov, who had served in Beijing as a KGB agent, was even more fluent in the tongue.

The work was routine and had been going on for several weeks without results. It was continued only because totalitarian Red China had replaced the former Soviet Union as the center of suspicions, and was a natural target for MI5. The Russians were cooperating with the British, as they were with the Agency. Arch was sure it was only because the Russkies wanted to soften up the Allies and their pocketbooks.

"Andrei, can you make out anything?" Arch asked impatiently.

Voshkov was now a member of Makrov's Foreign Intelligence team at the Russian Embassy, on loan to MI5, setting a precedent in the post–Cold War world.

"They're talking in the ambassador's office," Voshkov explained to his British partner. "Dr. Li is discussing the party at our embassy the other night. Seems he knows quite a lot about John Davidson. He's telling the ambassador that he's concerned about the American's arrival in London."

"Any mention of covert activity?"

"I can't tell. But the conversation has turned cryptic."

"Here, let me have the earphones," Arch said, impatiently taking the set from Voshkov.

"Listen to this." The British operative amplified the sound into the room. "They're discussing a Russian named Tolstoy—obviously a code name. Now, wait . . . . Dammit, someone just pulled the drapes shut. The sound has shut down. Can we switch to the telephone bug in the room?" Arch asked, his hand moving rapidly to the alternate equipment.

"No," Voshkov answered. "They swept the entire embassy a few days ago. There's not an operating bug in the place."

Arch shook his head. "I'll have the central office put static onto their telephone lines, then we'll send in repair men in the morning to replace the bugs. Steiner tells me our new ones are almost undetectable."

"OK. But let's call it a night." The Russian yawned. "The new shift is coming in soon. I'd like to leave a little early—have a date with a barmaid in Pimlico."

The MI5 man nodded agreement. "By the way, Voshkov. How does it feel to be working with us against the Chinese Communists? Any pangs of regret for the once-great U.S.S.R.?"

Voshkov frowned. "I try not to think about it, Arch. Those were great salad days for us. Why it all collapsed, I'll never know. But don't count us out. I have something to look forward to. We might someday be enemies again. Meanwhile, I'll see you tomorrow."

Arch waited twenty minutes before the second shift of two—one of Makrov's men and a fellow MI5 agent, Charlie Baker—took over.

He left the office, whose door bore the cover name Marylebone Electronics, and descended the elevator from the fourth floor. He went out onto Portland Place, a wide street punctuated by three statues of now-obscure characters from British Empire history.

Arch pulled on his black trenchcoat, typical wear of the U.K.'s lower middle class, and strode over to his reconditioned Rover taxicab, which had been repainted a bright white and had 190,000 miles on its odometer. On the windscreen was a parking ticket for twenty pounds, which he smilingly deposited in the trash can.

Inside the Rover, his mind turned over rapidly. He had to reach Sir Malcolm right away. What did the code name Tolstoy mean? Were the Chinese somehow in contact with outlaw Russians? And why? It was all beyond him, but he was sure Sir Malcolm could use the information.

He'd drive over to the Strand, then to the Irving Theater, where Asprey kept his clandestine office. If Sir Malcolm wasn't there, someone would know how to reach him.

Arch started the car ignition and pulled out onto the street. The Rover was approaching Marylebone Road when the engine suddenly stopped dead. He turned the key several times, importuning his favorite car. But the old Rover refused to move.

Had he flooded the carburetor? He'd wait a few minutes with the car stuck in the center of the road, until any excess gas had evaporated.

Again, he turned the key. This time there was ignition. But not the one he had expected.

The normal engine turnover lasted only a brief second. It was followed by a roar of such monumental proportions that the car levitated off the pavement. Arch could see orange flames start at the front of the bonnet, then sear toward him with gale-like velocity.

The second explosion was gargantuan, followed by a nothingness that simultaneously enveloped him and his car. Arch's last thoughts were ironic. Had he outlived the Cold War only to expire in the middle of London in sweet peacetime?

15

AT FIRST THE President thought John Davidson's critics might be right.

The Baptist's suspicions that the X-30 scientists were being systematically murdered were, they said, the by-product of his "overprofessional obsession" with conspiracies.

But the death of Professor Burns, coupled with the theft of his computations on the X-30 scramjet, convinced President Briggs. Davidson was right.

Apparently, these were not unorganized attacks. But if it was a murder conspiracy, who had orchestrated it? And why? Brigg's first response was that his former enemy, Russia, might be involved. But again, why? Surely his good friend, President Malinovsky in the Kremlin, wouldn't be part of such a plot. And hadn't the hardliners in the KGB and the military been neutralized by Russia's new democratic administration?

"Les, could you get Moscow on the horn?" President Briggs called into the intercom. "I want to talk to President Malinovsky personally. I'd rather not struggle through his English. See if Vladimir Greenstein is in his office. Get him hooked to a conference call with simultaneous translation. OK?"

Within fifteen minutes, Les had arranged everything.

"I have President Malinovsky on the phone," she called through the intercom. "Pick up the red phone."

"Hello," Briggs answered loudly. It was a habit borrowed from FDR, who had the early twentieth-century view of the telephone as a hollow tube. "Dimitri, I have a problem, and I wonder if you could help."

"Surely, anything, Mr. President. We appreciate the aid you've given us, even if we sadly need more. But that aside, what's your problem?"

When Briggs described the killing of the three X-30 scientists, the Russian was incredulous.

"Mr. President, I swear I know absolutely nothing about this. I'm also sure no one in my government is involved. Do you think that in our precarious economic position, we'd be interested in hypersonic travel, or advanced military aircraft? We need all the help we can get from the West just to survive, let alone advance."

"I understand, President Malinovsky." Intuitively, Briggs trusted Malinovsky. "But you still have a large core of hardliners, some of whom—my people tell me—have infiltrated your government. Can you be sure they're not manipulating this? All I'm asking is that you look into it. Who knows? Maybe you'll find evidence to nip another coup in the bud."

"OK," the Russian responded in English, adding a self-amused laugh. "See you at next month's summit."

President Malinovsky's inquiry had come to General Gregori Vorichenko at the headquarters of the MVD, the gray-uniformed national police who had taken over the old KGB building on Dzerzhinsky Square. In front of it was the vacant column that had once held the statue of Felix Dzerzhinksy, Polish-born founder of the Cheka, later the OGPU, then the NKVD, and finally, the KGB.

From Vorichenko, the query had gone to General Ivan Basiloff, the head of the incorporated old KGB Internal Security unit. From him it was passed on to his deputy, Colonel Arkady Tasinev.

Tasinev, a short, almost skeletal man, with a shaved head and sharp cheekbones—looking more Tartar than Russian—stood reading and rereading the inquiry from his president on the X-30 affair. He placed the memo down and moved into the kind of immediate action that had earned him the nickname of "Sprinter," a name his enemies embellished as "Sadist Sprinter."

First, the colonel dictated a memo, which he faxed to the presidium building in the Kremlin.

It read: "Dear President Malinovsky, I cannot deny that our agents in Washington, London, and San Francisco are seeking technical information on the X-30. That is their job. But as to *mokroye dyelo*, that deadly 'wet business' has disappeared with the Cold War. Like all dedicated Russians, we seek only harmony with our allies, the West. Colonel Arkady Tasinev."

Having dispatched his denial, Tasinev took a heavy set of keys from his tunic pocket and moved into the corridor outside his office. Selecting one key, he opened the first door and walked into what appeared to be a large closet. Only recently, it had been converted into a shortwave radio transmitter and receiver station. Along the wall was an impressive array of American-made equipment, including a precision Mil Spec 1030 transceiver, which, stripped, cost $25,000, and advanced peripheral CD recorders.

He sat at the console and withdrew his logbook, which he studied. Expertly, he dialed a transmitter frequency in the 40-meter band, 11 megahertz, aimed at the Shanghai headquarters of TEWU, the Red Chinese secret police.

"Hello Jade Palace. This is Tolstoy," he called into the microphone in clear, accented English, now the international patois of diplomacy. "Repeat. Jade Palace from Tolstoy. If you are not in attendance, please record this message: Mary, Mary, quite contrary, how does your garden grow?"

16

THE COUNTRY AIR was refreshing, Davidson thought, as was the eclectic mix of weekend guests at Hollow Oaks, Sir Malcolm Asprey's country house near Cambridge.

Davidson found himself assigned to a corner room on the second floor, furnished in comfortable, dowdy British style, as if nothing had changed in the 150 years of the house's existence. The chintz curtains were faded, as was the matching bedspread. Davidson unpacked his wardrobe: one tuxedo and two identical gray herringbone tweed suits. Washington summer or chilly London winter, that was his entire wardrobe.

That evening, with everyone dressed formally as if for the Covent Garden opera, Davidson entered the drawing room to join the others. Never was he fully at ease among the class-conscious British, but professionally he always appeared relaxed.

"Welcome to Hollow Oaks." Sir Malcolm Asprey rushed to Davidson's side. "Come and meet my friends."

As he was waltzed around the room by Sir Malcolm, Davidson was given the introductions, one at a time.

"You know Sergei Makrov. And this is Sir Albert Simmons, one of our self-made, quite liberal, press lords. And here we have Antony Riddle, a Conservative MP."

To each one, Davidson was introduced as former CIC of the Agency and, Asprey stressed, "a longtime friend of the American President." Before the intros were complete, the Baptist had met a vital slice of British society, including the Viscount Hampshire, heir to one of Britain's great real-estate fortunes; John Acroft, a Liberal Democrat MP; Dave Goodman, a defense affairs writer for a London daily; and Alison Mason, an attractive West End actress in her thirties.

"And John, you've never met my wife, the loveliest flower in my garden, Victoria Asprey."

The old spy stared at Lady Asprey. The woman was apparently in her early fifties. Davidson stood awkwardly, his mouth slightly parted, his mind and eyes transfixed. Never since the death of his own wife seven years before had he seen a woman of such obvious magnetism. Not that she was plastic-surgery perfect, but the fit of features and expression were overwhelming, at least to Davidson. The smile—if it were forced, the insincerity was concealed—was so radiant that Davidson felt his dormant libido reasserting itself. Lady Asprey's hair was dark blond and curled short, appropriate for a woman her age. Her figure was full but not heavy, her bosom discreetly buxom.

"Beautiful" was an inadequate description, Davidson decided. Her femininity, plus the intelligence in her eyes, was overwhelming.

He suddenly had the childish sensation that he had fallen in love. Would her voice break the magic image?

Davidson drew himself up sharply. He reminded himself that not only had his time passed for romance, but this mature vision of loveliness was married to a colleague and friend.

"Lady Asprey, your husband pays you due homage." Davidson was trying out his rusty gallantry.

"Oh, Mr. Davidson. The honor is mine. You are all Sir Malcolm talks about. The epitome of his profession, whatever that is. He talks so little of his work."

Davidson strained to fight off primitive urges. The guests mingled and the Baptist with them, purposely keeping his distance from Lady Asprey. But he couldn't help notice. Her eyes sought him out as well.

Soon, the professionals had exchanged their pleasantries and gathered in a cozy corner to talk shop, out of easy earshot.

"Beastly news," Makrov said in his broadest English. "That accident—if that's what it was—of your Arch fellow. He was assigned to eavesdrop on the Chinese Embassy, along with my man Voshkov. Am I right, Sir Malcolm?"

"Yes. Has Voshkov told your people anything that would shed light on the situation?"

"No. He reported that it was an uneventful night. He left early, but says that he heard nothing of value—if he's telling the truth."

"Can't you trust your own man?" Davidson asked.

Sergei laughed, his jowls shaking in enjoyment. "Oh, John, where is your usual paranoia? I still say you Americans are naive. Trust? Do you think a revolution as enormous as ours—coming after seventy-five years of tyranny—could be accomplished without holdouts? I tell you this: I trust no one in my outfit except myself. Don't you know about the *falshivi*?"

"Just rumors that the KGB still has its bad boys."

"Rumors? More than that, John. They are organized and everywhere, these *false* agents. That's the meaning of *falshivi*. The *nastoyashchi*, the 'genuine' or 'trustworthy,' are the only ones I can rely on. I think you use the same word—'nashi'—in your Agency as well. But who can truly tell whom from whom?"

"I don't know about Voshkov, but I don't trust the Chinese," Davidson answered, "and I'm sure they arranged Arch's murder. He must have learned something they didn't want out."

"Really, John?" Sir Malcolm asked. "What do they have to gain?"

"Gain? Why, everything. The Chinese are the last

giant power outside the Western framework. I'm convinced they intend to replace the U.S.S.R. as the Communist leader of the future. You heard Dr. Li. They're timeless. They're waiting for the West to expire from it's own errors—excess, greed, and immorality. Then they'll step in and take over, just as we did in the U.S.S.R. Meanwhile, they're not against giving history a shove."

"But why the X-30? Why would the Chinese want to hurt the American effort on that?" Asprey asked.

"It's not only to hurt us, but to compete," answered Davidson, who had just completed an intelligence report on Chinese war technology for President Briggs. "While we focused on the U.S.S.R. all these years, the Chinese have been making enormous advances in missile and space technology. They have the H-bomb, and at least a thousand warheads on their intermediate and ICBM missiles—aimed, I must warn you, not only at Japan, Taiwan, and Singapore, but at the United States and Western Europe. And, Sergei, at Moscow as well. They've become the major arms supplier to the Third World, especially to the terrorist nations."

Davidson was reciting what his colleagues mainly knew, but had supressed in recent years. He feared the world was yielding to the concept of a supposedly calmer New World Order at the same time that the Chinese were feverishly expanding their military technology.

"They've been selling their short-range Silkworm missiles, which are much more reliable than the Soviet Scuds, to Iraq, Algeria, Tunisia, and Iran," Davidson continued. "Now, they're offering their intermediate-range ballistic missiles as well—accurate up to seven-hundred miles and easily as good as the Russian SS-20s and the Pershing missiles we've scrapped by treaty. While our nations have been disarming at a rapid rate, they've been doing exactly the opposite. Doesn't that remind you of the 1930s?"

Sergei laughed. "John, I see you haven't changed a bit. Bully for you. But what would they want with the X-30—either stopping it or getting it? Isn't its technology beyond the Chinese?"

"Don't underestimate them, Sergei. General MacArthur did during the Korean War, and we took a real beating near the Yalu River. Their science is first rate, the result of thousands of their people studying at MIT, Cal Tech, and elsewhere in the States for two decades now. The Chinese scientists are putting their energy into the military, just as you Russians did for fifty years. They've built an excellent missile program, and now they're even offering—for cash—to send other nations' satellites into space. Their aviation industry has also come of age. They've copied your MIGs, and now they're expert. If they can stop the X-30, or better still, get their hands on it, it would be a Great Leap forward—just like the one the U.S.S.R. made when they stole the A-bomb back in the 1950s. Gentlemen, don't ever talk down the Chinese. In ten years time, you'll turn around and wish you hadn't."

Silence followed Davidson's comments.

"Very interesting, John." Sir Malcolm finally spoke up. "I'm making my small contribution. I've got my two best men—Steiner and Lauder, my nashi—investigating Arch's death. I've invited them for the weekend as well. They should be up here tomorrow."

The trio split to fulfill their social obligations. Davidson went from one guest to the other, casting occasional glances at Lady Asprey, who was busy organizing the upcoming dinner. For a few moments, John spoke with Simmons, the press lord, and his dinner companion, the lovely West End actress, Alison Mason.

"So, Mr. Davidson, I understand you're a former spook," said Sir Albert. "And considering world peace, I presume you're unemployed—and happy about it all. Am I right?"

Davidson surveyed the press lord. Simmons was tall, bulky, about fifty-five, and despite his peerage, spoke with a crude accent. Davidson had heard that he was a product of the poor East End of London and carried his near-Cockney origins as a badge of honor.

"No, Sir Albert, I'd gladly retire if the world would let me. But it seems that the death of hostility has been greatly exaggerated. Not until there's a Pax Americana-Europa will there be peace. And my guess is that we're looking at another fifty or even a hundred years. If the planet survives that long."

"But the fall of the U.S.S.R. has changed things, hasn't it?" Simmons asked.

"Oh, yes—if that change is permanent, which we're still not sure of. But there are tensions everywhere, ethnic wars and new realignments, all of which keep me fully employed."

"Mr. Davidson, you seem like such a nice man for a spy. That's what they call you, isn't it?"

This comment had come from Ms. Mason, whose voice was BBC perfect, and even exaggerated for stage presence.

"What's a nice man like me doing in a job like mine? I suppose you're asking," Davidson said, rhetorically. "Well, I guess someone has to protect you privileged people and your beautiful lives. It seems I've been elected."

With that, Davidson turned and moved on to the dining room, where the guests were now assembling.

"Here, John, sit here, next to me," Lady Asprey called out. "Don't worry. Sir Malcolm won't mind," she added, reading his hesitation.

Davidson happily settled in on Lady Asprey's right.

"We have just one rule at my dinner table," Victoria Asprey announced once all the guests were seated. "There is to be no talk of politics or war or any subject that involves tension. It's bad for my complexion. We'll restrict conversation to nice things like literature, and art, and gossip. Be as raunchy as you like. But no politics, please."

Throughout the dinner, Victoria and Davidson chatted animatedly in a lighthearted vein, and as his own worries dropped away, he began to appreciate her dictum. "Delightful" was barely the word to describe her, he thought. Then, as his happiness soared toward dessert, Victoria reached beneath the table and warmly squeezed the old spy's knee.

He had survived Makrov and the Cold War, but he wasn't sure he could handle this.

"JOHN, WOULD YOU like to go for a walk on the grounds? Parts are quite beautiful."

Davidson looked up from a copy of the morning's *London Times*. He was in the sun room, where he had seated himself after breakfast Saturday morning, and was now staring up at Victoria Asprey. She was decked out in a wide-brimmed straw hat, peasant skirt, and scooped-neck blouse, and looked enchanting, he thought.

"Everyone else has gone out riding," she murmured, a touch of coquettishness in her voice, "but I can't abide that beastly sport. I'm hoping you can keep me company until they return."

The Baptist rose quickly from his wicker chair and nodded. "Oh, yes, I'd love to see the grounds. Sir Malcolm tells me they're quite historic."

The twosome left the house and started down a flag-stone path that cut through the hundred-year-old lawn, as tightly woven as any fine golf turf.

"Over there, beyond that clutch of trees," Victoria pointed, "is where the Roundheads and the Roy-als fought a pitched battle during the 1642 Civil War. We occasionally dig up some of their old guns and skeletons. The King's forces came this close to Cambridge, a Roundhead center. But since then, thank God, it's been beautifully peaceful. I can't abide violence."

As they walked and chatted, Davidson stole glances at Victoria, who looked even more stunning in the morning sun.

"The grounds are immaculate," he commented. "Not only the grass, but the shrubs and trees. Is that all your doing?"

Victoria laughed. "Oh, no, John. I've never touched a garden in my life. My interests are strictly literary and artistic. I leave all that to Sir Malcolm. He's a real flower and tree buff, you know. We have a gardener—a true horticultural specialist—but Malcolm gets as involved as possible, time permitting. He's not as obsessive as Prince Charles, but he's there whenever he can be." She paused and stared at Davidson. "How about you? Do you love beautiful things—I mean, flowers?"

Davidson blushed. Not only was Victoria delightful in face and figure, but soft of voice and laced with an unpretentious charm. If he hadn't known better, he'd have thought he was in love.

They continued their walk through the extensive grounds, which seemed to run at least a quarter mile in each direction. Parts of the place were lev-el. Others were undulating, punctuated by patches of grass, then shrubs, followed by small enclaves of trees. At the extreme end of the property, which faced a small lake, Davidson spotted a tree whose base was covered with the fallen petals of its white flowers.

Davidson bent down and picked up a handful. He had to check his surprise. The flowers were about an inch in diameter and bell-shaped. He had crossed the ocean only to find the *halesia* with its blossom of silver bells.

"What do you have there, John?" Victoria asked. "I've never really noticed this tree. The flowers are quite pretty."

"Yes, we have them in the States. They're called silver bells."

"Mary, Mary, quite contrary," Victoria answered, throwing back her head and laughing.

"Why do you say that, Victoria?" Davidson was surprised.

"Because literature is something I do know about. 'Mary, Mary, quite contrary, How does your garden grow? With silver bells and cockleshells, And pretty maids all in a row.' "

Victoria paused and smiled, again with enormous warmth.

"John, it's been passing all these years as a nursery rhyme, but historians are really not sure if it ever truly was about a garden—or a flowering tree, as you've now shown me. They believe it has historical ramifications going all the way back to Mary, Queen of Scots, who is ostensibly the 'contrary' one. But I don't think we'll ever really know the rhyme's true origin."

Victoria picked up a handful of the petals as they started back to the house. They were silent for a few minutes, then suddenly, without warning, Victoria dropped the flowers and grasped Davidson's hand in hers. He could feel his emotions surge. Without warning, she kissed him, almost passionately, on the lips.

"I hope you don't find me too forward, John, but I feel you are a *sympatico* soul—even though I can't abide politics. And how do you find me?"

Davidson paused to recover his equilibrium.

"I find you magnificent, Victoria. But also off bounds. You are, after all, the wife of my good friend. And the two of you make such a perfect couple."

Victoria was quiet for a moment. "John, you're experienced enough to know that things have a way of being different than they appear."

"In what way different?"

"Well, Sir Malcolm and I had a wonderful marriage, until I found out that he had fallen in love with his secretary—a woman twenty years his junior. And I must say, quite a beautiful and intelligent person. He refuses, or hasn't been able, to give her up."

"Then why haven't you divorced?"

"I've asked myself the same question, as has Malcolm. I suppose we've shared a long life, and despite all, we are such good friends. So we've made an arrangement. From what I understand, that was quite common in Victorian times, when divorce was scandalous. He has his mistress, and I have carte blanche to do what I want." Victoria turned silent, in seeming contemplation. "But to be honest, John, until now I haven't been interested in using my freedom."

That Saturday night, the second evening of the weekend, there was a heightened sense of gaiety at Hollow Oaks, as the guests became better acquainted. After dinner, they played charades. Guy Lauder, the theatrical director and Asprey's MI5 associate, had arrived from London garbed in a houndstooth sports jacket and ascot. He directed the game, encouraging all to throw themselves into the spirit.

When he first arrived, Lauder and Sir Malcolm had discussed the Arch "accident."

"Steiner and I went over Arch's schedule for the night," Lauder reported to Asprey. "But we could find nothing wrong. There was no conversation on the recorder—either because they got nothing out of the Chinese Embassy surveillance or because someone erased it. We interviewed everyone in the three tours of duty, but they knew nothing. Said the Chinese were being particularly closemouthed. We talked to Voshkov briefly, but he went off soon after to Moscow. His yearly leave, it seems."

"So what do you think, Guy? What's behind it all?" Asprey asked. "Davidson is convinced the X-30 scientists are being systematically murdered by a coalition of Red Chinese and hard-line Russians."

"Beats me, Sir Malcolm. But maybe Steiner has some information. Seems he picked up a clue on the recorder in the Portland Place apartment and wanted to have it scrutinized. He took it back to the Irving Theater HQ and gave it to Simpson, the audio technician. The two of them were looking it over when I left."

"So where is Steiner? Shouldn't he be here by now?" Asprey asked, his voice betraying some concern.

"Yes. Why don't I give him a call?"

The theater director checked with the London MI5 office, then reported back to Asprey just before dinner.

"I reached Simpson at home. He says Steiner left there about three hours ago. He should be here any minute."

Asprey relaxed. "Good. I'd like to know what the hell is going on."

Lauder threw himself into the charades game, prodding the self-conscious guests to become animated. He had the help of fellow thespian Alison Mason, much to the displeasure of Lord Albert, who seemed annoyed by the easy intimacy of the couple.

Davidson decided he would play spectator, as did Victoria, who discreetly grasped his hand, out of view of the others.

"John, could you please meet me on the veranda at midnight? After everyone has gone to bed?"

Davidson stammered in hesitation. " . . . Do you think we should?"

Victoria laughed in her soft way. "Oh, nothing so adolescent, John. I just want to talk. Something I should have told you before."

At midnight, Davidson, still in his formal attire, quietly slipped down the enormous Victorian mahogany staircase and walked out to the terrace, where Victoria was waiting.

"Beautiful night, isn't it, John?"

Davidson stared up at the country sky, then at Victoria. Impulses dormant since his wife's death were being awakened. With a vengeance.

"Yes, as you are, Victoria."

"Flatterer. But that's not why I asked you here. This morning, when we were talking about my arrangement with Sir Malcolm, I didn't tell you the entire story."

"Yes?"

"Just that this is nothing new. Sir Malcolm has been unfaithful for many years. His secretary is not the first. I heard it from friends and didn't want to believe it, but now—"

Victoria's sentence was suddenly suspended, interrupted by a shrill scream that pierced the night air. Davidson thought it was coming from a quadrant of the grounds a few hundred yards away. First, a loud cry, then a softer, more pitiful wail.

"Stay here!" Davidson ordered Victoria.

He raced down the flagstone path. Immediately, the lights went on in darkened bedrooms. Within seconds, Sir Malcolm and several male guests were following in Davidson's footsteps onto the darkened grounds.

Davidson arrived at the point where the screams seemed to have come from, but the lawn was dark,

barely illuminated by a quarter moon. Spotlights from
the roof of Hollow Oaks suddenly came on, flooding
the area with light.

"Over there!" Sir Malcolm, in his nightshirt, pointed
to a group of shrubs.

Davidson and the others raced over, then stood, staring
down, their faces drained.

At their feet was the body of George Steiner, dressed
in his usual Daks blue blazer. His tortoiseshell glasses
were stuck at an ungainly angle at the end of his nose.
His throat had been cut in a precise swipe. The grass
around him was stained an ugly reddish brown.

"What's this?" Asprey asked, bending down. He picked
up a sprig of white flowers that lay on Steiner's
chest.

"Mary, Mary, quite contrary . . . ," Davidson hummed.
" . . . With silver bells and . . ."

"My God, man, let's not play nursery rhymes," Asprey
shouted impatiently. "Maybe there's a chance our killer
is still on the grounds. Let's spread out and search the
property. Make sure you stay in earshot of one another.
We don't want to lose anybody else tonight."

Davidson decided to scour the ancient six-foot-high
boxwood hedges, which, like a green fence, bound the
house in from the rest of the estate. He walked some two
hundred feet along the hedges' perimeter, and was just
turning in toward the patio off the dining room when he
heard it. The rustle of a bush, as if a small animal were
trapped inside the hedge.

"Anyone there?" Davidson called out.

When there was no response, he moved quickly to a
large tree nearby and searched the ground till he found
a long, leafless twig. He picked it up and raced back to
the boxwoods, where he had heard the noise.

"Anyone in there?" Davidson repeated. His Beretta 9-
mm was now drawn and aimed at the hedge. He lifted the
twig and thrashed the bush with a series of bold strokes.

Suddenly he heard a moan, this time more human than animal.

"Stop it, damn it! I'll come out," a voice called. The accent was decidedly Eastern American. Probably Connecticut, Davidson thought.

The Baptist moved back in surprise as a tall young man, obviously in his early twenties, emerged from the bushes. His hands were raised as if he were being arrested.

"Don't shoot! I was just walking across the grounds when I heard all the yelling and—"

"And who in the hell are you?" Davidson began, then caught a glimpse of the intruder's face in the moonlight. "Why, of course, you're Tony Alcott, the Cambridge physics student. What do you know of this murder?"

"Murder?" The young man seemed stunned. "God, I know nothing. And how do you know who I am?"

"From your picture. I'm John Davidson of the American Embassy. I got it from the Cambridge people after Professor Burns drowned. We assumed you were dead too. Where have you been all this time? And what are you doing here at Hollow Oaks?"

"One question at a time, Mr. Davidson," Tony said, lowering his arms. "I came here to find you. And if you give me a chance, I'll explain everything."

18

"VOSHKOV, PLEASURE TO see you."

Colonel Arkady Tasinev welcomed his colleague into his birch-paneled office in the old KGB building on Moscow's Dzerzhinksy Square, now converted to headquarters for the MVD. "You did a wonderful job on Portland Place."

Tasinev's eyes scanned the room, as if searching for the presence of electronic bugs. "Come, Voshkov, it is a nice day. Let's make a tour of Red Square, about all that's left from our heritage. We'll talk there."

Andrei Voshkov had been called back to Russia, ostensibly on family leave, but actually to report to his "alternate" boss, Colonel Tasinev.

Tasinev, a short man who wore a fur hat indoors to disguise a balding scalp, was deputy chief of the security section of the MVD, which had incorporated most former KGB agents, border guards, and KGB police. In the formal chain of command, the old KGB spy apparatus had been placed under the Foreign Ministry. In the open table of organization, Voshkov's superior was Sergei Makrov in London, responsible for the still-active spy forces in the Western world, from Berlin to Washington, with *rezidents* in each national capital under him.

But that was the "nashi" or "genuine" remaining KGB organization. Secretly, Voshkov was one of the *falshivi*, the "false" intelligence agents whose loyalty lay with the past—with their memory of the old Communist U.S.S.R. and their hopes for its revival.

The duo left the MVD building and headed out to the paved open terrace of Russia—Red Square. Surprisingly, it had not been named for the Communist empire as many believed. The adjective "red" was derived from the word for "beautiful" in the old Slavonic language.

The Square, or *Ploshchad*, was located just outside the Kremlin, surrounded by crenellated walls joining fourteen towers built for the czars by Italian masters in the sixteenth and seventeenth centuries. The fortress, once wooden, and now mainly red brick, had been constructed on a small rise in the Russian plains in order to hold off invading hordes. Still, it had been sacked several times, first by the Mongols, then by the Great Khans of the Crimea and Central Asia, followed by the Swedish and Polish invaders of the seventeenth century. Napoleon was the last foreigner to rule its halls, though Hitler had come within seven miles.

Its most recent invasion had not been one of arms but of philosophy. With a minimum of bloodshed, the great empire had been toppled by a simple idea, that of freedom. That new revolution sickened Tasinev, who desperately longed for a return to the orderly, predictable, even more prosperous, days of Communism.

"Voshkov," he addressed the Foreign Ministry operative, "you handled that British fellow Arch nicely. After that, we decided the MI5 man Steiner had to be eliminated as well. I hope our path is finally clear."

Voshkov nodded, pleased to be garnering kudos from a leader of the anti-democratic *falshivi*. "And how is our movement progressing?"

"Very well, Voshkov. We grow every day as the democrats become weaker. We're forming a coalition of 'reds' and 'browns,' the 'reds' former Communist officials and military men who've been stripped of power . . ."

"And the browns?"

"The nationalists—what the enemy calls 'fascists.' There is the *Pamyat*, or 'Memory,' which wants a strong Greater Russia, and a return to orderly government, even a czar. Then there is 'Motherland,' and the *Soyuz*, or 'Union,' a group led by young Army colonels who were active in the old Supreme Soviet. They too, want a reborn nation. Patriots all. Voshkov, the people are suffering under democracy and warming to us each day. They've lost their pride, and that's more essential than all the so-called freedom."

"And what about Red China?" Voshkov asked his *falshivi* mentor. "Why am I protecting their interests in London?"

"Ah, they're our trump card, Voshkov." The colonel's voice turned eager. "We made a great mistake in the 1960s and '70s by not making peace with Red China. Together, with our technical skill and their masses, we could have been unbeatable. Now they are the only large Communist power left in the world, and growing stronger every day. By working covertly with Beijing, we'll be bringing strength back to the Communist cause. Then, after we regain power in Moscow, we shall have an invincible alliance with the Chinese. And you, Voshkov, are important in that scheme."

Voshkov pumped up his meager chest. "Colonel, I'm on my way back to London in a few days. I am at your command."

"Good. Be ready for instructions, by radio. They involve our British contact, 'Mary.' Be on the alert."

The two men started back across Red Square, passing the historic Spassky tower and its huge clock. Tasinev looked longingly at its summit, from which the symbol of seventy years of tyranny and glory, the giant red star, was missing.

19

"DAVIDSON, THIS IS Makrov. I need to see you right away."

The Baptist had returned to London and was in his cubbyhole at the American Embassy reading the latest issue of *The Economist* when he answered the phone. Makrov's strange British-Russian diction was laced with anxiety.

"What's up, Makrov? Why the emergency?"

"I can't talk on the phone. I'll drive around to your embassy and pick you up in front of the FDR statue in ten minutes. Be there!"

With that, the Russian hung up. Davidson had an appointment scheduled with the ambassador, but he sensed that Makrov's call was more urgent. He was waiting outside when Makrov drove up ten minutes later, tooting the horn of his Jaguar.

"OK, now what's up? And where are we going in such a damn hurry?" Davidson asked once he had gotten in on the passenger's side.

"One of my trusted nashi, Sotanov, just called me from a pay phone. He started to tell me that two men from my office—apparently *falshivi*—are the ones who drowned Professor Burns. They're holed up in a small house in East Anglia, and they're plotting another murder."

"Yes?" Davidson asked. "Who are they?"

"I asked him that, and he started by saying, 'Mary . . .'"

"Then?"

"Then the phone went dead in the middle of his sentence. I think we'd better get out there right away."

"Where?"

"I had the call traced, and it came from a phone booth in the village of Harston, not far from Cambridge."

As they traveled the sixty miles from London on the M11 motorway, Makrov gave Davidson his view of events.

"I feel in less-than-command of my own operation, Baptist. The Commonwealth idea in the old Soviet Union is not working out. Instead we're experiencing a kind of anarchy. The hard-liners are not about to lie down and die. In fact, they're mobilizing more strongly—I suppose in the hope of another coup. And with our bad economic conditions, the next one could succeed."

"Is the opposition that strong?" Davidson asked.

"Oh, yes. The *falshivi* are everywhere in the intelligence areas, and they're working hand-in-glove with the TEWU, the Red Chinese secret police. For all his smiling pretense, and his supposed cooperation with you Americans, Dr. Li is hoping we democrats in Russia fail, and our new government with us. And he's not beneath giving it a shove. Now we have this 'Mary' agent spreading death among our people. So far we can count four murders—three X-30 scientists and a British agent. Who's next?"

Makrov paused and looked imploringly at Davidson. "Do you have any idea who this 'Mary' could be?"

Davidson had been asking himself the same question.

"I don't have a clue, except . . ."

"Yes, Baptist?"

"Except I'm pretty sure it's a British national. Three of the deaths have taken place here. If you were to push me, I'd say that 'Mary' is an upper-class Englishman—of the ilk of Burgess, McClean, or Philby, and the fourth man in that old Red spy ring, Sir Anthony Blunt. He'd been one of Queen Elizabeth's aides and was kept on by the Crown even after his disloyalty was uncovered in the 1960s. All the spies were Cambridge people, which exactly fits our locale. For some peculiar reason, Communism has a strange attraction among the British upper-crust. I suppose it's a question of guilt. That kills more civilizations than warfare. This 'Mary' is probably one of them and has hired a professional hit man to boot."

"But who's paying for all this?" Makrov asked.

"My guess is the Red Chinese, or the hard-line Russians with gold the old Communist Party has stashed away in Russia and in Swiss banks. They're surely working together with your *falshivi* renegades."

The powerful Jaguar, pushing the speed limit, was soon in Harston. At the local police station, a constable took Davidson and Makrov—after they had shown their diplomatic passports—to the phone booth in question. Nothing was evident. There were no signs of struggle.

"What's our next step?" Makrov asked, his frustration showing. "I'd love to get my hands on this Mary bastard."

"So would I, but it'll take some noodling. I do have an idea. Since they're holed up in this town—and probably holding your man Sotanov as prisoner—they could be in a rented house, the same headquarters where they planned Professor Burns's murder. Let's try the estate agents."

Their first call was at McKenzie's, off the high street.

"Can I help you?" an old displaced Scotsman with briar pipe asked. "Looking for a nice summer cottage?"

"Yes," Davidson said, but quickly added that it was for later in the year. "Could we see some houses already rented? We could take over one of them when the present people leave."

The list was of four homes rented in the past few weeks. In the Jaguar, they zipped from one to the other. The first three were obviously legitimate city people, mainly from London, on short leases for holiday.

At the fourth house, a brick Victorian at the outskirts of town, they were struck by the rundown condition of the property. The trellises on the outside were broken. The ivy ran helter-skelter up the old facade. The long front windows were cracked in several places, and the flagstone walk to the door was missing several pieces, with uncut weeds growing in their place.

They mounted the porch, which was no longer on its horizontal, and entered the front door, which was ajar a few inches. The house not only looked deserted, but as they walked through the parlor, it gave off the appearance of both neglect and a hasty departure. Packing materials and empty boxes were strewn around. In the downstairs closet, they found a plaid mackinaw. Was someone still hovering about, or had they left the coat in error?

Davidson leaned toward Makrov's ear. "You go around the outside to the back and check out the rear door. Have your Mauser ready."

With that, Davidson advanced slowly up the steps, his own Beretta 9-mm semi-automatic drawn. He quivered at the creak emitted as he made contact with the first step. He moved to the edge of the circular staircase, half supporting himself on the banister to relieve stress on the aged wood. So far, so good. He had gone a third of the way up when he stopped—abruptly.

From the landing above, he heard noises, as if someone were moving about. The amorphous sounds now crystallized into voices. Two people were talking: one in broken English, the other in Mayfair tones. Quickly, Davidson grasped the edge of the banister and climbed over its side, dropping softly to the floor, where he lay prone, out of sight of anyone above.

Within seconds, the two men rushed down the stairs. Peeking out, Davidson could see their backs and drawn guns.

"Did you hear that?" the Englishman asked the other. "First I heard a squeak, then a thud."

"Maybe you imagined it," the other man, whose voice was tinged with an Oriental flavor, responded. "But we've got to get out quick. They've been to the police, and could be coming here now."

Davidson waited until the two men had left by the front door. He started back up the stairs, but halted abruptly midway. Two gunshots filled the air, followed by the roar of an accelerating car. He raced to the landing and opened the window.

"Makrov," he shouted, spotting the Russian in the rear just below the window. "Get after them, quick!"

Davidson turned rapidly, running to the front door, where Makrov had already come around.

"Whose shots were those?" Davidson asked, his eyes scanning the scene. He was answered by the sound of a small Ford racing away from the house. "Let's follow them."

Makrov's face drained. "Oh, look at that, Baptist. We're not going anywhere. They've shot out two of my tires."

They reentered the house and mounted the stairs together, Davidson in front, gun still drawn.

"When we hit the landing, you go left," Davidson instructed. "I'll take the right corridor."

On the landing, the two past-their-prime intelligence men moved like athletes through the cavernous house, racing down the long halls, kicking in doors, then immediately pressing themselves protectively against the outside walls before peering in. One at a time, they covered the eight bedrooms and baths. Davidson was advancing on the last bedroom, apparently a maid's chamber, when he saw Makrov enter the hallway, his arms out and palms up, the international symbol of frustration.

Davidson signaled for silence, then pushed in the door. He advanced through the small, bare bedroom, then into the bath.

"Makrov!" Davidson screamed.

The Russian came running, halting at the threshold. The two men advanced to the bathtub, then recoiled. There, floating facedown in the reddish water, was the body of a man. Makrov moved forward and twisted the figure faceup. A sharp, now bloodless, bullet hole punctuated his forehead.

"My God, John, it's my man Sotanov. The bastards have killed him."

Makrov nudged Davidson's elbow. "Over there, John, look."

Davidson turned toward the sink. On the bathroom mirror, shaving cream had been sprayed into a legible message: BAPTIST. HOW DOES YOUR GARDEN GROW?

Davidson swiveled back to the tub, where his eyes caught the second symbolic message, which he had missed. Floating on the surface of the water were two sprigs of white silver bells.

"Let's get to the police right away, Sergei," Davidson said, then paused. "Oh, I forgot about the car. The phone's not working either. I tried it in one of the bedrooms. That means a walk back to town, or a neighbor's phone. Let's go."

As they left the house and were approaching the disabled Jaguar, Davidson saw a car turn the corner with abnormal speed.

"Hit the deck! Down!" he shouted.

Davidson leapt toward the Jaguar, pressing Makrov in front of him. The maneuver was just in time. As the small Ford raced by, the sound of automatic gunfire filled the quiet street. Davidson grimaced as Makrov pressed protectively closer, the scent of the Russian's

French cologne overwhelming.

In a few seconds, the gun bursts had ended. From his vantage, Davidson could see the Ford exiting the street. Unfortunately, the license plate was only a blur.

"Well, Davidson, you saved this old *rezident*'s life. How do I repay you?"

Davidson smiled at his one-time adversary.

"Sergei, just remember that the next time—especially if we end up on opposite sides of the fence again."

"THAT'S THE WAY it stands, Tony."

On his return from Harston, Davidson filled in young Alcott on the geopolitical puzzle that had resulted in five deaths to date. Tony's own would have made it six, if he hadn't survived the drowning attempt on the Cam.

"As I told you, I want to help out, Mr. Davidson. I have no experience, but I'll do what I can—if you want. I've spent the days in my hotel room, trying to reconstruct what I saw on Professor Burns's computer. My diagrams, from memory, are still crude, but I'm going to keep at it. It's coming back to me a little at a time."

"Good. Do you have enough money to stay in London and continue to work on it?"

"Not really. I probably could get a job as a physicist, or go back to school at Cambridge, but I can't afford to stay here in London at a hotel, even this dump, and do this."

Davidson entered a short trance.

"OK, Tony. On my own, I'm going to commit some of the government's money. We'll put you up at the Lancaster Hotel—it's not too expensive. I'll include you on my expense account for now. Then I'll get you on the Agency budget, and clear it with the President."

"The President?" The young man was astounded. "Do you actually talk to him?"

"I'm afraid so, Tony. Now, you get to work, and I'll have the embassy pick up your hotel tab. Just sign for your meals." Davidson opened his wallet. "Here's fifty pounds for walking-around money. Get to work and strain that good head of yours. Try to remember everything you saw on Burns's supercomputer. And be careful."

Alcott found the next week somewhat dull, but challenging. He enjoyed the luxury of the hotel, especially signing for meals. He made sure he wasn't underfed.

There was no magical breakthrough in his memory, but each recalled item on the X-30 design led to another, not unlike the fortuitous chain of a child's puzzle. He kept in touch with Davidson, advising him on his progress.

For diversion, he did little but watch BBC television, and occasionally sit in the small hotel lounge, decorated in Edwardian style.

It was there, one Monday evening, while he was reading the *London Times*, that his eye was caught by the sight of an attractive woman seated opposite him. He had forgotten that all his energies had been wrapped up in physics. Tentatively, he smiled at her. She was seated, immobile, with her hands folded in her lap, like a schoolgirl, which made her all the more appealing.

She was staring ahead, partly at him, it seemed, and

off into space at the same time. Her clothes were tasteful; in fact, she seemed to belong to another generation. She wore a brown tweed suit over a discreet tailored white silk blouse. She was ladylike, looked intelligent—and sexy. Since she was seated, he couldn't tell her height. But judging from her long legs, stockinged in silk and mostly exposed as her skirt rose, she was taller than average.

The woman was not pure English. He could tell that at a flash. But as he studied her face for racial, or ethnic, clues, hoping she wouldn't object to the obvious scrutiny, he remained mystified. Occasionally his eye caught hers, and she smiled, very slightly. Not quite inviting, but not hostile. The eyes? Yes, there was a hint of vulnerability in them. They were unusual: iridescent blue, but less than rounded. In fact, they showed a hint of the Orient. He was no ethnic detective (as was Davidson, he who could tell a Czech from a Frenchman at thirty paces) but he had reached a conclusion. The woman was at least a quarter Oriental—Chinese, Korean, or Japanese. The rest was some form of European. He guessed English.

The more Tony studied her, the more intrigued he became. He noticed a full bust pushing up against the suit, and even a hint of strong thighs hidden by the thin woolen skirt. Her hair was long, soft, and black, her complexion strangely white, almost ghostly. Did that destroy his theory of Oriental blood? Or was it merely a layer of chalky makeup?

He was caught up in the puzzle, and increasingly intrigued by what he decided was an exceptional beauty. Not that of a screen star, but a quiet beauty, enhanced by extraordinarily intelligent eyes.

Unfortunately, she was obviously waiting for someone, and it wasn't him. Tony continued to read the *Times,* with an occasional unsubtle glance at his Eurasian—if that's what she was—beauty. After ten minutes, her patience

seemed to dissolve. She began checking her watch. At
least twice, she got up and walked toward the front door
of the establishment, only to return. She seemed more
annoyed than bored.

"Damn," he heard her mutter after a half hour of
waiting.

Tony felt bold. What could he lose? He was getting
tired of nothing but physics and television. Maybe she'd
share a drink with him while she waited.

"Excuse me, miss," he said after a tentative cough as
he approached. "I couldn't help but notice that you've
been waiting—unsuccessfully—for someone. Maybe I
could help break the monotony. Could you join me in
a drink? As soon as your guest arrives, I'll disappear
just as I appeared. Magically. OK?"

He waited. The young woman tilted her head up toward
his. Her expression was unrevealing. She stared at him
for a full ten seconds, then allowed herself the smallest
of smiles.

"You are nervy, I must say," the woman began. "My
escort has a habit of being late. Though I appreciate
your solicitude"—now her voice displayed a touch of
sarcasm—"I think I can wait another ten minutes without
company. That is if you don't mind."

Surely a rebuff, Tony thought. But he continued the
quest.

"I understand your reluctance to talk to strangers.
That's a smart policy for a beautiful young woman.
But let me introduce myself. I'm Tony Alcott, from the
States—Connecticut to be exact. I'm a doctoral candi-
date in physics at Cambridge, and I'm here in London
for a week while I do some work for the home secretary.
Perhaps we could wait out your ten minutes together. As
the encyclopedia salesmen say—'No obligation.' OK?"

This time he got the desired response. First she stared,
her expression neutral. Then she broke into a broad
smile.

"You are *very* nervy, Mr. Alcott. But perhaps you're right. I'm not the most patient person. In a few more minutes, I'll be biting my manicured nails. All right, let's get a drink—I'd like some iced tea—and we can talk until my escort arrives. I'll give him twenty minutes, then I'll assume he's not coming. He's not the most reliable person I know."

Tony was elated. What a wonderful break in his routine. The couple were soon seated at a cozy table, exchanging CVs. Her name was Tina Waltham, from St. John's Wood, near Regent's Park. She had originally come from Hong Kong, and yes, her grandmother was Chinese. The rest of her heritage was English. He was pleased, and surprised, by her background. She was a botanist by training, but was now in the wholesale flower business. He offered his own, less exotic background, and she kept asking questions about America. Surprisingly, she had never been there.

The twenty minutes passed, and still no escort had shown.

"I think I'll go home to my flat, Mr. Alcott. But I want to thank you for passing the time with me. Not only are you nervy, but you're very nice. At least that's the impression you give. Is it true?"

Tony laughed. "I'm even nicer in real life. May I take you home by cab?"

He watched her face as she considered the offer. As he waited, he felt the same emotions as some-one drawing to an inside straight. He was no longer just curious. He had been raised on imma-ture and/or tough American women, and turned off by the bookishness of Cambridge bluestockings. Now, faced with a woman whose sensuality was overwhelming, he prayed this would not be the end of it.

What about Burns's work? For now, that could go to hell. His pulsating loins had taken over. What was that old saw about the stiffness of passion having no conscience?

"Mr. Alcott, I'd be honored if you'd take me home. But can a physics student pay the cab fare?" She laughed and gave him a soft peck on his cheek.

He feared his exhilaration was showing. Women, he found, liked their men hot, but outwardly restrained: the bandit-gentleman. He'd play the role for her. In fact, he'd play any role.

Tina lived in one of the large modern apartment houses facing Regent's Park. Her flat was on the ground floor, with a garden patio in the rear. He didn't have to ask her if he could come in. She just opened the door and graciously waved him ahead of her.

They sat and watched the television for about twenty minutes. Tony was so aroused that he had to hide his feelings, and more. But her sweet, secure smile made him realize he was fooling no one. The couch soon turned into an arena for lovemaking. Tony caressed her breasts through the silk. His hands madly explored her thighs as his mouth searched out hers.

"Tony, Tony. Easy. You're mussing me up. Hold off, and I'll be back better prepared for your aggression. You told me you're an athlete. We shall see."

Alcott waited, now past the point of no return. Ms. Waltham's beauty had captured his senses, and he hoped—really prayed—that she was ready for more.

Three interminable minutes passed before Tina returned to the living room. She still wore her high heels, but otherwise she was naked. Her hair, which had appeared to be shoulder length, was no longer tied up. It cascaded down until he could see the ends peeking out from behind her hips. She caught his eye surveying her, then quickly swiveled in place. From that angle, he could see that her hair reached to the edge of her bare buttocks.

"I'm a little embarrassed, Tony. I don't usually parade

my body, but I thought you—above all—would like to see me in the altogether. I'm really flattered by a fan like you. Every woman likes to be considered beautiful, and you look most appreciative. Am I right?"

When Tony nodded, once, then twice, she turned in slow sinuous circles until every millimeter of her white skin had been exposed several times. She lowered her half-Oriental lids and smiled—elegantly.

Alcott just stared, his eyes dazzled by the sight. She was taller than he had thought. Her legs were also longer and were now spread apart defiantly in imitation of a fashion model. Her pubic hair was jet black, a massive forest of intrigue. Her breasts were full, perfect and upright, as if the bra she had taken off were an unnecessary accoutrement.

He advanced toward her, tentatively, half expecting the vision to vanish. As he approached, Tina suddenly turned so that her rear faced him. She bent slowly, as if bowing to invisible gods, until her soft genitals were fully exposed.

"Would you like to start here, Tony? I like it that way."

Alcott moved toward her, fearful his heart wouldn't hold out. No sculling contest had ever sparked him so emotionally. He reached his fingers toward her buttocks, and for the confluence between them.

"Tina, you're so beautiful," Alcott murmured, then prepared for the test of his life.

21

"BAPTIST!"

It was Makrov shouting on the telephone, shattering Davidson's equanimity.

"Yes, Makrov," Davidson said sotto voce in contrast. "What can I do for you?"

"Meet me at The Turk's Head pub. I have great news."

The Turk's Head, along with The Antelope, was London's poshest watering hole. Situated in Belgravia, that select quarter that housed more aristocracy and money than any other locale in the U.K., the pub had once been the gathering place for English intellectuals and wits. Today it was the hangout of upper-class youths, more knowledgeable about the Who rock group than the why of civilization.

"So what's the news?" Davidson asked when they met over a pint.

"It's right here, Baptist." The Russian leaned across the small booth and handed Davidson a large padded envelope. "See what's inside."

Davidson pulled open the package and took out two black plastic discs.

"Yes, Baptist, they're the ones—the hard discs stolen from Burns's supercomputer at Cambridge. Apparently the same people who killed the professor had stolen them."

"My God, Makrov, this is some find. Where did you get it?"

"After we left, I sent two trusted men back to Harston. They worked with the local police and virtually tore the rented house apart. The discs were under a floorboard, under the linoleum, in the bathroom. Quite a present, eh? Maybe now we can get X-30 to fly? No?"

Davidson smiled in appreciation, then grimaced at Makrov's lapse into Russian linguistic structure, in which there was no definite article. "I go to store," Russians said, and Makrov had said "get X-30" without the "the." This surprised Davidson. Except for that occasional error, his English was impeccable.

"Such a waste," Makrov was fond of saying. "Who needs a 'the'? And French is even worse, with *la* and *le*." Then he would smile. "But of course, maybe that's the secret of the West. Foolish subtleties that make no sense."

"In any case, Sergei," Davidson said, handling the discs. "This is absolutely wonderful. I'll get them right off to our wind-tunnel people in Arizona. Maybe with some new calculations and tests, they'll be able to take the scramjet up to Mach 20, maybe even 25."

In the Arizona desert, the arrival of Burns's hard discs was exhilarating news. The murdered scientist's earlier calculations had taken them so far, but his death had virtually stopped progress on the super-Mach tests at the giant facility.

Now the crunch had come. They had to convert Burns's equations into nozzles, valves, and parts that would allow the liquid-hydrogen engine to function in especially thin atmospheres, at temperatures in excess of 20,000 degrees, and speeds in excess of Mach 20. That done, the X-30 could fly into space under its own power.

Jack Langer had the contents of the discs printed out and the information fed to his project leaders. If Burns had fixed the error, the full-size scramjet would "fly" at Mach 25.

The design changes took a week. On the appointed

morning, Langer stood in the control booth of the world's most powerful wind tunnel. The 400-megawatt arc jet, the centerpiece of the facility, was waiting to fire up. At his order, it would create the man-made lightning that would bring the engine heat up past the 20,000 degrees needed to simulate flight at 300,000 feet altitude. In the last test, they had reached Mach 14 before the engine faltered. Now they would try for Mach 20, then 25.

"OK, fellows, steady as we go," Langer called. "Nine, eight, seven, six, five, four, three, two, one. Fire!"

As the arc jet spewed out its hot bolt, the scramjet roared through the simulated heavens—Mach 12 at 200,000 feet; Mach 14 at 250,000 feet; stretching for Mach 25 at 300,000 feet. Then, once more, it happened. Langer wiped his brow as the engine began to fire in irregular rhythms, then sputtered and shut down, just as it had before.

"Damn it!" Langer called over the intercom. How in the hell, he thought, was it possible for Burns to make the same mistake twice—especially since the second time he was safely in the other world?

DAVIDSON FELT BOTH at home and awkward at Hollow Oaks. He was at home because of the longtime friendship with Sir Malcolm and their current work together; awkward, because of his attraction to Asprey's wife, Victoria—and her obvious reciprocation.

"John, so good to see you," Victoria said. "You look

a little peaked. Too much worry for someone your age, I venture. Why you and Malcolm want to get involved in such a ridiculous and dangerous business is beyond me. What beauty is there in politics or espionage? Seems more like an excuse for grown men to engage in little boy games. Am I right?"

Sir Malcolm and Davidson laughed.

"Who knows? The reality of war and intelligence work has always been with us," Davidson said, "but on the other hand, maybe that's all part of the male biology, boys' games played out by adults. In which case, we are hopeless. You may be right, Victoria, but there seems to be no alternative."

"I don't know about that, John," Victoria responded. "I prefer to paint and read, and Malcolm prefers to garden. Maybe your trouble is that you have no hobbies. In any case, I'll leave you boys to your meanderings. I have a date with a romantic novel."

Victoria gave her husband a hug, then pressed her lips strongly into Davidson's cheek. "Cheerio!" she lilted.

The two men were left alone in the red-walled library, a room out of the nineteenth century, with English pine bookcases, a faded, frayed Oriental rug, a tan leather chesterfield, and sporting prints galore.

"A brandy, John?"

Davidson nodded, and the men sipped as they talked.

"Do you have any thoughts about who Mary could be?" Davidson asked. "All is not going well, you know. I presume you've heard about Burns's discs failing in the Arizona test. Frankly, I'm getting worried."

Asprey looked out the large garden window and shook his head in contemplation.

"Yes, I've heard. And I'm trying to narrow the field a little, but it's not easy. Remember the party we had here? Well, virtually everyone I invited, even Viscount Hampshire, is a suspect as far as I can make out.

That's why I brought them together. That includes John Acroft, the MP; the writer Dave Goodman; press lord Sir Albert Simmons; even Antony Riddle, the Conservative MP. Some of them had longtime flirtations with the U.S.S.R., which was a common affliction here. Now I'm worried that they've shifted allegiance to Red China, which could become as large a problem as the U.S.S.R. It seems there's no end to controversy in the world—and just when we thought there would be a Pax Americana."

Asprey halted, then suddenly switched thoughts. "We might also be dealing with some leftover Soviet illegals."

"Soviet illegals in Britain?" Davidson asked. "Do you think they're still active? I'd think they'd have been defused once the U.S.S.R. went out of business."

"Yes, so would I. But the Russians had at least four hundred planted over the years, all with faked British ancestries and papers. Some have become highly respectable, with important jobs. Of course, no one knows their true backgrounds. They might miss the regular money they were getting, and maybe they've secretly taken up with the *falshivi*, or even the Red Chinese. That's where the new cash for espionage is coming from."

Davidson smiled his agreement. "And how about Guy Lauder? Is he reliable?"

"Yes, John, as good as gold." He paused.

"And how about Alison Mason, the actress? Is she a loyal subject of the Crown?"

The British intelligence man turned away from the window and stared at Davidson. "We think so, but why do you ask, John?"

"Just a small thing, but it's gotten me thinking. I have some men trailing all your suspects. They recently saw her arm in arm with Antony Riddle, the MP. I thought she was Simmons's girl."

Asprey pursed his lips in surprise. "Really?" Quickly, he seemed to change the subject. "Are you feeling any great pressure yet from the White House?"

Davidson shook his head disconsolately. "So far, just some subtle words from the President. But I feel it in my bones. All hell is about to break loose."

23

ALISON MASON FELT enriched by her contacts in the political world of the United Kingdom. It wasn't just her fame as a legitimate theater actress (her newest play, *Lady of Chelsea*, was playing to packed houses in the West End), but also her friendship with both Sir Albert Simmons, the press magnate, and Sir Malcolm Asprey, ostensibly a Ministry of Defense official, who, everyone whispered, was really a top agent at MI5.

As a poor girl growing up near the Elephant & Castle, and whose proper Mayfair accent came strictly out of the Royal Academy of Dramatic Art, Alison Mason (born Meg Thimble), was still in awe of the rich history of the nation, especially the workings of Parliament. Today, she was making her first personal visit to the House, escorted by none other than the prominent Conservative MP Antony Riddle.

A tall, angular man in his forties, Riddle picked Mason up at her elegant flat on Harley Street in Mayfair. She opened the door to what seemed like an apparition from the past. He was dressed in the ultra-formal style of Neville Chamberlain, wearing wide chalk-striped flannels and an antique wing collar and narrow black tie.

"I'm really looking forward to the tour," confessed
Alison, who was obviously excited at the prospect of
seeing Parliament in the company of an MP. Riddle
was a bit stiff, but a pleasant man, she had found.
More important, he had a particularly good brain, if she
was any judge, and she thought she was. The American,
John Davidson, for one, struck her as brilliant. When, at
another country weekend, she had attacked the common
practice of IQ testing, someone protested: "But then how
would we know who is and who is not intelligent?"
Alison didn't mean it as a put-down but it came out
that way: "Intelligent people have no trouble discerning
the trait in others," she had answered.

Before she made the "date" with Riddle, Alison had
read up on his CV, dug out of the library morgue of
Simmons's left-wing daily newspaper. Checking up on
people, she admitted, was one of her more paranoid habits. Alison claimed it stemmed from a desire to learn the
truth about parvenus who sidled up to her only because of
her fame. Riddle obviously didn't fall into that category,
but she thought it best to know his background anyway.

Strangely, Riddle's biography began at age twenty-
two, when he entered Oxford as a student of political
science. It made no mention of his birth, or his parents,
or his early schooling, but was full of detail of his life
since: researcher for an MP after graduation, then a Tory
party hack working in the organization, then finally a
candidate. At the age of thirty-three, he entered Parliament, and he was now—insiders gossiped—a candidate
for a ministerial post, probably in the Foreign Office.

The bio held no mystery except that one: where and
what was he before he was twenty-two? Alison's devil-
ish curiosity was working overtime. She'd try to worm
something out of him today.

In his Range Rover on the way over to Parliament,
they chatted animatedly.

"So, will your colleagues mind having a simpleminded actress bothering them during their deliberations?" Alison asked.

Riddle laughed, exaggerating his already broad upper-class accent. In fact, it was so impeccable—even broader than that of the Prince of Wales—that for a moment she got the odd impression that Riddle had learned English as a second language. His was not unlike the supra-perfect diction of the late actor Richard Burton, who had spoken only Welsh as a boy. But of course, she finally reasoned, that was nonsense.

The day went beautifully. Alison met with Riddle's colleagues and was even introduced to the Prime Minister.

"Miss Mason," the PM cooed. "I've just seen you on the stage in the West End, and you're even more beautiful in person!"

She smiled, thrilled, and was reminded how much more diplomatic, if not brighter, than other people politicians were.

As she walked through the sacred halls while Riddle gave her a running historical commentary, Alison subtly probed for information.

"Antony, you speak so beautifully," she commented. "Was it Eton or Harrow before you went up to Oxford? Does that account for it? Or were you to the manner born? Perhaps the second son of an earl?" She laughed.

"No, nothing so glamorous. Just a simple grammar school background in the south."

That's all he said.

Once the session was opened by the bewigged Speaker, she watched as Riddle rose to speak on the hotly debated issue of immigration.

"Hear, hear," his Tory colleagues shouted in agreement as Riddle opposed what he called "suffocating immigration" into England. Meanwhile the Labour Party members shouted their opposition, including one resounding call of "Fascist!"

"That wounded me," Riddle told Alison on the way home to her flat. "I've always been concerned about working people. It's just that foreigners are taking the jobs of our own people."

Alison smiled and agreed. But as he spoke, she couldn't help but concentrate on the cadences of Riddle's diction. What was it that kept coming into her mind? Somehow this defender of the native-born Britons seemed to be, in some strange way, a foreigner himself.

24

"MISS, COULD I see copies of a few horticulture magazines?" Davidson asked the clerk in the reading room at the British Museum.

He was in the very place where Karl Marx had researched *Das Kapital*, the document that had, not so indirectly, set Davidson on a lifetime of intelligence work.

"Certainly. We have about a dozen of them. Which would you like?"

"I'd like one of each, just to peruse. Is that all right?"

"Yes. Find a desk and we'll call you when they're ready."

Within fifteen minutes, Davidson had an assortment of periodicals spread out before him. Could they make a green-thumb scholar out of a hopeless gardener? He browsed quickly through each, settling on one impressive trade publication, *The Horticulture Week*, formerly *The Gardener's Chronicle*. First published in 1841, it had the solid look of the English countryside in its pages.

This excursion into horticulture had begun earlier that morning in a series of "thought experiments" Davidson had conducted in his small cubbyhole at the American Embassy on Grosvenor Square.

Placing his feet up on the desk with a Churchill biography in front of him, he had reached the point in the late 1930s when the old Tory war-horse was being rebuffed by Parliament because of his "warlike" attitude toward Adolf Hitler, a stance that was later to bring him immortality.

By reading—and moving his mind away from his present concerns—Davidson had found that he could sometimes make a breakthrough in reasoning.

As he read, he pondered his dilemma. The hard discs Makrov had found in Harston hadn't worked out. Either it was because Burns had made another mistake, or the *falshivi* in the Russian Embassy had set Makrov and him up for a supercomputer sting.

Who was handling this whole X-30 operation on the other side? The Red Chinese—particularly Dr. Li Chen of the TEWU—had the most to gain by stopping, or securing, the technology of the X-30, a feather in their burgeoning aerospace cap. Davidson had frankly been surprised by the growth in their missile business, as well as by their international military traffic for hard currency.

Allied with Dr. Li were undoubtedly the *falshivi* operating out of the Russian Embassy in London. Their local coordinator was the elusive "Mary," but Davidson doubted if such an exalted agent would risk dirty hands. The weakest link in that chain was surely the executioner, a versatile hit man who had already taken five lives.

What leads did he have? Only a nursery rhyme and some sprigs of *halesia*, the silver bells.

He turned it over. The killer was probably the least circumspect of all those involved. In fact, the inflated ego that forced him to leave his calling card in half scanned lines from the nursery rhyme, or a sprig of white flowers, made him vulnerable. But only if Davidson could find a way to connect the leads to the hit man.

Though Davidson had little interest in horticulture, he had to assume that the killer was an amateur gardener, if not a professional.

Davidson put down the Churchill bio. He picked up his jacket and headed out of the Grosvenor Square embassy, for the Underground, or, as Londoners prefer, "the Tube." At the familiar red circle, he descended. After one change, he got off at the Russell Square station, close to his destination, the British Museum.

Now seated at a cozily lighted desk in the reading room of the museum, in the midst of seven million volumes, Davidson was carefully examining *The Horticulture Week*. After articles on crossbreeding, including one on the search for the "True Blue Rose," and wads of ads, he scanned the notices of upcoming exhibitions. One caught his attention: a horticulture show right outside Cambridge, the site of so much activity in the still-clouded case.

It was scheduled for next Saturday. Davidson decided he would buy a pair of walking boots and a smart woolen cap. With his perennial gray tweeds, he might even fool the locals into believing that he was truly a country squire in love with English gardens.

The red-and-white "HORTICULTURE SHOW" banner waved over the fairgrounds, the empty land between a local cemetery and the sixteenth-century Anglican Church of St. John the Lesser.

Davidson paid his two-pound admission, picked up a

catalogue, and started through the maze of booths, not knowing what to expect or who to look for. It was an excursion in serendipity, which he had learned was often as important as reasoned investigation.

This was not the first garden show of his life. His late wife had been a born digger. Though he didn't enjoy gardening himself, he had appreciated her smile of gratification when she picked a full pound tomato off the vine.

Davidson went from booth to booth, his eyes serving two causes. The first was to learn something about horticulture; he even took in a quick lesson in grafting fruit trees. The second was to keep his senses keyed to the area, always searching.

About forty minutes into the fair, he found a target. Standing outside a booth perhaps a hundred feet away were two faces he recognized. He decided to keep his distance and observe. One was Guy Lauder, the West End theater director and MI5 aide to Asprey. As usual, he was dressed casually in a sports jacket, checked shirt, and mismatched tie. His honey-colored hair, long on all sides, was almost tucked into his back collar. With him was Alison Mason, the tall, attractive blond actress, perhaps five years his senior. The two were cozily close, their hands entwined. At Hollow Oaks, Davidson had thought she and Sir Albert Simmons were a twosome. But one never knew.

What was Lauder's interest in the show? Horticulture? Or had Asprey sent him there on a lead of his own?

Davidson moved in the opposite direction and was studying a dwarf bamboo plant when he heard it.

The announcement came over the loudspeaker, like a declaration of war.

"Attention everyone. A two-year-old child is lost. We are going to search the adjoining woods behind the grounds. Volunteers, please line up, twenty feet apart.

Thank you. We will suspend the show and start the search immediately."

Davidson dropped the potted plant and raced to the search starting line. The sun was waning a bit in this late afternoon, but there was still light enough to see, except—he noted as he squinted ahead—in the darkest part of the woods.

"All right, at the starter gun signal, everyone advance and beat the bushes."

Davidson stayed up with the group, occasionally glancing to his left and right to maintain contact. The area was deeper than he had thought, and as he advanced, the forest thickened. Here, no more than fifteen miles from Cambridge, he had walked into what surprisingly resembled a primeval scene. The light from above was growing fainter, the air more humid. After twenty minutes, he looked to his sides and realized he had lost contact with the others. He wasn't exactly disoriented, for the sun was peeking through at the far right and he could retrace his steps. But he was undecided. Should he try to find the others, or continue on his now-lone pursuit for the missing infant?

"Ooowww." He heard a soft moan, either that of an animal or a child. Davidson listened, as if honing in on radar, and moved toward the sound, picking up his pace as it got louder.

It seemed to be coming from behind a low-branched tree with a stout trunk. Davidson's step was now resolute. Had serendipity come to his rescue—if not in leading to the killer, at least in an errand of mercy?

He approached right up to the tree and was starting to circle its trunk when he felt it. A hand came like a swift snake and wrapped itself around his neck.

"No nonsense now, Davidson. I have a gun in your back."

In that instant of fear, the Baptist reflected how readily he had entered Mary's trap. The voice was decidedly

British, with the slight inflection of East Anglia, educated, upper middle class, and high-pitched, though not
feminine. Apparently he had come, not-face-to-face but
back-to-front, with the killer he had been seeking. Only
now, the advantage was not his.

"You've been a nuisance, Baptist. So I suppose you'll
have to resign yourself to sixth place in the elimination
contest."

The man with the gun gave out a small chortle. "Meet
your maker, Davidson. Mary sends her love."

The sound of the gunshot was like an artillery barrage
against the silence of the forest. Davidson first jumped
at the retort, having said his own last unction, then fell
to the ground, the timpani reverberating like a series of
drums in his ear. From the corner of his eye, he could
see a tall shadow, gun in hand, flee into the depths of
the forest. His hand searched for his wound, tracing his
neck and back for the expected torrent of blood.

"Don't bother yourself, Mr. Davidson. You'll find
nothing there."

He stared up. Standing over him was a woman. He
squinted in the near dark. She was blond and smartly
dressed in a plaid woolen suit, with a small beret on
her head.

"Yes, it's me. Let me give you a hand up."

On his feet, Davidson stared at Alison Mason, West
End actress, her outstretched fingers still holding a smok-
ing lady's-size, double-barreled derringer, appropriately
sided in mother-of-pearl.

"I only shot in the air to disrupt his rhythm," she
apologized. "Had I fired at him, I might have hit you
instead. The second one would have been my desperation shot."

For all his savoir faire, Davidson stood openmouthed,
hardly understanding the swift flow of events.

"But how . . . ?" The question finished itself.

Mason laughed. "How? Simple. As should be obvious,

I'm working with Guy Lauder for Sir Malcolm in MI5. And how did I get here in time? Well, we spotted you puttering about in the garden booths. When the lost child announcement came over the loudspeaker, I had a hunch that perhaps it was a lure to attract you into the woods. We're all vulnerable these days."

"And where is Lauder?"

"Oh, he finked out. Not the woodsy or robust type, you know. Lets this fragile woman do much of that work. I followed close behind you, and became alert when you veered from the main group."

"Did you see my assailant? He's the one with the killing streak, the hit man for Mary."

"I caught only a fleeting glimpse in the half dark. Could only make out that he was tall, with a gaunt face. Do you have any other clues?"

"Perhaps. He said a few sentences, and I could tell he was local, and educated. I also think he was disguising his voice a little—had made it higher-pitched. But it's something. I might be able to recognize it again. And . . ."

"Yes, Mr. Davidson?"

"Thank you, Miss Mason. I'd like to finish this case before I go anywhere. You were most intrepid." He leaned over and kissed the young woman on her cheek.

"Good." Alison smiled, taking Davidson's arm in hers. "Shall we return to Mr. Lauder? He might be worried about my safety."

She laughed as they moved back through the English woods, surely an incongruous pair of intelligence professionals.

25

TONY ALCOTT COULDN'T believe his luck. His work on reconstructing the X-30 material stolen from Dr. Burns was coming along. Not perfectly, for he had been careful—for security reasons—not to take notes when he was hacking through the supercomputer files at Cambridge.

But mostly he was lucky because Tina, his part-Oriental lover, had wandered into his life, willy-nilly. Bar pickups were supposed to be disastrous, but this one had defied all the rules. She was smart, loving, and an amateur athlete in bed. No, he wouldn't say that she was a nympho. But she did seem as eager for sex as he was, which was an accomplishment in itself.

"What is it that you do all day long while I'm at work, grinding my nerves at the wholesale flower market? Don't you go absolutely mad in this hotel room?"

Their usual rendezvous was Tina's apartment in the Regent's Park area, but tonight she had come to his hotel room in central London for the first time.

He had resisted the idea, but she had started to cry, claiming he wanted her only like a call girl, in her abode, and not as a lover in his own home. "If you want to get laid tonight, darling, it'll have to be in your bed." Quickly, she had won that argument.

As soon as Tina asked the question about what he did with his time, she spotted the computer on a small makeshift desk, surrounded by manuals and books.

"Oh, I have my answer. You told me you were a physics whiz. So I suppose that's how you spend your time, playing with the computer. Am I right?"

Tony laughed. There was something so direct, so simple about her personality that it thrilled him. Unlike other woman he had met, she seemed without complications, without connivance, without calculation. What entered her mind came out her mouth, and she seemed to hold, or have, nothing in reserve. He found the directness refreshing.

"Yes, I'm playing around with a small project for the Home Secretary. Nothing really important, but it does keep me busy."

Tony felt a touch of unease as Tina shuffled through the printouts on his desk.

"What have we here?" Her voice had a lilt. "Something to do with airplanes?" She fondled a computer diagram of the X-30, then held it up to the light. "Or is it a spaceship?"

Tony raced over to his desk. "Here, give me that. That's not for your eyes—or anyone else's!"

She handed him the paper sheepishly. "Sorry, darling. I had no idea you were such a big shot. I'll never peek again."

Tony apologized for his temper outburst. "Let's forget it, and get down to real work."

The couple spent the evening in lighter pursuits, preferring to stay at the hotel. They played a game of whist, then watched the BBC on the telly, before Tina leaned over and casually massaged Tony.

"Oh, now things are getting interesting," she murmured, pushing her breasts against him. "Come on, let's see your real manhood."

In bed, Tony couldn't restrain himself, exploring every inch of her firm, naked body as first she mounted him, then rolled over onto her knees, raising her nude buttocks up in the air again, her long hair hiding all but the vital parts. The sight tantalized him.

"This way in," she whispered, "through the warm back door. OK?" Tina moaned as Tony, slowly, softly, but resolutely obliged her.

"Just right, darling." She laughed. "Let the festivities begin."

The festivities were better than ever, he felt sure, and lasted almost an hour. Afterward, they turned over, and still joined, the exhausted lovers slept.

"Oh, my God, it's late," Tina said, startled as the morning sunlight stabbed into the room. She stretched her hand toward the night table.

On it was a note. "Darling, I had an early meeting this morning. I'll be back by 9:30 A.M. See you then if you're still there. If not, I'll see you tonight. I can still feel you. Love and Lust, Tony."

Tina smiled at the thought. She checked her watch on the table. She had overslept. It was time for her appointed call to a pay phone near Portland Place. She should have been dressed and making the call from the street, but she guessed the hotel phone was secure enough.

She dialed the number and waited. One, then two rings. A man's voice answered, his diction barely tinged with the singsong of the Orient.

"Chui," she said. "Tell Dr. Li that I have made contact, intimate contact, if you know what I mean . . . Yes, he has the material here in the room, and it seems significant. You want me to check? . . . OK. Hold on."

Still nude, Tina walked across to the computer desk and rifled through Tony's papers. No, the X-30 material was missing. She opened the disc drives and peered anxiously within. No, his floppy discs were not there either. She searched all over the area, but none were in sight.

"Chui," she said, returning to the phone. "Should I check the hard disc?" She laughed to herself at the adjective.

"Yes, please, and hurry."

Tina sat at the computer and tried to bring up the list of files, but nothing came onto the screen. Apparently, Tony inserted a password to actuate the menu. It was now almost 9:15. She had no time to play hacker. Tony would soon be back.

"Chui," she said, resuming the call, "I can't get into the system right now. I'm going to leave before Alcott returns. The next time, I'll make more practical plans. Don't worry, I know what I'm doing. Tell Dr. Li I'll deliver everything he needs tomorrow."

"MR. DAVIDSON, NOW that you know who I *really* am, can I come over to see you? It's something important. Maybe a lead to the X-30 hit man."

The caller was a pleasant interruption, the Baptist thought. Better to be bothered by a pretty young woman than by the sometimes overbearing Russian, Makrov.

Actress and MI5 agent Alison Mason arrived within the hour. Davidson met her, not in his closetlike office, but in the gracious embassy sitting room, where VIP guests were received.

"I can only thank you again, Miss Mason, for saving my life. That's as close as I ever want to come. I've a few years left to play out my little scenarios, and I'd hate to miss the endings." He paused. "And to what do I owe this visit?"

"I might have a clue to your search for Mary."

Davidson perked up. "Yes? And how?"

Alison first told of her little dates with Conservative MP Riddle, then of her suspicions. "His English is too perfect, yet occasionally he makes the smallest, simplest mistakes," she told Davidson, "almost as if he's perfected his English from scratch. But not as a boy. Not native, if you follow me."

Davidson wasn't sure he did. "Does he have a foreign accent when he trips up?"

"No. Absolutely not. But for someone who speaks so perfectly and went to Oxford, he makes the strangest grammatical errors: you know, who for whom. But most important, once or twice he dropped the definite article 'the.' And besides, his diction is *too good*. Like Richard Burton."

Davidson thought of Makrov's attempts to imitate the likes of Riddle and laughed.

"So what are you trying to say? What are your suspicions?"

"Well, I had the people at HQ check out his file—yes, we keep them on all politicians—and it's strangely thin. There's no checkable past before he was twenty-two. Says he was born in Sevenoaks, but his birth certificate was burned. He supposedly went to an old public school, Cheshire Common in Yorkshire, but the school has been closed for twenty years now. No one has the old records. His parents ostensibly died in a car crash while on vacation in Italy, and he has no relatives. I'm not sure I believe any of it."

Alison was now talking Davidson's language: a paranoid scenario of someone who was not who he seemed to be. The Baptist's whole history at the Agency was such a tale—one in which the old spy proved not to be a "paranoid" as some colleagues hinted. Instead, many of his deepest suspicions had proved to be on target.

"So, what do you, our most attractive spy, believe?" Davidson asked.

Alison laughed, now convinced that men—of whatever age—had horny blood, which flowed almost until they died. She pecked at Davidson's cheek.

"Thanks, John. What I think is that Riddle is a leftover 'illegal,' one of the hundreds of undercover Soviet people who were settled here when they were young and were given fictitious backgrounds so they could rise in British society. He's certainly done that. Then he'd be ready to come out of the closet when needed."

Davidson was surprised, if not shocked, by Mason's idea. Riddle seemed to him to be so English, almost a caricature. But then again, that itself was reason for suspicion. He doubted that the new Russian Republic would wake the U.S.S.R.'s illegals from their sleep, but the *falshivi* or the Red Chinese might take over their control.

He stared at Mason. Not only was she beautiful, and brave, but she seemed to have the instinct of the naturally skeptical soul, a chip off the old block.

"Brilliant, Alison. If it's true, he could be Mary, or at least part of the conspiracy. Will you have a chance to check it out further?"

"Oh, that's already in the works, Baptist. We're locating some teachers at his supposed old school, and we'll see if any of them remember him. I'll let you know."

"Good. Call me anytime," the Baptist responded. "Day or night."

27

"DARLING, YOU PROMISED that tonight you'd stay away from your computer. Will you keep your word? I want to show you something."

With this comment, Tina stood smiling after Tony opened the door to his hotel room.

"Come in. Yes, tonight I'm just entertaining the thought of entertaining you. And what do you have to show me?"

Tina brushed her lips against his, then walked resolutely to the couch.

What's she up to now? Alcott asked himself. He felt elated by her presence, but a bit anxious at having to stop his work at a crucial point. He had made a breakthrough in logic, and Dr. Burns's equations were being reborn in his brain. One solution had led to another, and he was finally confident that he had the key to the brilliant X-30 repair made by the Cambridge scholar before he was killed and his files pilfered.

But if he had to delay his work, he could think of no better way than a few hours with the lovely Tina Waltham, English by way of Hong Kong, and her extraordinary lovemaking.

"Come sit next to me, Tony. You'll enjoy this."

He was soon looking—he felt like a Peeping Tom—at enlarged color photos of Tina in the nude, in a variety of provocative poses. Holding her full breasts in her hands was the most innocent. His eyes drank the photos in.

He knew he was obsessed with the woman, but for
a moment a wave of prudishness, the memory of his
mother counseling temperance in all things, including
sex, overwhelmed him. He was torn between shame and
unabashed ardor.

"Tina, why the pictures? We don't need that to stimu-
late us."

"Oh, Tony, trust me. I want you never to forget me,
and how much we had together. Who knows? Maybe
the pictures will be more permanent than me."

Now Tony was confused.

"Why? Are you going somewhere? Are you going to
drop me as abruptly as I picked you up at the bar?"

She laughed. Her eyes closed momentarily as she
kissed Tony fervently.

"Don't be such an American fool. I'm only going on a
small trip back to Hong Kong to see my relatives. Soon,
they'll be under Communist control, and I want to try
to get them out to England. But I'll be back in two
weeks. The pictures are just in case my plane crashes,
or I'm kidnapped and disappear into the Communist
swamp."

He laughed. "My God, Tina, you are clever. More
than I'll ever be with all my Ivy League education."
He paused. "Now let me take another peek at those
pics. Darling, you never looked lovelier, except in real
life."

She started to disrobe, and Tony began what turned
into an uninterrupted interlude of caressing, kissing,
massaging. "Let's go to bed. I've forgotten all about
my computer."

Tina removed her clothes as they walked into the
bedroom. She stared quizzically at him.

"Speaking of your computer, how has the work been
going?"

Tony was surprised. "Why do you ask? You always
seem so bored by anything technical. In fact, I've avoid-

ed talking about computers and physics for fear of driving you away."

"Silly boy. Sure, I'm no mathematician and I couldn't handle a computer if my life depended on it, but I am interested in you and in *anything* you're doing—in or out of bed."

Alcott stared at this unusual woman, who he was afraid he loved, yet couldn't fully understand.

"Actually, Tina, my work is coming along beautifully. I think I've made the breakthrough I was looking for. Soon I'll have more time for us."

He studied her face. A glow now illuminated the smile.

"Why, that's wonderful, Tony. I'm so glad for you. And all that's on that little computer?"

"Oh, yes. It's a powerful dynamo, lent to me by Cambridge. It can handle several hundred million computations a second, as fast as the old mainframes that once filled a whole room. Do you want me to show you how it works?"

Still nude, Tina scampered over to the computer. "Oh, yes. Start at the beginning. I don't know the first thing."

Tony's eyes wandered, first from her exquisite body to the computer, then back.

"All right. First I turn the switch to on. Then I type in 'MW' for memo."

He went through the opening ritual, then hesitated. Should I type in the opening password? He laughed at his discretion. What would Tina know or care about his work?

"See here. If I want the directory of files to come up, I have to type in this password." His fingers hit the keys slowly: C-A-M. "See, now I can call up any of the files." He hit the most innocent of his secrets, the file "WING STRESS," then smiled at Tina. "That's all, young lady. After that, it's all top secret."

She reached down to his chair and moved her bare

breasts into his face. He extended his lips like a suckling child.

"Enough of computers," Tony breathed.

In bed, Tina first excited Tony, then, as usual, dropped to her knees and turned around with her face to the wall. Her rear was extended almost to his face while her long black hair played mysteries on her buttocks. Her moist genitals were proudly revealed.

"You know my weakness, darling. Mount me, tender but hard."

Tony obliged, then once the act was consummated, collapsed on the bed. Within minutes, he sensed himself falling into sleep, that respite of active males.

Reality quickly shifted to a dreamlike stage. Tony dreamt he was back at Cambridge, wearing a starched white shirt and university blazer with white chino pants. He was at a dance organized by the American Club and soon found himself staring across the room at a Eurasian girl with a breathtaking figure and the smile of a Giaconda.

Of course! It was Tina. She came rushing across the floor toward him, arms outstretched as if to hug him. As she approached, he could see the smile change, from the warm grin of a potential lover, to that of an angry hellion. She came within a few feet, her arms now poised like the wings of a bird, her features distorted, the nose beaklike. Her legs had turned to those of a giant bird, and her fingers had twisted into talons. She was sweeping in, like a vulture, aiming for his eyes, seeking to blind the bewildered man.

"Stop! Stop!" he screamed. He thought he had called out only in his tortured sleep, but then as his eyes opened, he shuddered. It was not an idle nightmare. His dreams had been prophetic. Tina—naked as a child—was rushing toward him, a large-bladed kitchen knife in her hand.

She leapt toward his still-sleepy body, the space

between them rapidly closing, the knife high in her hand, then sweeping downward with the speed of a thrown javelin.

"My God!" Tony screamed in terror, rolling his body violently aside just as the blade's trajectory came within inches of his heart. He fell to the floor as Tina's knife thrust into the soft mattress that only moments before had been the site of their lovemaking.

"Damn!" she screamed, pulling the knife out and raising it again for a second attack. Calling on the instinct of an athlete, Tony blocked her arm with his left hand and reached with his other to dislodge the knife from her grasp.

Never had he fought such a determined adversary. Tina pulsed and weaved her naked body, pulled away, then thrust again with the knife.

Wrestling this time in search of life, not love, Tony finally grabbed her wrist and twisted it with the strength of a rower's arm. The knife fell on the bed, where Tony picked it up. Without thinking, as if he were fighting off a rattler, he thrust it back without aiming, without understanding, only seeking to protect his life. The knife seemed to enter on its own, finding its mark between Tina's breasts.

The blood poured from the wound. Tony had struck a major artery. Tina breathed heavily for seconds, then, as she had so often done in passion, she whispered:

"It was fun while it lasted, darling. Wasn't it?"

28

DAVIDSON'S INTUITION WAS on target. He sensed Washington was getting anxious, perhaps even panicky.

The next morning, in his near-bare office at the embassy in Grosvenor Square, he spotted a sealed envelope centered neatly on his desk.

He opened it. It was a notice that a coded message was waiting. He walked the stairs to the code room, filled with computer and cryptographic instruments of every dimension. In here, shortwave radio messages, satellite transmissions, coded faxes, teletype messages, and letters were decrypted for the embassy staff.

Once he presented his notice to a clerk, he was handed another sealed envelope. He opened it and scanned the message.

"NEED YOU HERE. BRIGGS. HURRY.

Though among the briefest of missives, it was clearly urgent. Speed meant transport by military aviation. Davidson called ahead and learned that the White House had already made arrangements. He'd be taking a DC-9 out of a U.S. Air Force base forty-seven miles from London at 13:00 Greenwich Mean Time, which would get him into Andrews Air Force Base eleven miles outside Washington at 14:00 local time, or 2:00 P.M. His appointment with the President was for 2:45. A White House chauffeured Lincoln, one of twenty-nine maintained for the President and his staff, would pick him up.

The trip was uneventful. Davidson spent the time reading a biography of Ben Franklin's illegitimate son, William, who later became governor of New Jersey and a British sympathizer who was arrested by the Americans. The Baptist's only discomfort was his uncertainty. Why was he being called back so suddenly? Was the President angry at his lack of progress?

From Andrews AFB, the limo took him past a clear view of the Tidal Basin and the Jefferson Memorial, then over the Fourteenth Street Bridge and down Pennsylvania Avenue to number 1600, where he entered by the Northwest Gate. The guard took a perfunctory look at his ID, then waved him on.

"Welcome back, Mr. Davidson."

They had made good time, so after his hell-bent trip across the Atlantic, he had to sit and wait for the President. He remained for ten minutes in the small anteroom, smiling occasionally at the two Secret Service men, until he was rescued by Les Fanning, whose raven-haired beauty and gracious manner came as a welcome diversion.

"Mr. Davidson." She took his hand in hers and pressed it warmly. "Always a pleasure. The President is waiting."

These visits to the Oval Office were like gas stops in the desert, a chance to rekindle his enthusiasm and put his work in broader perspective. He had begun his efforts on behalf of American Presidents with Ike, and had spanned the reigns of Kennedy through Briggs.

As he advanced up the Agency ladder, Davidson's involvement had become deeper. But since his forced retirement from Langley, his covert efforts had paradoxically become even more significant. In this era of a sanitized Agency and leaky Congressional oversight, his unpaid efforts had become the most important work of his life. He laughed at the idea of retirement. A dedicated life ended not with a resigned exit, but with a resounding professional bang.

"John, welcome back to the Colonies." The President greeted him at the fireplace. "How's Mother England?"

"I always enjoy my visits there, Mr. President. I'm an old Idaho boy, but Princeton and Virginia have turned me into an Easterner. Britannia touches my racial unconscious. Everyone there sends their respects. You know, underneath the anti-Yankee talk, there's still great feeling for our young nation." Davidson paused. "But I'm sure I interrupted you. Why, sir, this hasty call home?"

"It's China, John. Red China and your X-30 mission. That enormous sleeping giant of a nation is acting restless, and that makes me nervous."

"Anything special?" Davidson asked, pleased the President was zeroing in on the geopolitical threat of a billion-population Communist nation that dominated the Asian land mass.

"Yes, the Chinese are roaring ahead economically— with our help, I must say. This year, they're into double-digit growth. And, John, they have us in a bind. They play capitalist by setting up islands of free enterprise, then they pull back when they feel like it, never upsetting their generally Communist totalitarian operation. Their trade balance with us is now $15 billion a year and growing. But damn it, our manufacturers want them for cheap production, and they'll soon be a good market for our manufactured goods. Should we clamp down too hard, they'll take their business elsewhere in the Pacific rim. Their cagey ambassador, Teng Shi, never says it to me directly, but that's the implied threat. Meanwhile, they're taking over Hong Kong in 1997. That will double their economic power in one fell swoop."

Davidson was happy his directives on the Chinese economic threat were getting through.

"You've served in China, haven't you, John?"

"Yes, sir, I was Agency chief of station in the Beijing Embassy not long after it opened."

"Then you know that they're richer and more confident and starting to flex their political muscles. They're giving us trouble—guess where."

"I'd presume the Asiatic republics of the former U.S.S.R.—Turkmenistan, Uzbekistan, Tajikistan, and Kirgizstan, all on China's western border."

"Exactly, John," Briggs responded. "These new countries pay us democratic lip service because they're looking for Western money. But most of them are mainly totalitarian fiefdoms, carryovers of the old Communist Party. And they're starting to play footsie with the Chinese. We're talking about 60 million Muslims cut loose from Russia, who are looking for new sponsors. Iran and China are rushing in to fill the void."

The President's expression turned pensive. "I don't know if we haven't made a mistake being so nice to the Chinese. The theory was that a little appeasement would go a long way. Now we're into heavy appeasement. I'm not so sure it's the right course."

The President rose and strode over to the federal eagle woven into the rug. "Since you're an old China hand, John, what do you think?"

"I think your concerns are justified, maybe even a little understated. These new Chinese are smarter than Mao, and we underestimate them. They've sent thousands of students here to study science and technology, which has given them a leg up in one generation. And as they get more prosperous, they get more repressive. My people tell me there are thousands of political prisoners in jail and that they execute scores of dissidents a year. Mr. President, we're dealing with a wily new enemy."

"What do you make of this X-30 escapade?" the President asked. "Do you really believe the Chinese are behind the whole thing? What's his name—Dr. Li Chen of the TEWU Secret Police?"

"Absolutely, sir. But that's only part of their whole munitions and intelligence activity. When we lifted the ban on high-tech transfer to China in early 1992, they moved forward another step. With our high-speed supercomputers, they can handle advanced projects like the X-30. My people tell me they're also working hand-in-glove with the North Koreans—their client state now that the Russians are out of business. Together, they're developing the new SCUD-C, an advanced version of the Soviet-designed SCUD-B we fought against in the Gulf War. The North Koreans are shipping these new missiles everywhere. They have a range of 360 miles and are more reliable and accurate than Saddam Hussein's. Now the Chinese have developed the M-11 missile, which has almost a 1,000-mile range. They've promised not to sell it, but they've consistently broken their word. Besides the North Koreans promise us nothing. They'll surely get their hands on it, and offer it for sale. And that's only the beginning of our problem with the two strongest remaining Communist countries in the world."

Briggs continued to pace. "That's why China's involvement against the X-30 bothers me so, John—if you're right. Years ago they wouldn't know what to do with that technology. But now, their MIT- and Cal Tech–trained scientists are among the best in the world. If they get their hands on that technology, it'll turn up in superior fighting planes, in missiles, and more. John, you've got to stop them."

Davidson was heartened by the urgency in the President's words. The sense of the Red Chinese threat had finally reached the Oval Office.

"I'm trying, Mr. President, and I'm getting help from Makrov. He's a former KGB general who now heads the Russian foreign intelligence in Britain. But the Chinese are secretly using his people, renegade Russian *falshivi* agents still hoping to bring Russia back into the Communist fold. I feel that things are starting to break, and I'll report back soon."

"Excellent, John. Now I have some good news for you."

"Yes?" Davidson hadn't expected any on this trip.

"Our people in Arizona have taken Tony Alcott's notes that you sent me, and they've been doing some noodling on their own. The result is that they've found the solution to the scramjet problem. The bird has been taken up to Mach 25 in the arc jet out in the desert. The X-30 came through beautifully, and we're soon going to make an experimental flight at Edwards Air Force Base. Then we'll bring her to London for the air show in August. It'll startle the world, and show them that America is still Number One."

"Very good, Mr. President," Davidson said, knowing that the White House was relying on him to insure the plane's security in Britain. He watched the President rise, a signal that the meeting was nearly over. "One last thing, sir."

"Yes, John?"

"Young Tony Alcott wants to join my team. He's a brilliant physicist and, by accident, a great athlete. Could I press him into service, ex-officio, but with your blessings. I think he'll be an asset."

"Of course, John. You're not getting old—none of us are. But at the same time, a little youth at your side, with steady legs, won't hurt your operation. Get him a desk at the embassy and anything else he needs. I'll wire ahead."

29

"MR. DAVIDSON, ARE you sure you know what you're doing?"

On this warm Saturday night, actually at 1 A.M. on Sunday morning, Tony Alcott, newly enlisted in the cause, had arrived dressed in a dark gray sweat suit. After jogging twice around the block, he had made his rendezvous with the Baptist, who had arrived in a Rover driven by an accommodating file clerk from the embassy.

The thought of Tina's death had been dogging Tony, even bringing on short bouts of depression, which he was still fighting off. Fortunately, the Metropolitan Police had thoroughly investigated the incident and come away convinced that he had acted solely in self-defense.

"I've heard about your exploits, Mr. Davidson, but this idea seems too much for an amateur like me," Tony said when they met that morning, just a few days after Tina's demise. "I don't mind telling you I'm scared—even with the Beretta you gave me."

The duo, which spanned several generations, had met at High Street, just hundreds of meters from the Russian Embassy on Kensington Palace Gardens.

Davidson laughed solicitously at the young man, who was now an agent duly installed in the Grosvenor Square embassy, with the State Department cover of a visa officer in training. He tapped Tony on the shoulder, smiling as his fingers inadvertently touched the pistol holster under his sweatshirt.

"Are you comfortable using a gun?" Davidson asked. "You can be a champion athlete and still be too cockeyed to hit a barn door."

"No, that part doesn't bother me. I was on the pistol team at college, and I've checked out the Beretta. What bothers me is the possible public exposure." He squinted quizzically again. "I'd hate to get caught by the British police and have my folks in Connecticut hear about it."

Davidson smiled, moving toward his goal on the small, sequestered street that ran close to Kensington Palace. Despite the late hour, the scene was far from deserted. People were coming and going to parties, and a few tourists strolled on the balmy early summer eve.

"I sure hope you're right, Mr. Davidson," Alcott said as Davidson reassured him, then filled him in on the origin of this unprecedented diplomatic caper—born the day before in Sergei Makrov's office at the very same Russian Embassy.

"MAKROV, I'M STILL a little shook up by my near miss in the woods," Davidson had told his Russian colleague. "Mary almost retired me permanently. So far, all I've had is a quick glimpse of the killer, and some hint as to his voice. But we need more, and soon. I've just been back to the States, and the President is pressing me hard. I've also learned that the people at Cal

Tech have finally made the breakthrough. The X-30 has gone through its paces at the Arizona facility at Mach 25."

Davidson and the *rezident* were seated in the elegant Russian Embassy, in a room that put Davidson's rabbit-warren office to shame.

"So what are your plans, Baptist? I must confess, I'm a little stymied myself. Perhaps you should advise your President not to hold his X-30 trials here in England. At least until we apprehend Mary."

Makrov rose from his grand leather chair and paced. "And have you asked President Briggs to put more pressure on the Chinese? Like you, I'm convinced that Li Chen and his miserable TEWU are behind the mayhem. Do you think Beijing is aware of his scheme? Or is the Mandarin bandit operating on his own?"

"The President asked me the same thing, Makrov, but he refuses to delay the X-30 operation. Says he's confident I'll take care of the problems. On Beijing, he promised to put pressure on Prime Minister Peng. Whether that'll do any good, I don't know. The Chinese are proving shiftier than you people used to be."

As Makrov laughed at the insult, Davidson became embarrassed. "I'm sorry, Makrov, but we've been on opposite sides so long, I forget that we're now friends. Hard to change an old dog's way of pissing. So what do we do now?"

Makrov continued his pacing, then stopped and veered toward the Baptist.

"John, I may have an idea. Mary's identity is obviously known to the sneaky *falshivi* operating right out of this building. And—"

"Sorry to interrupt you, Sergei, but do you have any suspicions who their contact is in your embassy?"

"Yes, that's what I was about to say. The MVD people in Moscow—Deputy Director Arkady Tasinev to be exact—have checked everyone out, but who can climb inside the soul of a Russian? Gregori Dazindov, my second secretary, keeps making noises about the old glory of the U.S.S.R. He gets agreement from a handful, but his gloom over our new, shall we say weaker, position is truly deep and painful. I can tell. I believe you've met him at embassy functions."

Davidson pondered. "Oh, yes, a slight, bespectacled intellectual type. Am I right? Doesn't seem like the kind who'd run a secret spy outfit out of his own embassy. But you never know."

"Exactly, Baptist. He could be our culprit. I'm going to put one of my best nashi, Voshkov, on Dazindov. When I get a full report, I'll pass it on to you. Meanwhile, I have an idea."

"Yes?"

"Somewhere in this building are documents that will surely confirm the tie between the *falshivi* and Mary, and probably the Chinese as well. But the ambassador would never let me conduct the kind of ruthless search we'd need. As far as he's concerned, all the Foreign Ministry personnel support the new Republic of Russia, and the Commonwealth as well. That's why . . ."

Davidson smiled. "What are you thinking, Sergei? Do you want me . . . ?"

"Yes, that's just what I'm thinking. Why don't I help you break and enter the embassy during a weekend night when few people are here? Most of the staff will be at our country estate near Hastings having a good time. Perhaps you and your MI5 friends could ransack the embassy and come up with something. I could arrange everything." He paused. "Is your Russian up to snuff?"

"A little rusty, but I can manage."

"How about your sidekick, young Alcott?" Makrov asked anxiously.

"Oh, he took three years of it at Princeton. He's ahead of me."

"Good." Makrov smiled condescendingly. "And

should anything untoward happen during your mission, my hands will be clean."

"You want me to ransack your embassy? You'd permit that?"

"Permit it? My good American friend, I insist on it. What better way to snatch the *falshivi* foxes?"

Once told of the plan, Sir Malcolm had arranged for Davidson to do his work with full MI5 cooperation. He set it up so that the American duo could gain entry to Kensington Palace Gardens on a simple ruse. They were visiting Alistair Marcus, a department store magnate, a close Tory friend of Asprey's who owned an elegant home on the exclusive street.

Davidson and Alcott made their A.M. call on Marcus, who wished them Godspeed. "I have no idea what you fellows are up to, but if it's in the service of the Crown, I'm all for it."

From the back quarters of Marcus's home, the two "burglars" changed into dark clothes, scaled the five-foot brick fence, then silently traversed a neighbor's rear lawn. Guided only by the moon's half-light, they stealthily approached the left side of the Russian Embassy.

Inside, Makrov was preparing to follow the scenario. To enter the compound, Davidson and Alcott had to climb the embassy fence, which was electronically wired to a central alarm system inside the main building.

Makrov positioned himself at the left rear of the mansion and scanned the fence with infrared binoculars. Waiting until the appointed time—1:15 A.M.—he searched the area. At first his glasses showed no one, but just two minutes later, he could make out Davidson lying low on the ground outside the fence, garbed in black, holding up the prepared signal, a small rheostat searchlight turned to its lowest brightness.

Makrov instantly raced to the central hall, then down

the stairs to the basement. At its far end were the circuit breakers, cable, telefax, electricity, shortwave radio, satellite receiver, and alarm connections, all bunched together. He smiled, knowing that Sir Malcolm had long ago received the blueprints of this secret communications inlet by bribing—with hard currency—the Russian engineers who had come from Moscow to maintain the system.

Now his concerns were more immediate. He released the alarm switch, turning the small red register to green. The outside fences were now disarmed, as were the motion detectors inside the private offices.

Makrov quickly ascended the stairs, and without having to fake anxiety, he raced into the security guards' room, his chest heaving. Three plainclothes MVD men were watching British television, laughing at a BBC situation comedy.

"Gregori!" he nearly shouted at the sergeant in charge. "I just heard noises outside at the back right-hand side. Take a look, quick. I'll go out and check the left side myself."

The men exited. Makrov studied his watch. It was now 1:19 A.M. Davidson and Alcott should already be over the disarmed fence and waiting at the large side window. He nervously raced back to his original position, then relaxed. Davidson was peering over the sill. Quickly, Makrov opened the window, bringing the Western cat burglars into the once-holy sanctum of Communism.

"Baptist! Tony! Follow me!"

The three men rushed into the central foyer and up the long staircase.

"In here," Makrov instructed. "This is the ambassador's office. Start here. The rest of the rooms are off this corridor," he said, pointing. "I'll go back downstairs and try to keep the MVD people busy after they get back. That shouldn't be too hard. They love British telly. Then I'll return and try to get you both out—in one piece."

• • •

"Let's split up," Davidson told Alcott, whose prepos-
terously light blond hair was covered by a ski mask. "I'll
take the ambassador's office. You search the next one. I
think it's the chargé d'affaires. Then we'll meet in the
second secretary's office—that's Dazindov's—the one
Makrov suspects."

Davidson stood at the threshold and admired the
ambassador's suite, a combined office and small rear
apartment. Not only was it elegant, but he was struck
by how disparate were the living conditions of average
Russians and those of Russian officials. The same trend
was overtaking America as well, the Baptist feared.

Davidson walked on the old Uzbekistan rug, slowly circling the room, appraising the possibilities. There
were shelves of books, with cabinets below. He moved
to the desk, a large walnut affair of British design,
and rifled through the drawers. Nothing of significance
there.

The drawer at the bottom was locked. He tried his
all-purpose key, but this lock was apparently a pick-proof
mechanism embedded in a conventional wooden facade.
From his pocket, he withdrew a miniature lockpick device
($298 retail, but supplied free by Asprey) and inserted the
drill-like bit into the keyhole. He pressed the button and
the pick raced until it reached the "sheer line" where the
tumblers were lined up. With a quick turn, the drawer
opened.

Inside, there were small bundles of five-pound notes,
obviously for emergency expenses, a code book, which
Davidson knew Sir Malcolm had anyway, and folders
of private correspondence. He rifled through them, but
none mentioned either the X-30 or Li Chen or Mary.

After a second tour of the room, poking randomly,
he removed some books from the shelves and searched
for hidden openings. Finally, Davidson decided that the
ambassador's office was too obvious a place to hide

secret materials. He moved on to the chargé d'affaires's quarters next door. After twenty minutes, he concluded that that search had come up empty. What about Alcott? Was he making better progress? Perhaps younger, less impatient, hands could do the job.

Davidson headed for the second secretary's office, a relatively small room, but still larger than his own at Grosvenor Square. The tyro agent was hunched over, poking through a file.

"How's it going, Tony?" Davidson asked, then answered his own question. "My God, you've taken this place apart."

Every file drawer was open; most of the books had been taken off their shelves. The small rug was rolled up. The room looked as if it were being readied to be boxed and shipped elsewhere.

"Well, you said you wanted it searched," the younger man proudly answered. "Did you have any luck?"

Davidson shook his head. He watched as Tony continued his ferreting. The Baptist stood guard at the door as Alcott searched through every piece of paper. He opened the small wall safe, then removed the remaining books from the shelves.

"Baptist," Tony whispered, pointing to the edge of a fluted pilaster that ran down one segment of the bookcase. Davidson could see a distinct crack in the wall, as if it were the leading edge of a small trapdoor.

"Move your hands around the area," Davidson instructed. "Maybe the damn thing will open with the right touch."

They both worked the area with their palms and fingers, trying every combination of pushing and pulling. But without success.

"Look over there." Davidson's tapered fingers were pointing to a large nail sticking out of the pine border of the bookcase.

Alcott reached up and pushed against the metal. A

trapdoor, no more than a foot square, creaked open, obviously powered by a small motor hidden in the wall. Alcott reached his hand into the tight space and pulled out the prize: a notebook computer.

"Good, good." Davidson smiled. "Now we have to get out of here, quick."

The two men descended the elegant long staircase into the marble foyer. From the corner of the study, Davidson saw Makrov, partially hidden by the double door, signal to them. They moved quietly across the open area. Once in the room, Makrov, his face sweating in the air-conditioned atmosphere, motioned again.

"I see you found something," he said, noting the computer in Tony's hand. "Get out the way you came in. I'll close the window after you, and retreat to my office upstairs. Then I'll put the alarm back on."

The three men moved in concert. Once on the side lawn, Davidson surveyed the scene. Were any of the guards still outside? Without binoculars, he could see the answer. Two Russian security men, garbed in black leather jackets, were standing casually at the rear, talking. The Baptist and his new aide crouched low against the building, where they could hear the Russians.

"Makrov says the coast is clear, but we have to look out for ourselves," one guard, a burly, crevice-faced man, was saying. "If anything goes wrong here, it'll be our hide, not his. Let Tiktonov watch the telly. I say we should make another round right now. Just to be sure."

Davidson touched Alcott's elbow. "We have to wait them out," he whispered. "Take my Beretta and give me the computer. Let them walk around. If they miss us and the coast is clear, I'll make a dash for the fence. You can cover me from here. If necessary, you know what to do."

The wait was less than three minutes, the time ticking off painfully in Davidson's head. The guards started in the other direction and circled the building.

"My God, Tony, they're coming at us from the other side. I'm going to make the rush. Wish me luck!"

With the computer stashed under his black cable sweater, Davidson rose and raced for the fence. He had just reached his goal and was straining to get his hands to the top when he heard it. A loud pistol shot rang out, followed by another, shattering the tranquility of the neighborhood, reaching even to the Prince of Wales's palace close behind.

The Baptist kept climbing the fence, finally tumbling over onto the grass at the other side, hugging the dirt horizon for safety. He wasn't wounded, but he feared for Tony. In the weak slice of moonlight, he could see Alcott coming toward the fence. Behind him, he could see the two Russians lying on the ground.

Hand over hand, Alcott climbed the once-electrified fence, and just as he reached the top, Davidson could see one of the Russians stir, then reach toward his gun.

"Tony! Watch out! Behind you."

Alcott swiveled, and with one hand anchoring him to the fence, he swung the Beretta toward the danger spot and fired without the luxury of aiming. The Russian moaned and dropped a limp gun arm on the ground.

"Are they dead?" Davidson asked, concerned about stretching his Presidential mandate for action too far.

"I don't think so. I shot one of them in the thigh to slow him down, and the one that almost finished me took a slug in the arm. They'll survive. Now, let's get the hell out of here."

The Marcus house, farther down Kensington Palace Gardens, was a welcome refuge. Still, Davidson didn't want to involve the prestigious Tory in any political hassle. Within minutes, three Metropolitan Police squad cars had arrived at the Russian Embassy, called in by neighbors who had heard the gunshots. From the Marcus porch, the Baptist and Tony, now dressed in their regular clothes, could see one unmarked car separate from the police wagons and advance down the street toward them.

"OK, John, Tony," Sir Malcolm called from his Jaguar at the curb. "Get in here quick. I'll take you through the police lines and back to your embassy. Did you find anything?"

Davidson waved the notebook computer. "Here it is. I'll let you know what's in it after I have my technical people do their thing."

The two night bandits quickly entered Asprey's red Jaguar, and the chauffeur closed the rear door.

"Good night, Alistair." Sir Malcolm waved to Marcus, who was standing open-jawed. "Thanks. The Crown appreciates your efforts. If the police question you, just give them my name. I'll clear everything. Cheers!"

"ARE YOU SURE?" Davidson asked Frank Schiller, the technician at the Agency. "Is that all you found on the notebook computer?"

"Yes, Mr. Davidson. We checked all fifteen files, and then the backups. We even looked for traces of erased material. What you have there is a complete printout of its contents, with file names first."

Davidson waited until Schiller had left, then examined the material. First, he scanned it, then zeroed in on one line.

The file names covered Russian Embassy housekeeping; sweeping of electronic bugs planted by MI5 and the Chinese; contacts with Foreign Intelligence HQ in Moscow; a short note from Tasinev, the deputy minister of the MVD; then an enigmatic one-word file.

It was labeled "MARY." Under that, in caps, was the cryptic sentence "CONTACTS: SIR MALCOLM ASPREY AND THE GARDENER."

Davidson stared, then closed his eyes. He tried to wish the whole thing away. Angrily, he threw the printout on his desk.

Could it be true? Could his old friend and colleague truly be "Mary," the operative, probably of Li Chen, who had now killed five scientists and others?

Or was this a *falshivi* connivance? Had Dazindov learned beforehand, perhaps from a source in MI5, that Davidson was planning a foray into the Russian Embassy? Had the file been manufactured disinformation to throw dust in Davidson's eyes?

Which was it? Asprey, friend or foe. If he were Mary, it would explain a lot, particularly the excellent advance intelligence on the X-30 and its scientists.

Davidson desperately wanted to give his colleague the benefit of the doubt, but he was equally obligated to check out Asprey. And that's exactly what he planned to do.

That same morning the phone rang.

"Baptist, Malcolm here. What in heaven's name did you find on Dazindov's computer? I'm agog with curiosity."

Davidson had decided to say nothing. The file was not concrete evidence that Sir Malcolm was playing double, only a tantalizing possibility. If Asprey were a double, it was surely not the first time in the history of MI5, an agency riddled with the likes of Kim Philby, Burgess, et al. But neither was it wise for Davidson to reveal his doubts.

"Malcolm, the most curious thing. There's nothing on the disc at all, except some housekeeping and other worthless intelligence. It seems our plan turned dust. I'm sorry."

Davidson listened intently for some hint of disbelief in Asprey's reaction, but the MI5 veteran seemed to share his disappointment.

"Better luck to us next time, John. Something will turn up, I'm sure."

Davidson decided on the same course of silence with Makrov. Any "sting" required the smallest number of conspirators. Even Langley would be left out of the loop.

"Sorry, old chum," he told the Russian on the phone. "The file was empty of leads. We wasted a lot of energy and danger to get nothing—and wounded two of your men in the process."

"Are you sure, Baptist? Nothing at all?" Makrov's voice was tinged with suspicion.

"Why would I lie to you, Sergei? Were you expecting anything special?"

"No, but I figured Dazindov would have secreted something incriminating about his *falshivi* contacts. I've put a special tail on him."

"Good," Davidson said. "Let me know what you learn, and I'll do the same."

Davidson hung up, knowing he could only share his suspicions with young Alcott, who would help him execute the planned sting.

32

"JOHN, I HAVE big news," Sir Malcolm Asprey said on the phone.

Davidson listened intently.

"We checked out Antony Riddle, and Alison's suspicions were right. He's an illegal. He's confessed all. Was put in place twenty-five years ago by the KGB, waiting for *Der Tag*. If the Commies had taken over Britain, through war or subversion, Riddle—a respected Conservative—was to take over as Prime Minister. A real sleeper."

"What's he been doing now that the U.S.S.R. is *fini*?" Davidson asked, intrigued by the news.

"Just waiting for someone like Makrov to contact him and tell him what to do. But he says no one has. He's been in limbo, and lucky to be an Englishman— by adoption. As a boy, he was a star English student in Moscow, so they decided to get him into the U.K. when he finished college. And as you can see, it all took. Riddle seems to be the perfect Englishman—even a caricature of Colonel Blimp."

"Does he know anything about Mary?" Davidson asked.

"He says not a word."

"So what do we do with him now?"

"Baptist, that's just what I was about to ask you."

Davidson pondered. God, he was talking to the very man the Russian Embassy files had implicated as being either "Mary" or the main contact. Sometimes, he was infuriated by his own position in life—trusting, then not trusting, then not knowing what the hell to do. Suddenly, he had his answer. He'd use Riddle against his old friend and colleague. To either help implicate or clear him.

"Malcolm, let's enlist him as a double agent," Davidson said, now slightly confused as to who would be watching whom. "We'll get him totally involved and see (a) if he's telling us the truth, and (b) who contacts him, if anyone."

"Splendid idea, Baptist. But I'd prefer that you talk with Riddle. After all, it's a little embarrassing for me. You know, we *were* in the same social circle."

Davidson waited in the small lobby of Brown's Hotel in London, where he had arranged to take tea with Antony Riddle. He was dressed as always in his gray winter herringbones. He could only smile as Riddle arrived in a houndstooth-checked sports jacket, garbardine slacks, and a paisley scarf at his neck. Quite the Englishman—by way of Russia.

"Riddle, how are things at Parliament?" Davidson asked. Both he and Sir Malcolm had decided not to publicly unmask Riddle yet, so he still held his seat in the House. Riddle as *Riddle*—not as Anatole Resmenev, his real name—was useful. As an unmasked illegal, he'd be of no value in the hunt for Mary.

The Tory politician sat down and faced Davidson, his voice somewhat tremulous, his expression showing embarrassment.

"I'm sure no one will believe me, but the English transplant took so well I had no intention of helping the Russkies even if they called me out of deep cover. I love this adopted country of mine."

"Good. That's a head start, because I want you to lend a hand in uncovering a killer. He's taken five lives so far, and unless I'm wrong, there are several more in jeopardy. Probably including myself."

Riddle pursed his lips in an expression characteristic of the upper classes. "Re-al-ly!" he said, stretching the simple word into a seeming paragraph.

Davidson explained what had transpired to date, leaving out his suspicion of Sir Malcolm.

"I want you to send out feelers to your old handlers at the Russian Embassy, and at the Chinese, as well, if you know anyone."

"Oh, yes, I'm an old friend of Dr. Li's. He only knows me as an MP. But then again, I may be wrong. As a parting gift, the hard-liners in the KGB may have handed over the records of all illegals—including myself—to the Red Chinese. Their secret police, the TEWU, are really active over here, I understand."

"Excellent. Do whatever you can, including dropping hints to Dr. Li that you'd like to be helpful in any way. I'll leave it to you, but you might let it be known that you were once a deep-cover illegal. The worst that can happen is that he'll turn you in to British intelligence. But of course they already know."

Davidson paused, then smiled at Riddle, whose sitting stance gave away his discomfort. From having been a pillar of London society and a possible deputy minister, he was now subject to disgrace, heavy penalties, even imprisonment.

"Mr. Davidson, I suppose you're asking me to serve as a double agent, for MI5 and the Agency. Am I right?" Riddle asked.

Davidson tried not to show any emotion. "That's an indelicate way of putting it, Antony, but I suppose you could say that. And although I speak without full authority of the British government, I'm sure the Crown will forgive at least some of your old sins in exchange for your help. And besides, the Cold War is over. Or at least one of them!"

33

AT 8 A.M., Colonel Charlie Dressler mounted the stair
ladder at Edwards Air Force Base in the Mohave Desert.
Just before entering the cockpit, he cast his eyes upward
and turned in a slow circle. The sky and the air had
served up a perfect windless day for this historic flight.
He would have welcomed even a small cumulus cloud
to break the perfection, but the horizon was that soft
crystalline blue seen only in the desert, the motherland
of experimental aviation.

This was the culmination of all such voyages. There
had been several lower-speed trials of the plane, but
this was the ultimate test flight of the X-30, the $20
billion NASA–Air Force vehicle that would revolutionize both air and space travel. The stubby-winged—not
particularly pretty but not truly ugly—ship sat like a
lonely cat waiting to be petted. As Dressler motioned, his
navigator-copilot, Nat Bowman, boarded next, equipped,
as was Charlie, with a protective pressure suit and self-
contained emergency life support system, just in case.
But despite the precaution, they knew that at 250,000
feet, or in space, there was little chance to escape the
cold, the vacuum, or the heat of reentry.

If anything did happen, Dressler mused, it would be
best if it took place below 100,000 feet, the ceiling for
the SR-71 and other experimental predecessors. But fate
seldom asks victims for their druthers.

An assembly of officials, from NASA, the White

House, the Air Force, the Pentagon, the consortium of five corporations that had built the plane, even the Vice President, stood on the tarmac—a safe distance away— as the liquid-hydrogen engines started up. The noise was strong but considerably less offensive than many had expected from this fire-breathing machine.

The X-30 taxied down the runway in a conventional manner, then stopped in place for several minutes for its fuel tank to be capped off. That done, it revved up speed and lifted off the ground. Dressler was surprised by the ease of its handling. Looking out of his cockpit, the short wings, almost one with the body, didn't seem long enough for the lift. But the computer simulation and the wind-tunnel work proved accurate. The plane flew with the felicity of a Boeing 727, which was about the same size.

The engines, each with more than four times the power of a conventional jet, quickly brought the plane up to 75,000 feet, where Dressler put it through its paces. The initial speed at that altitude was Mach 1, then once the sound barrier was broken, the X-30 pushed ahead to Mach 3, 5, to Mach 6, reaching past the limits of conventional aviation. It soon became hypersonic, as it flew at 5,000 mph, almost twice the speed of any prior aircraft.

Dressler pointed the nose upward at a medium climb angle that was unprecedented for a plane its size. The X-30 reached 100, 150, then 200,000 feet above the earth, almost thirty miles into the sky, almost to the point where the atmosphere met space. At this altitude, the molecules of oxygen were scattered and the air could no longer fully fuel the engines. Dressler released stored oxygen into the liquid-hydrogen scramjets, and the X-30 throttled ahead to Mach 10, or some 7,000 miles per hour.

He was now ready for the ascent into space. The engines were fully fueled by a mix of oxygen and liquid hydrogen, and the nose was again pointed skyward. As the X-30 advanced to Mach 15, then 20, then to the escape velocity of Mach 25—17,500 mph—the heat rose to almost 20,000 degrees. The special titanium–carbon matrix body turned white hot, but never significantly altered its shape as the X-30 transmuted from airplane to spaceship, traveling smoothly through the vacuum.

Using his rocket steering jets, Dressler placed the X-30 into orbit, where the ship floated effortlessly in the heavens.

After thirty minutes of silent, eerie passage that placed him back over the United States, he energized the rockets. The aerospace plane moved out of orbit and headed for reentry into the atmosphere. Unlike on prior missions, the heat of reentry was the least of concerns. There were no ceramic tiles to fall off, and the metal-carbon fuselage sheath had already withstood higher temperatures on its *ascent* into space.

Seventy-five minutes after it had taken off from the old dry lake bed at Edwards, the X-30 landed, to a tumultuous welcome from the congregated officials and a crowd of fifteen thousand surrounding the field.

The first Mach 25 flight of man, and the first air-to-space voyage of a winged aircraft, had been accomplished.

In the White House, a pleased President Hawley Briggs made his phone calls to world leaders. Most were of the friendly variety, but two of the calls were designed to convey a special message.

"President Malinovsky," he said to the President of the Russian Republic. "I want you to know that the X-30 has flown, and I also want to thank you for the help given us by your London operative, Sergei Makrov."

Briggs waited, accepting the congratulations of the Moscow leader, then firmed his tone.

"But, Dimitri, I also want to warn you. We will not

tolerate any interference in this program. My man in London tells me that your renegade KGB men—the *falshivi*—are involved in a plot to stop the X-30. I want that halted. Right now."

At the other end, Malinovsky was taken aback. "Mr. President, I assure you that the last thing my country needs is an X-30, or to stop your efforts. We have more basic problems. Yes, unfortunately, we do have our *falshivi*, in every segment of our government. But who do you believe they are cooperating with?"

"The Chinese, and possibly the North Koreans."

The Russian was pensively silent. "Mr. President, I will instruct Makrov to increase his trusted personnel and root out the *falshivi*. I promise to do all I can. But please understand my own dilemma. Who can and who cannot be trusted in Moscow?"

The President hung up and called in Les Fanning.

"Les, next I want to talk to Prime Minister Peng of Mainland China. Please—"

Abruptly, he halted. "No, I've changed my mind. His assurances will mean nothing. Forget the phone call."

To himself, Briggs muttered that Davidson's success would accomplish more than all the false promises from Beijing.

In the Russian Embassy in London, Makrov lowered his glass of hot tea. He stared out the window at Princess Diana's palace at the end of the street. The phone had just rung.

"Yes, this is Makrov. Who is this?"

His esophagus tightened. It was his President, calling from the Kremlin.

"Makrov. I've just received word that the American X-30 has flown. Yes, I have congratulated them. And President Briggs sends you his best. But we can no longer wait for results. He is angered by the betrayal of some of your intelligence men. I want all spying and

anti-American activity by the *falshivi* to stop, immediately. I'd also like a sign—a gesture of some kind—
that we are helping the Americans. And soon. Do you
understand?"

"Yes, Mr. President. I have a plan that will please
them—very much."

"Good," Malinovsky said as he clicked down the
receiver.

Makrov nodded into the dead phone, then repeated
his promise. "Very much indeed."

AT THE CONSORTIUM headquarters for the X-30, Computer CAD specialist Jack Kendrick pulsed with excitement.

An expert at digital miniaturization, he had worked
around the clock transposing all the essential body-wing
configurations of the X-30 onto floppy discs less than
two inches in diameter.

The effort was not an assignment from the project
director. Rather this was free-lance work for himself.
Kendrick, a twenty-year veteran of the aerospace industry, was frightened by the cutback in personnel over the
past few years, watching as the supposed "peace dividend" came to mean mainly layoffs and aerospace close-
downs throughout the southwest of the United States.

He considered himself a "good" American. Kendrick
was conservative politically, voted Republican, and had
cheered the Gulf War. But that was all impersonal.

Personally, he had a new family to care for; he had already made one split in his "community property" after a divorce; and his NFL betting losses had left him hopelessly in debt. He had his future—even his present—to worry about. The so-called "military-industrial complex" didn't seem particularly concerned about him.

The overtures had been by a Czech fellow worker with less than secret clearances. "It could mean a lot to you, Kendrick. Why not meet with my people?"

At first, he had brushed aside the invitation. But just yesterday he had read disturbing news in an aerospace publication. Now that the X-30 was a reality, there would be cutbacks in the "development team." That sounded as if they were spelling out his name. He spoke to the project director, who only shrugged. "You do good work, Kendrick, but what in the hell do I know about Air Force or NASA plans? Besides, I'm worried about my own job."

Kendrick approached his contact, who explained the terms. He agreed to a rendezvous.

He was to meet his potential enrichers at the Nevada Inn on Interstate 15, just beyond the California border, less than a mile inside the land of legalized gambling. The rendezvous would be at the crap table; the contact was a player called Rushkov, who would be obvious from his accent.

What in the hell would the Russians want with the X-30? Kendrick wondered. They could barely feed themselves. Surely, Rushkov was merely an intermediary for someone else. But who? The more he thought about it, the more he realized he didn't really care. The less he knew about the technology transfer he was about to make, the better.

All he needed to know was the price and the delivery terms, and they had been spelled out by the Czech. He had brought along half the disc information in his pocket, in a small plastic case. Rushkov had been told to bring

$250,000 to his hotel room in hundred-dollar bills out of numbered sequence—the down payment on half a million.

The smallest pangs of guilt nagged at Kendrick, but he successfully pushed them aside with dreams of a debt-free existence. He knew capitalism was the best— really the only—possible way of life for a free man. But his debt and fear of losing his job were crippling his mind. Maybe once he made the transfer, he could think again.

Besides, dammit, wasn't the Cold War over?

"TONY, WE'RE GOING to have to do some retail intelligence work," Davidson told young Alcott as the two men shared coffee and strategy in the embassy cafeteria. It was one of many exercises searching for clues to the identity of "Mary," and the at-large killer who Davidson felt sure was a professional hit man.

Davidson could see Alcott warming to his new job. Only the memory of Tina Waltham seemed to haunt him from time to time. But the Baptist understood that Tony believed it had been a matter of his life or hers.

"Good, John. But tell me again. Did the President himself personally approve of my joining this mission?"

Davidson laughed, recalling the pride of his own first intelligence assignments, in the OSS under General Wild Bill Donovan—starting in France, then with Tito's left-wing guerrillas fighting Hitler in Yugoslavia. Now this young physicist was playing a similar role, and he had been surprised by Alcott's proficiency—and bravery— the other night at the Russian Embassy.

"Yes, Tony, I was right in the Oval Office when President Briggs gave me the go-ahead on you. You're on the federal payroll. And for all I know, you're in some secret 'finding' given to the Senate Intelligence Committee. The reason is I need you for a job right away."

"What's up?"

"I'm convinced our hit man is somehow tied to gardening. He showed up at the Cambridge show, where he tried to finish me off. And there are other clues that point to it as well. I got a quick glimpse of him. He's somewhat unusual looking: tall with a very gaunt face." Davidson smiled. "I want you to find him, single-handed."

"How?"

"Easy, Tony. First, work up a list of the nurseries and horticulture outlets within a fifteen-mile radius of Cambridge. Then visit them one at a time, and look for the executioner. I'll fill you in on everything I remember about him. When you get a lead, bring me in."

"Thanks, John," the young physicist answered facetiously.

Before Alcott left, Davidson told him about the unusual messages the killer left with his victims, and what he knew about the *halesia*, or silver bell, blossom.

Alcott began his trek by looking for a car. He found the right-handed wheel on British cars uncomfortable. "Stanton," he asked an embassy colleague, "I've got to go scouting in the countryside. Could I borrow your U.S. Ford Escort for the trip? Just for a day or two. I promise I'll be careful."

Stanton stared at him quizzically. "You look like a jock—not the careful type. You can have it, but I'll charge the government if anything happens."

Tony smiled his agreement, then arranged to remove the diplomatic plates and replace them with ordinary British ones. He handled the assignment with scholarly thoroughness. Dividing the map of East Anglia into eight pie slices, he placed Cambridge at the center. From a London direct-mail firm, he secured a list of the garden establishments in the area, then cross-checked them against local phone books.

Daylight was just forming when he left his studio flat in Pimlico. Tony started up, then drove through East London toward the M11, the motorway that connected London and Cambridge. The sixty-mile trip took only seventy-five minutes. From Cambridge, eating up petrol at four dollars a gallon, he made his way through the countryside, stopping at every establishment on his list. He also checked out some other nurseries—either new or too small to have been listed—that he spotted on the side roads.

By four in the afternoon, he had covered more than twenty places along the Cambridgeshire byways. In each case, he scanned the shop and the nearby grounds for a tall, gaunt-faced man.

Some six miles outside Cambridge, he looked at his list. The next place, about a quarter mile down the road, was the establishment of "Michael Cavendish: Horticultural Specialist." He cut abruptly across the road and drove into the gravel turnaround. The house was small and delightfully Victorian, with gingerbread and red brick painted a relieving white. Vines ran up over the front door, which held an enormous carved brass knocker. The windows were bay-shaped and filled with a clever assortment of potted plants and flowers.

The bell on the door tinkled softly as Tony entered. He smiled at the woman behind the counter, then checked briefly around the shop before approaching.

"Is the manager in?" he asked the clerk, a short, attractive woman with blond hair tied into a bun. It was the same opening query he had used all day.

"No, I'm afraid Mr. Cavendish is in Cambridge for the day. Holding a symposium at a garden club. Can I help you?"

"Perhaps. I'm looking for American boxwood bushes, about a dozen of them, each about thirty-six inches high." Tony had made that same request at every stop, relatively sure no one in England would stock them.

"American boxwoods?" The clerk looked surprised. "No, we don't have any, but when Mr. Cavendish returns, I'll ask if he can order them. Could you call back? Here's our card."

"Thanks. I might need some other things. Could I walk around your nursery outside?"

"Of course. Take your time."

Alcott trod the gravel path, past rhododendrons, hemlocks, Bradford pear trees, then he stopped short. He was face-to-face with a quartet of fifteen-foot-tall trees. The ground below them was a soft blanket of white, bell-shaped petals. Silver bells.

It struck him hammer-hard. He remembered Davidson's instructions about the executioner's signature—"Mary, Mary, quite contrary."

Until now his voyage into the British hinterland had come up empty. But perhaps knowledge of these trees, property of Mr. Cavendish, would interest the Baptist. He got back into the Escort and headed toward the M11, a distance of four miles on curving country roads. Most were no more than twelve feet from shoulder to shoulder—when there were shoulders.

He tried not to hug the center hump of the road, which would make the driving easier but more dangerous. An oncoming car, or worse yet, a lorry, could push him off the road or force a head-on collision. He really didn't know how the English managed these country roads, especially at night. And the Escort didn't have an air bag.

A mile from Cavendish's nursery, as he started up a small hill, Tony eased the car just a little left of center, fearful of what he couldn't see over the crest. His anxiety was justified. As soon as the Ford cleared the top, he could make it out. A large maroon Mercedes— he guessed a 500SL—loomed ahead. At first, he guessed that the two cars would pull to opposite sides of the narrow road as they approached. Alcott quickly did his part. He jerked the Ford so far left that his inside wheels trod down the brambles that made up the shoulder.

But as the cars came closer—the oncoming one almost twice his size—Tony froze. The Mercedes was riding the middle of the road, accelerating its engine on a collision course. He pressed down hard on the horn. A screech of panic filled the country air, but the Mercedes kept coming. It didn't waver as the ground between them closed from two hundred to one hundred yards, then less.

Was the madman playing chicken? That thought was followed by a swift decision. Tony pulled the wheel hard left and drove the Escort more than four feet off the road just as the Mercedes passed him. The wind pressed through his open window. He stared, his eyes dilated, as a large oak tree, at least two feet thick, shot up into his path. He made another quick turn to the left, just missing the trunk by inches. Pumping hard on the brake, he brought the Escort to a stop in a patch of woodland.

The chirp of a bird brought a spontaneous laugh from the frightened intelligence man. He had just escaped death at the hands of an unidentified enemy. Was it tied to today's excursion and the gaunt-faced killer?

Alcott got out of the car and pressed his heels into the dirt. He looked around. He had driven about thirty feet off the road, but the ground was dry, hard, and relatively level. Could he restart the engine and weave his way back to the road?

The engine coughed, but came on. In first gear, he advanced slowly, twisting between the trees. When only ten feet from the road, he came up against a tall beech blocking his way. He reversed, then pushed ahead until he came out on the road. The Escort had picked up several dents and a legion of scratches. Stanton wasn't going to be happy.

Once again on his way to the M11, Tony was pondering whether the *halesia* trees meant anything, when he saw something that he didn't believe. Or want to. The same Mercedes was now *behind* him and rapidly bearing down. Tony pushed the accelerator to the floor and formed his lips in prayer. He was soon traveling at seventy miles per hour, rounding each curve with a bravado born of desperation. But the 245-horsepower Mercedes continued to close in.

Tony pressed the horn, and held it down. This time it was not to warn the Mercedes, which was only seventy feet behind him. It was a signal of panic. Maybe the noise would alert someone. A constable. A helicopter. The inane idea passed quickly through his mind as he felt a jolt. The Mercedes had hit his left rear bumper. First once, then again. The two cars were now virtually joined, one at the mercy of the other. Tony feared he was headed toward oblivion.

He stared out the rearview mirror, and suddenly saw the Mercedes pulling back. It slowed so that the space between them grew to fifty yards. Were they giving up the chase? As soon as the thought entered Tony's mind, he could hear the whine. The Mercedes's engine had revved up. This time it was coming at him in one accelerated, continuous swoop.

The 500SL hit the rear left of his Escort with a force that literally lifted the small car into the air. He could feel himself first flying, then tumbling, over and over. The roof of the car came down to meet him, then turned so that it became his floor.

The Escort came to a stop, again in a wood. But this time it was some ten feet below the road. Tony was upside down, his body hanging like a skydiver's in the harness of his seat belt.

"Help!" he called out. "Help!"

But who could hear him here? he asked himself, just before he moved into welcome unconsciousness.

THE RUSSIAN EMBASSY was no place to make this phone call.

Sergei Makrov, former KGB general, left Kensington Palace Gardens and walked down High Street. The night was so pleasant that he decided to stroll all the way to Hyde Park Corner, as distant from his colleagues as possible.

There was little danger in making his call from any pay phone, but discretion had become an instinct. As he walked, Makrov—dressed in impeccable Savile Row flannels—stopped at a shop window and waited. It was a tradecraft cliché, but still the best litmus test of whether one was being shadowed.

He halted first at a jewelry store and stood virtually immobile, pretending to look in the window. In reality, his eyes were focused on the glass, using it as a mirror. He spotted a man, wearing a fedora, 1950s style, standing behind him.

Makrov waited a minute, then moved on. He skipped three stores, then stopped at the fourth, a haberdashery shop. The window was filled with male mannequins garbed in subdued British tweeds. Again he pretended to look at the merchandise while watching the man, who had just made the same stop.

Obviously, he was being followed. But by whom? And why?

The man had a square face with Slavic features. He guessed he was Russian, but Makrov didn't recognize him. In any case, he was not a member of his embassy. Perhaps someone from another Russian organization. There were many in London, and despite supposed deemphasis on foreign intelligence, old habits died slowly. The Soviet maxim was apparently still in force: duplicate your forces and don't let one side—in this case *Rezident* Makrov—know what the other is doing. Probably a *falshivi* from some other group, perhaps TASS, the news agency, Makrov thought.

Meanwhile, he intended to deliver his present to the West, just as he had promised President Malinovsky.

At Hyde Park Corner, he entered the phone booth and took out his AT&T calling card. On a piece of paper, he had scribbled a phone number in San Francisco. After reaching the overseas operator, he gave her the call number and his account.

"Whom do you wish to speak to, sir?" the operator asked.

"Anyone. A station-to-station call." A good mimic, Makrov made his voice even more British, concentrating on each consonant and remembering to use the definite article.

"Hello, is this *the* FBI headquarters on Golden Gate Avenue?"

"Yes, whom do you want to speak with?"

"Anyone—any FBI agent, that is."

"One moment. I'll put you through."

An American voice, with a soft Southern tone, came on.

"This is Agent Sam Barker. What can I do for you?"

"I can't give you my name. I must remain anonymous. But you should know that an engineer at your X-30 plant in Southern California—his name is Jack Kendrick—has stolen the specifications of your aerospace ship and is delivering them to a spy named Rushkov. It's not for the Russians, though. He's working for the Red Chinese."

The voice at the other end maintained its even demeanor.

"When is the delivery being made, and where?"

"Tonight, at the Nevada Inn near the California border. In Rushkov's room at midnight. Good hunting."

With that, Makrov hung up and abruptly left the booth. His shadow, who was burly and a foot taller than he, smiled and started in lockstep as Makrov approached the curb at Piccadilly.

The light was just about to change. Makrov moved a few inches off the curb to get a start, careful not to put himself in the way of the oncoming traffic. Even though he had lived in London for a few years, he often forgot to look to the right instead of the left.

Suddenly, he could feel someone press on his back. His legs were moving involuntarily into the street. He couldn't stop either his forward motion or the trajectory of the black Rover taxi, which was rapidly closing the distance between them.

In a few moments, it was all over. The taxi had screeched to a stop, but not before its bumper had thrown the Russian *resident* two feet into the air. Makrov lay on the asphalt, immobile and too paralyzed with fear to try to move.

"Call an ambulance, quick!" the burly man shouted, then disappeared into the gathering crowd.

37

"WELL, TONY THAT'S one car you owe Stanton—though I've put in a requisition for the Agency to pay for it. It's only junk now."

Fresh from his encounter with the Mercedes, Alcott was still somewhat shaken. He had hung upside down for a few minutes, then regained consciousness and managed to release the restraints. After falling down onto the roof of the car, he had crawled out the open windows and hiked into the nearest village, where he placed a call to Davidson. An embassy car was sent from Grosvenor Square to pick him up.

Moments after his arrival, Tony told Davidson about the silver bells at Cavendish's place. The two were now ready for a second expedition into the East Anglian hinterland, this time in a heavier Volvo. The next morning, they reran the M11 route to Cambridge, but Davidson—excited by the report on Cavendish—decided to make the horticulture shop his first stop.

"Tony, if he's the man, he'll recognize me in a minute. So when we get there, you go in and I'll play possum by lying low in the car. Get a good look at him, then try to have him come out with you so I can make an ID."

Tony walked into the shop, the bell tinkling behind him.

"Hello. Remember me? I came in the other day and asked for American boxwoods," he said to the clerk. "Is the manager in now?"

The woman's face, blessed with the soft pink of the moist English clime, suddenly turned red.

"Why . . . Yes, Mr. Cavendish is here. Do you want to see him?"

Alcott waited a few minutes before a tall gaunt-faced man—fitting Davidson's description—came out into the shop.

"American boxwood? No, I don't have any, but I can show you some English variety. Actually a finer leaf, you know."

Tony smiled. The two men walked out, then followed a flagstone path to the back nursery, where Alcott pretended to be interested in the British plant.

"Well, let me mull it over. I need a lot of them," he murmured, then strode back to the Volvo.

"What do you think, John?" he asked the Baptist, who had returned to his slouched position in the passenger seat.

"That's him. I have no proof, but it sure seems like the same man. What was his speech like?"

"Pure Mayfair. Upper class and well educated, just as you remembered."

"Good, let's—" Davidson halted in midsentence. "Look behind you, Tony. There's Cavendish getting into his Jaguar. I'll stay down until he leaves, then we'll follow him. But please, play it cautious. We don't want to be spotted."

Alcott played the game like a pro, altering the distance behind Cavendish from moment to moment. At one point, he even permitted the lead car to reach the outer edge of his vision. That risked losing him, but it created the sense of detachment needed for any successful tail. The Jaguar kept moving in the direction of Cambridge, then made a sharp left into a country road.

"My God!"

Davidson, who had almost dozed off during the twenty-minute trip, came alive.

"Down at the base of this small hill is Hollow Oaks, Sir Malcolm's place. Do you think . . . ?" Davidson swallowed his sentence. Was this further evidence that Asprey and Mary were connected? Or even one and the same?

"Make this first right, quickly, Tony. Let's keep out of sight. I don't want to stop Cavendish if he's going to visit Sir Malcolm. We'll wait here until he leaves. Then I'll go in and check out the situation."

Davidson's voice was strained. "Maybe I'll even go in and confront Asprey."

Ten minutes later, from their hidden vantage point, they watched as the Jaguar moved away from Hollow Oaks. Davidson judiciously held his place for a few minutes, then asked Tony to pull up into the gravel courtyard.

Tony stayed in the car while the Baptist banged the ornate brass knocker. The old spy stood on the flagstone landing and surveyed the gracious environment Sir Malcolm and Lady Victoria had created in the Cambridge countryside. It more than rivaled Virginia, he decided. Davidson gave England the edge because of the age, the cultivated landscape, and the sharp separation of forest and countryside. In Eastern America, the two were often still entwined. Sometimes, back home, he sensed that three-hundred-year-old Indian settlements were hovering just beyond the next clump of trees.

He smiled appreciatively and waited. In a moment, the butler answered the door.

"Is Sir Malcolm home? Tell him it's John Davidson."

The butler had little chance to respond.

"John, darling!" came a call from the back of the entrance foyer.

Lady Victoria Asprey half raced toward the door, then stood for a moment facing Davidson. Suddenly, she placed her lips firmly on his. Her hands encircled his neck, her breasts and thighs pressed against his body.

"Darling, what a distinct pleasure. Please come in." Victoria turned. "Alfred, some tea, please."

In the sun room, with the early afternoon light playing patterns on the chintz and bamboo furniture, Victoria Asprey pulled her chair up close to Davidson's. Her knees blatantly rubbed against his.

"Tell me, John, why this delightful visit? You have to excuse me, but lately I've had thoughts only for you. And I understand from Malcolm that you've been handling some dangerous assignments. And at your age! You should be ashamed. Or at least frightened."

"More frightened than embarrassed, Victoria. One of my enemies seems determined to eliminate me, and one of my aides from the States as well. We've both been attacked. Myself with a gun; he by a rampaging Mercedes."

"Really, John? Who would want to do that?"

"That's why I've dropped in to shake up your tranquility, Victoria. I suspect that the man who was just here is part of the conspiracy."

Lady Asprey laughed. "Why John, that was Michael Cavendish. Conspiracy? My God, no. He's just a gardener. Actually, a graduate horticulturist—a specialist who handles Malcolm's bushes and trees. A very gentle Englishman if truth be known. What could he have to do with your—and Malcolm's—business?"

"What did he want just now?" Davidson asked, avoiding her comment.

"Just wanted to see Malcolm. I think an overdue bill. Sometimes I fear my husband is obsessive about these grounds, and too extravagant. Although I must say they are beautiful."

Could Victoria have overheard any conversations between Malcolm and the Gardener—Davidson's name for the suspected killer?

"Have you ever heard Sir Malcolm mention anyone called Mary?"

Victoria's expression turned quizzical. "Mary? Is that one of his girl friends? If so, I've never heard the name. Why, John?"

Davidson explained that it was a code name, then brought himself up short. Best not to reveal any more.

"And, Victoria, I'd appreciate it if you wouldn't mention this visit to Sir Malcolm. He might be jealous."

Lady Asprey rose and stood over Davidson. She bent her ample body down until her bosom virtually surrounded his face, then kissed the surprised widower softly on the lips.

"I'd be much happier, John, if you'd really give him something to be jealous about." She laughed again in her musical tones. "But of course I promise to say nothing. I'd rather not know anything about your work anyway. So unbeautiful."

DAVIDSON FELT THE world was revolving poorly on its political axis.

Here was Sergei Makrov, his longtime adversary in foreign intelligence, in the hospital with an injury—fortunately minor—after being pushed into the way of a taxi. Surely it was the work of a *falshivi*, angry at him for turning in one of their spies to the FBI. Lenin, as long as he remained in his pink marble tomb on Red Square, would have geopolitical conniptions.

Makrov had boasted to Davidson about his "splendid cooperation" with President Briggs and the FBI, who had apprehended Kendrick with the X-30 plans in the Nevada hotel.

"Tell me, Sergei. Wasn't Kendrick one of your own men?" Davidson had asked Makrov. "I appreciate that you're helping us find the X-30 killer, but have you stopped all your American spying on the project? What I mean is—are you hanging up your gloves?"

Makrov responded with a bear hug. "John, you are wonderful. So expert, and so naive at the same time. I throw you a little fish, so you think I've given up the sport. Just wonderful!"

Meanwhile, Davidson's longtime ally, Sir Malcolm Asprey, had now twice aroused suspicions about his loyalty. Once in the secret record-keeping of Dazindov, who Makrov believed was head of the Red Chinese–*falshivi* Axis. The second incident had taken place just yesterday, with the appearance of Cavendish, the Gardener, at Hollow Oaks.

The Baptist had promised himself to test Asprey. He was pensively doodling on a pad to devise a sting when the phone rang. As it turned out, it was pure serendipity.

"Mr. Davidson," the embassy operator said, "I have the President of the United States on the phone. Please use the scrambler. I'll switch the call."

"John, this is Briggs." Davidson heard the voice once it had been scrambled and descrambled, an audio process that took less than two seconds. "I have important news—and instructions."

"Yes, sir. What is it?"

"Now that the X-30 has flown successfully at Edwards AFB, I've arranged with the British Prime Minister to have the plane exhibited to the press and test flown at their Northolt Royal Air Force Base in Sussex, just outside London. As a sign of our friendship, I've arranged for a British Officer—Wing Commander Terrence Beame— to fly copilot with Colonel Dressler. I want you to insure security. Use some of the Agency men at Grosvenor Square if you have to."

Before he hung up, the President reminded Davidson to thank Makrov for having tipped off the FBI. Not only had Kendrick been easily taken, but the spy contact, Rushkov, working out of the Russian Consulate on Green Street in San Francisco, admitted to being a *falshivi* hard-liner, still angered at the demise of the U.S.S.R. He was willing to help any enemy of the U.S.A., especially Red China.

At dawn the next morning, the X-30 left Edwards in the California desert. At a restrained speed of Mach 4, or twice the speed of the Concorde, it flew without incident to the American air base in Greenland, some five-thousand miles away. The trip had taken two hours, beating the sun by four. The X-30 would remain there for two days for mechanical inspection. After that, it would make its maiden transatlantic voyage to Britain, cutting Lindbergh's twenty-seven-hour flight down to forty-five minutes, an achievement that had taken less than seventy years. The Royal Air Force base at Northolt would be cordoned off to the public for the historic landing, with only officials and a few press people meeting the aerospace plane. Security had been tripled, including the deployment of Patriot anti-missile defenses in case of a surprise terrorist attack.

The schedule called for a second shakedown flight from Britain. Dressler and Wing Commander Beame were to board the X-30 and fly a tight circle by heading first for southern France, then Norway, and returning on the third leg to Northolt. The five-thousand-mile journey would take less than an hour. After refueling, the two pilots would take the X-30 up to 300,000 feet, accelerate to Mach 25, then punch a hole into space. Once the plane was in orbit, the television cameras would be turned on, for the world to witness the historic event.

Meanwhile, Davidson had to put his sting into play. He still hoped that his suspicions about Asprey were wrong. Not only had he been embarrassed to confront Asprey with the evidence, but it would have been counterproductive. It might have frightened the MI5 veteran away from any action he might take on behalf of the conspirators.

Planting the honey for the sting came in a quick lunch with himself, Alcott, and Asprey at The Antelope pub in Belgravia.

"Congratulations, gentlemen," Asprey had begun. "I suppose, Alcott, that you're here to beef up security on the X-30. Quite noble, but don't fear—we have taken all necessary precautions."

"I'm sure you have, Malcolm, but we're going to double-team just in case," Davidson explained. "I've put Tony in charge of a special Agency team of two men who will settle into the hangar the night before the flight. We're disguising them as mechanics, and they'll stay close to the bird. It's an expensive one, you know."

"Really? Agency men in disguise?" Malcolm asked, surprised. "Expecting some kind of invasion?"

The three men laughed, but Davidson sensed a hollow ring in his own jocularity. He'd wait and see how—and if—Asprey acted on the bait.

39

"CHUI! COME HERE quickly!" Dr. Li Chen called from his inner office in the Chinese Embassy on London's Portland Place.

Eschewing interoffice electronics, he had called for his assistant in a loud voice. The words quickly reached Chui's little enclave next door.

Dr. Li moved aside his calligraphy paraphernalia and laid out the board for a game of GO, preparing for a contest with his unsmiling aide.

It pained him that the complex game had lost some of its popularity in China, where it had been invented some thirty-five hundred years ago and flourished under the rule of the philosopher-Mandarins. Nothing, not even the simplistic game of chess, so helped to develop the mind and build attack strategies for life and business—even war and politics—as GO.

The GO board held 342 squares (18 on one side and 19 on the other) and was played by two opponents, one with black pieces, the other with white. Each, in turn, filled up the board with the intention of surrounding and capturing the other's pieces, or soldiers. The game held infinite mathematical combinations and permutations, at which Li Chen was a master forced to grant huge handicaps to fellow players.

The tactics of GO, he reminded himself, were similar to the game China was now playing with America. Since America was still dominated by messianic Puritanism,

and involved in a constant campaign—even through
war—to impose democracy and capitalism on the
world, he had helped China steer a course through
those dangerous waters. The strategy was to give the
appearance of partial compliance with U.S. demands—
what Washington called the "New World Order" of
American hegemony.

For a spell, China had even played the democracy
game, but had returned to iron control when exchange
students brought the poison of dissent back home with
them. After the Tiananmen Square massacre, which Li
Chen had helped orchestrate, he doubted any group would
again be moved to such foolishness.

On economics, the West was playing into China's
hands. The special capitalist economic zone in the south
brought billions into the national coffers, making social-
ism all the stronger. That failure to develop two parallel
lines of economic strategy had finally sunk the U.S.S.R. he
was sure. Mao had been guilty of the same error, but Dr.
Li—and modern China—would never make that mistake again.

He smiled at the thought of the adroit Red Chinese use
of propaganda—including front-page editorials praising
capitalism in the *Guangming Daily*, the Politburo's official newspaper. When reprinted, they softened American
hearts. The result had been exactly as planned: special
treatment from Washington, from favored-nation status on exports to the lifting of the ban on high-tech
equipment, including supercomputers that made it possible to accurately target ballistic missiles on America
and Moscow.

Li Chen now faced a new challenge. Beijing would
officially denounce it, yet it would bring him secret favor
in the Politburo.

"Chui! Come here! We have a game of GO to complete." His impatience with his assistant surfaced as
the young man appeared. "Hurry. But first, you must

make contact with Mary. I want the X-30 stolen and flown to an air base near our border. Do you understand?"

Dr. Li's assistant broke into a wide smile.

"Stolen? Yes, I will start the wheels, General. That is wise strategy. A bold stroke. Little wonder we all fear to engage you in GO."

"BAPTIST, THIS IS Charlie Halleck out near Cambridge. I'm calling from my car phone. We've had this Cavendish fellow under surveillance around the clock. Nothing's been happening—until now. He left his place in his Jaguar and headed south, and he's on the M11 headed for London. Tell Tony to pick him up—registration number J513LBX—by waiting on the shoulder before the first London exit. I'll be right behind him in my Opel. OK?"

Davidson listened to the Agency man assigned to tail Cavendish, then hung up.

"Tony," he said, walking into Alcott's office in the rear of the American Embassy, "Halleck just called in. He's on the Gardener's tail."

After relaying that information, Davidson added: "The two new agents have just come from Langley. They've been posted as Air Force mechanics in the X-30 hangar. They're supposed to get there early tonight, in time to get things ready for the X-30 landing at Northolt tomorrow afternoon. I think you should check them

out—after you get through with Cavendish, whenever
that is. OK?"

Tony found that picking up Cavendish's red Jaguar was
simple. In Davidson's Volvo, he followed the Gardener
into London proper, then toward the Strand, past the
Savoy Hotel, and into the busy theater district. On a
side street, the Jaguar stopped in front of a large second-
floor store with the legend "OSBORNE THEATRICAL
COSTUMES" painted across its window.

Alcott waited outside as the tall man with a full head
of gray hair mounted the stairs to the costume shop. He
made a note to check with Osborne's after he finished
his tail of Cavendish. What in the hell would a killer
want with a theatrical costume?

Ten minutes later, the Gardener left the shop, a cord-
wrapped brown package under his arm. He got back into
his car and wound through the city.

"Halleck, this is Alcott," Tony called on his car
telephone. "I'm here in London with Cavendish. If he
heads directly back to the M11, I'll call you and you
can pick him up again. I've got a chore elsewhere."

Cavendish did just that. "Charlie," Tony phoned in
a half hour later. "The Gardener's already close to the
motorway, and he's all yours. I've got to head out to
Northolt Air Force Base."

"Can I see your credentials?" the Royal Air Force
guard at the gate politely asked. Alcott handed him his
diplomatic passport and a plastic-encased missive from
the Defense Ministry explaining that Whitehall had giv-
en him permission to enter the cordoned-off X-30 area.

It was now close to 9 P.M. The base was encased in
a deep fog, which had arrived with the darkness. All
planes had been grounded, which gave the huge facility
the feeling of a deserted World War II operation, lost
in time. But the weather had been good earlier that

evening, and Alcott guessed that the two Langley men should already be in place. They had been flown to Northolt directly from Andrews Air Force Base outside Washington in a passenger Boeing 707 operated by the 89th Airlift Wing, the same outfit that flew the President in Air Force One.

The RAF guard studied the passport and papers, then raised the wooden barricade.

"Go right ahead, Mr. Alcott. Good luck to you Yanks on the X-30 flight tomorrow."

Tony drove the Volvo down the road, then made a sharp right. Directly ahead was the X-30 hangar, a tall, sprawling structure that had been emptied of a half dozen Tornado fighters to make room for the aerospace plane.

"Yes, sir?" Another RAF guard stopped the Volvo. "Can I help you?"

After Tony again produced his documents, he was asked to park his car in the nearby courtyard and proceed on foot to the hangar.

"Have the two American X-30 mechanics arrived yet?" Tony asked.

"Oh, yes, sir. They came in two hours ago. Said they had some preparations to make."

"Are they inside now?"

"I think so. They've just had a visitor."

"A visitor?" Alcott was surprised. Perhaps Sir Malcolm.

"Yes, sir. An RAF squadron leader. Giles Turnbull, I think his name was. He went in about twenty minutes ago."

"What did he look like? A tall, gray-haired man? Long nose and gaunt face? High cheekbones?"

"Exactly, sir. That's him."

Tony raced to the front entrance to the hangar and then moved toward the rear of the empty, cavernous space, his Beretta drawn.

"Gallagher! Rossetti!" As he shouted the names of the Agency men, the words came back in a hollow echo from above the rafters, which seemed even higher than the several stories they were. But there was no answer. The hangar was draped in semidarkness. Tony continued on until he came to the rear, then he suddenly halted. On the concrete block wall, a legend had been spray painted: "MARY SENDS HER LOVE!"

Alcott stared up above the words.

Hanging from the steel rafters, their necks tied by nooses, were two bodies, swaying softly in the dim light. At their feet, as if in memoriam, were two small bouquets of silver bells.

"DARLING, DON'T WORRY. It's going to be an apple-pie easy flight. I've done it a dozen times in simulation, and it'll go right according to script. I promise."

RAF Wing Commander Terrence Beame, a silky blond–haired man of middle height, middle years, and middling life-style, was saying good-bye to Constance Beame, his wife of five years and the attractive young mother of his child. Remarried after a dreary, unsuccessful union, Beame had found happiness with this agreeable woman and his three-year-old son in a renovated old cottage less than four miles from his field, Northolt RAF Base.

Beame's countenance was all smiles. Today's flight on the X-30, as copilot to Colonel Charlie Dressler of the USAF, was the pinnacle of his career, a fast-moving enterprise that had been given a boost by the Gulf War. His laser pinpoint bridge bombing over the Tigris and Euphrates rivers in a Tornado fighter-bomber had won him the Victoria Cross, a promotion from squadron leader, and a short, pleasant visit with an appreciative Prince Charles.

Dispatched to Edwards Air Force Base in the California Mohave Desert, he had come back with an enviable tan and twenty hours of simulated flying on the X-30. Today was the real thing. Last night, he had attended a briefing with Colonel Dressler and the ground and communications crew, given by General Eddie Malloy of the USAF, the majordomo of this X-30 flight. In just two hours, he'd be in the air, ready to break all prior speed records. A half hour after that, he'd be in space. An eventful day in anyone's life.

Connie kissed him fervently. The happy man waved good-bye, then got into his Land Rover, which served equally well in the Kenya savanna or on the bumpy English country roads. Beame was driving along, rehearsing his initial steps for the X-30 flight, when about halfway to Northolt, he suddenly hesitated. Up ahead he could see a local constable energetically waving his hands for him to stop.

The constable peered into the car and spotted the three thick stripes of rank on Beame's jacket sleeve.

"Wing Commander, I'm sorry about the delay. There's been a bad car crash about two hundred yards up ahead, and we've temporarily closed the road until the tow people arrive."

"My God, Constable, I have to get to Northolt—soon."

"No problem, sir. Just turn left here and go onto the parallel road. It's about a quarter of a mile down. There's a detour arrow that will lead you back to the main route. Shouldn't cost you more than a five-minute delay."

Beame smiled and was about to move the Land Rover into gear, when the constable suddenly raised his hand again.

"Sorry to bother you, sir, but I have a request from this gentleman." From out of the constable's car appeared a fellow RAF officer, a squadron leader, one rank below Beame's own. "This is Squadron Leader Haversham," the constable said. "His car was one of those in the accident. Totally disabled. Would you mind giving him a lift? He tells me he's going to Northolt as well."

Beame surveyed Haversham. A tall man with a full head of dark brown hair, a mustache, and an almost painfully thin frame. Yet he had a surprisingly full, rounded face.

"OK, Haversham, Hop in."

Beame took a left, and once they were on the parallel road headed toward Northolt, he chatted with his passenger.

"Tell me, Haversham. Have you been at Northolt long?"

"No, sir. As a matter of fact, I've never been there. Today's my first day. I've been assigned to a Tornado squadron. And you?"

Beame's X-30 assignment was classified until the crew announcement was made later this morning.

"I'm a Tornado man myself," Beame answered. "Did you see duty in the Gulf War, Haversham?"

"Heavens no. I'm a retread, just coming in to do my reserve duty. Too old for real action, I suppose. I'm flying a desk and computer."

Beame glanced at Haversham's face. Yes, he guessed the man was about fifty, somewhat ancient for his rank.

"Well, we all serve as we can," Beame said graciously, then glanced up the road. My God, he thought, another interruption. Standing in the center of the lane, perhaps a hundred feet ahead, was another constable. His hand was outstretched, palm up, the universal symbol for "stop." Behind him was a striped orange-and-white wooden barricade. What now?

The policeman tapped on the window. As Beame rolled it down, the constable poked in his head and quickly studied both men.

"All right, Wing Commander, and you, Squadron Leader. Out of the car, please."

"Out of the car?" Beame complained. "But I'm late for an important briefing at Northolt."

The constable circled the car, striding officiously, then returned to the open driver's window.

"I'll have to see about that, sir."

"Well, at least tell me what's going on. Another accident?" Beame asked.

"No, Wing Commander. It seems an impostor entered the base last night and killed two American mechanics— on that new plane that's coming in from the States. So we're helping the RAF people, conducting a search of everyone headed that way. The same person might try something again today."

Beame nodded his understanding. "How can we help, Constable? I'll do whatever I can. But whatever it is, please make it quick. I have to get to the base early this morning."

Time was beginning to press. Beame had heard that General Malloy had a nasty temper and was intolerant of lateness. This morning, he wouldn't blame him. If every segment of the X-30 flight wasn't on time, it might have to be postponed, and wait for another ideal flying day.

The constable seemed to ignore Beame's concern.

"I'll have to ask both of you again. Please get out of the car and show me some identification."

Beame was getting increasingly annoyed, but he was pleased by the emphasis on security, especially after hearing about the murder of the American mechanics.

God, was there some plot against the X-30? And by whom? Surely the Russians wouldn't want the plane, or even bother to stop it. As ordered, he left the Land Rover, followed by Haversham.

"Here." Beame offered the constable his ID, as did the squadron leader. The constable studied both IDs and returned them to the flying officers.

"Good," Beame sighed, with relief. "Now, could you please remove the barricade, so we can go?"

The constable stood his ground and just smiled.

"Constable." Beame's tone was now loud. "I hate to repeat myself, but I have an important RAF mission. Do I have to call base headquarters and get them to remind you of it? Please remove the barricade right now." He could feel his anger rising.

The constable's grin only grew wider. He stood immobile in the center of the road. Then, without altering his expression, he drew a revolver from under his uniform jacket.

"This is my answer, Wing Commander. Get back into your Land Rover and do as I say, and no one will get hurt."

Beame was nonplussed. "What in the hell is going on, Officer?"

The last minutes had been totally confusing. He turned to Haversham, whose expression was neutral.

"Squadron Leader, you'll have to give me a hand with this crazy constable. He can't handle the two of us. Let's take the SOB, whatever his game."

Haversham moved quickly into his tunic and withdrew his own gun.

"Good work, Haversham," Beame shouted. "Now let's disarm the crazy bastard."

But slowly, the squadron leader turned his pistol away from the constable and pointed it at Beame.

"I'm sorry, Wing Commander. But he's with me. This is no game. We're all going to Northolt together."

42

"MRS. BEAME?"

The man stood at the threshold as the wing commander's wife answered the door to her cottage.

"Could I come in, please? I have to talk to you—it's about your husband, the RAF pilot."

Constance Beame stood resolutely in the doorway, suspiciously eying the uninvited guest. A bulky man, he had an East European accent of some kind—possibly Russian, she thought. Surely he wasn't from the RAF. What could he want?

"I don't know," she stammered, blocking entrance to the house. Anxiety suddenly overtook her. Terrence had been gone less than twenty minutes. "Is anything wrong? Has my husband been hurt in an accident?"

"No, he's all right."

"Then where is he—at his base?"

"No, he never got there."

"Where then?" she asked anxiously.

"He's in our custody."

"What do you mean—in your custody? Who in the hell are you?" Mrs. Beame's Scottish blood had started to roil. "Terrence is a decorated officer, a wing commander in the RAF, and he's on his way to Northolt for an important flight. How dare you come here and talk such nonsense! Now, you leave here immediately or I'll call the police!"

The bulky man smiled, somewhat sardonically, then

pushed against her, forcing his way into the cottage.

"I don't want to hurt you, or your child." The man's hand was now displaying a Mauser. "Bring the boy in here. You're both going with us."

"You're a madman!" she shouted. "This is England. You can't kidnap us."

With that, she lifted her foot in a swift arc and kicked his ankle, her shoe coming off in the motion.

"*Sukin sin!*" the man shouted in Russian. Then he repeated in English, "Son of a bitch!"

As he grasped for his leg, the gun clanged to the floor. Mrs. Beame dove for it, but the bulky Russian kicked his foot mercilessly into her stomach. She fell, the breath forced out of her. The Russian limped over and lifted the gun off the floor. He pressed it to the frightened woman's temple.

"Mrs. Beame—you've shown me your temper. Now, if you don't watch out, I'll show you mine. Get your child in here. We have a car outside. You're both going with us as hostages—to make sure your husband behaves and does what we tell him. Do you understand now?"

She waited, breathing heavily. The courage seemed to drain from her. Now she was sure that Terrence had been kidnapped. And what of her child? Would they dare hurt him?

"Now, that's better. Will you cooperate or do I have to hurt you in front of the baby?"

The threat quieted her. "Can I pack some things?" Her voice was filled with resignation.

When the Russian nodded, Constance got up off the floor and walked into the bedroom. Within a few minutes, she came out with her three-year-old, who was sobbing fitfully.

"Come now, Ian, don't cry. Everything will be all right. We're just going for a little ride in the country."

"Exactly right, Mrs. Beame." The burly Russian nodded. "Just a pleasant vacation."

The door to the cottage opened. Another man with Slavic features, this one thinner and more ascetic, came in.

"Comrade Voshkov. I've got the Mercedes waiting. Will we be going soon?"

"Yes, but first we have to wait for the phone call from the constable's car. We want Mrs. Beame to hear her husband's voice. Then she'll know she has to cooperate. After that, we'll all take a nice trip to Hastings."

At that moment, Wing Commander Beame was standing in the center of the barricaded road, two guns pointed at him. The mission had taken a strange twist. He didn't fully understand what was going on, but apparently both men were imposters. He seemed to be the victim of a conspiracy against himself—or more logically, the X-30.

"What if I refuse to cooperate?" Beame stared at his captors. "It'll do you little good to shoot me."

"You're right. And we have no intention of doing that, Commander, unless you try to escape. But we're sure you'll cooperate," the squadron leader said. Turning to the constable, he barked an order. "You cover Beame while I get his house on the car phone."

Within a minute, Haversham beckoned. "Over here, Beame. Someone wants to talk to you."

The wing commander picked up the phone, only to have his worst fears quickly confirmed.

"Darling, this is Constance," he heard his wife say. "They've got us prisoners, and they're going to take us somewhere in the country. This man—I think he's a Russian—says he'll hurt us unless you do what they tell you. But don't let them bluff you. I—"

Beame heard a sharp cry from the other end, then the phone went dead.

"You bastards!" he shouted.

The squadron leader pressed the gun barrel into the nape of Beame's neck. "You can curse us later, Beame. Now we're all going to Northolt. Get into the car, and please do exactly what we say. Otherwise, you won't have a family to come back to."

43

"ORLOV. ARTYBYSHEV. GET ready. We're going to Hastings.

"For the weekend?" they asked hopefully.

"No. Take your Pistola Markovas, walkie-talkies, dog whistles and receivers, and Uzi automatics. We probably have a tussle waiting."

Second Secretary Gregori Dazindov was organizing an action squad of these two men, and two others from the Russian Embassy, on Kensington Palace Gardens.

The train service from London to the coastal town of Hastings, where the invader, William the Conqueror, had fought the decisive battle in 1066, was an efficient two-hour ride, but he needed privacy for this mission. He would take the group by car. No one outside his squad, especially not Makrov, was to know his intent. Supposedly it was just another impromptu visit to the vacation estate, the gift to the U.S.S.R. from an English aristocrat grateful for their effort in fighting Hitler.

The X-30's arrival at Northolt was the spark that had set off this expedition. The seizing of Wing Commander Beame's wife and child had turned the whole affair into a serious game. By now, it should have been clear to all those still in the intelligence business that there were no rules left in the post–Cold War era.

Dazindov and his men were to rendezvous at three points in London at midnight—at the Sloane Square underground station, at Prince Albert Road at the edge of Regent's Park, and at the Elephant & Castle tube station. He would coordinate the operation and pick them up, consolidating everyone into two cars. After that, they would drive, separated by ten minutes, to Hastings.

The future of relations among the Russian Republic, the Commonwealth of Independent States (which was already crumbling), the West, and Red China—for better or worse—would depend on the efficiency of Dazindov's strategy.

But Dazindov felt confident. Whether as a KGB man in the old order, or now as a diplomat and part of the Foreign Ministry's Intelligence Group, he had always done his part with initiative and dispatch. He•had no intention of being compromised now.

44

"WHAT KIND OF madness is this?" Beame shouted from the driver's seat of his Land Rover as it approached the Northolt Base. "Don't you think I'll be able to identify you later on?"

Beame spoke with bravado, but in reality, he felt helpless with his family as hostages. Nor did he have a clue as to why he had been taken prisoner. But, he confessed, he was in fear for his own life as well. If not now, then after the conspirators were finished with him.

"You don't think this is my real appearance, do you?" the squadron leader laughed. "Not a single feature of my face is authentic, and that's true of the constable as well. All you'll be able to say—if you live through it—is that I'm tall. And there a lot of us in that club in England."

Beame zeroed in on the man's voice. It was decidedly upper class. Either an educated native of southern England, or he had been schooled somewhere at the university level. His tone was slightly high-pitched, but Beame wasn't sure if that was authentic or a cover.

"There's the gate up ahead, Beame. Now, do exactly as I instruct you. Tell the RAF policeman that I'm accompanying you on the flight. Don't worry. My papers are in order if they want to see them. I'll put my gun away, but remember—one false word and your wife and child will be killed. My people have instructions to do that automatically unless I contact them from the plane by shortwave radio."

"What do you mean you're accompanying me on the flight?" Beame was incredulous. "That's impossible. You're out of your mind. I'm flying with the American pilot, Colonel Dressler."

"We'll see about that, Beame. Now, remember, I'm banking on your ingenuity to get me on the X-30. And so is your family. Get to it."

At the gate, the guard approached the stopped Land Rover.

"Wing Commander Beame?" he asked as he peered in and recognized the officer.

"Yes, Airman. And this is Squadron Leader Haversham. He's my staff aide on the X-30 flight. Just been assigned to me."

As Haversham produced his own officer's credentials,

Beame peeked at them quickly, surprised. They seemed authentic.

"All right, you can go through. And good luck on your flight, Wing Commander."

Beame steered the Land Rover down the administration road, then branched off toward the X-30 area, which had been cordoned off. The tarmac and hangar were openly guarded by a half dozen air police with automatic rifles. Beame knew there were a dozen more in a nearby hut, on the alert. In addition, four American Air Force MPs stood guard directly around the plane.

But all the security was useless. His mission had changed. It had become a reverse one: to outfox security. He had to lie to his own men if he was to keep his family alive. Guilt suddenly overwhelmed him. Billions of dollars and decades of work invested in the X-30 were being sacrificed because of him. Wasn't the plane more important than his personal concerns? Quickly he brushed aside the thought. Perhaps that was true in the abstract, but he had a wife and child to protect. That was reality.

Beame halted the Land Rover about one hundred feet from the plane. From there, he could see the ground crew making their last-minute checks. In fifteen minutes, they were scheduled to start their engines, then become airborne fifteen minutes later. The field's longest runway had been kept unused all day for this takeoff.

"I don't care how you do it, Beame, but get me on that plane." The imposter's voice was firm. "And remember the consequences if I don't radio my people from the X-30. Do you understand?"

The wing commander nodded resignedly. "We'll have to walk the rest of the way to the plane. Act smart but let me handle any discussion."

The two men approached the aerospace plane, looking like any two RAF officers on their way for a flight. The X-30 sat silently on the runway, its engine not yet revved, its short wings forming an integral part of its body. Sitting on the tarmac, it seemed the obvious symbol of the future.

The uniformed duo moved ahead toward the X-30, but just as they reached the ascending ladder, they were stopped abruptly.

"Wing Commander Beame?" asked an American MP standing in the way. Apparently he had recognized Beame from the briefing the night before.

"That's right, Sergeant." He offered his RAF credentials.

"And who is this, sir?" the MP asked, motioning to Haversham.

Beame had been too flustered to concoct a cover story, but his mind now raced at survival speed.

"Oh, this is Squadron Leader Haversham, Sergeant. He's my technical aide on the flight. He'll be aboard with me for just ten minutes. We have to check out the operation of the computers."

Haversham quickly produced his false credentials.

"All right, sir." The sergeant saluted, then returned to his post at the perimeter of the guarded area.

"Good work, Beame. Now, let's get aboard. Are the pressure suits on the plane?"

"Yes."

"And how about Colonel Dressler?"

"He's probably been aboard for a half hour. Let's go up into the plane before we're stopped again." Beame suddenly realized he was still in the dark about the imposter's plans. "Why are you going up here with me? Can you fly the damn thing?"

The squadron leader laughed silently. "Me fly? My God, man, I can barely ride a bicycle."

"Then what's going on?" Beame asked in near-panic.

Haversham avoided the question. "Wing Commander, can you fly this ship by yourself—if you have to?"

"Yes, but I won't have to." Beame was confused.

"Dressler's the expert on the X-30."

"Good. Now, let's get on board. And remember. If you don't care about yourself, there's Constance and the boy."

LADY VICTORIA ASPREY puttered around the sun room of Hollow Oaks, an island of tranquility in a world she had learned to dislike. She halted in her small labors and placed her feet up on a flowered chaise, a copy of *Lady Chatterly's Lover* in hand.

Why would anyone want a gardener as a lover, she mused, when men like John "The Baptist" Davidson were available? He was of the right age, the correct intelligence, and apparently was smitten with her. Then why his restraint? She had done everything but seduce him. He was polite, even warm, but he still rebuffed her advances. The better-bred colonials like Davidson were strangely Puritanical for all their supposed sophistication, Victoria was convinced. Meanwhile, the upper-class English, like herself, had learned to free themselves of bourgeois inhibitions. At least she had.

Yes, she decided, she would seduce the Baptist, whether he was ready or not. It would be therapeutic for her and, though he might resist it, probably very good for the old spy as well.

"Oh, John, I was hoping you'd be able to make it," Victoria said as the Baptist entered the front door. "But really, gray herringbones in the dead of summer? Can't you change your ossified old habits?"

Davidson laughed, then surveyed the woman before him. She was not wearing trendy jeans, but was dressed in a halter top and a pair of tight shorts, with her midriff exposed. The outfit not only accentuated her body, but called up pleasant nostalgia for Davidson—as if he were a young man back in the 1950s, courting an attractive ingenue.

The longer he stared at Victoria, the more attractive she seemed. Her hair was blond, tinged with strawberry, and her bosom was full but not matronly. Her face was radiant, and her complexion the soft pink born of the moist English country air. So unlike the leathery face of many American women her age, who falsely believed a golf-course tan was feminine.

Feminine was the word for Victoria. As he stared at her, he sensed his loins react, a message that he—the widower—had learned to suppress. But not today.

"Victoria, you're absolutely beautiful." Davidson's lips were suddenly on hers, his arms fast around her waist. He traveled northward, caressing her breasts through the halter.

"John, you're naughty! I had no idea!"

Victoria's girlish giggle only inflamed his ardor. "I won't say 'stop,' John, only for fear that you will."

Lady Asprey folded her arms around Davidson's chest and pressed her hips into his groin, rotating in small, demanding circles.

"We don't want a premature accident, do we, John? Let's go to my bedroom. Believe me, my intentions are in no way honorable."

Davidson followed Victoria like a teenager being led into sex by the upstairs maid, which had been his own experience at fifteen in Boise, Idaho, in the large bourgeois house of his father, a successful mining engineer.

Seated on the edge of the bed, he watched while

Victoria performed suggestively in front of him. First she removed her halter, exposing her breasts to the light. They were large and upright, pink and red against white, defying gravity as if she were an adolescent.

"Don't stare so, John," she laughed, her manner pure flirtatiousness. "You make me feel self-conscious."

"Sorry, Victoria, but you are a magnificent phenomenon."

Lady Asprey removed her shorts, then her underclothes. Davidson thought it proper to look away, but he was transfixed by the light coursing through the large window, washing across her body, then settling on the blond forest at the confluence of her legs. Not only had he forgotten the sensation of such arousal, but he had never been so stimulated before in his life.

"Now, don't you go anywhere, John love. I want to put on my favorite outfit, just for you."

Davidson sat rigidly on the edge of the bed, still clothed in his herringbones, with his rep tie knotted tightly at his pulsating Adam's apple.

Victoria disappeared, but reemerged within two minutes. This time, she stood before him totally nude except for a long string of large pearls nestled between her breasts. She wore only a wide-brim straw summer hat, and her feet were shod in tall spike heels. Victoria stood there proudly, her body slowly undulating, first with her legs together, then wide apart.

"Now, sir, American intellectual," Victoria purred, "am I successfully seducing you? Do you want to enter the pearly gates?"

Davidson's mind whirled with pleasure and confusion. After all, this was the *wife* of his friend and colleague. He hesitated, but only for the moment. He rose from the bed, encumbered only by the tightening around his pants, and walked over to Victoria. Instead of expressing the unrestrained passion he felt, he merely kissed her softly on the lips.

"Thank you," he muttered.

"Does that mean you will?" she asked. "You are noted for your power of resistance."

"Perhaps usually. But not now."

Within moments, he had undressed, uncharacteristically throwing his clothes over a chair. He watched as Victoria took off her hat and shoes and moved onto the bed next to him. As he placed one arm around her, she put her head into the crook of his neck. His other hand slowly explored her body.

"John, you are such a dear man. I knew of your brain, but this!" Her soft fingers had found him.

The moment seemed suspended. Not since the days when Katherine was alive, had he felt such peace, as if lost years had suddenly been restored to him.

"Victoria, I really have no one to talk to—except you. I have something on my mind. Is this an appropriate time?"

"For what, John?" She had lifted her head off his chest and kissed him, once, then again and again. "Any time is good. We needn't hurry the festivities. Now, tell me what's troubling you."

"It's about Sir Malcolm. You know how closely we've worked over the years."

"Yes?"

"Well, I've discovered something that might implicate him in a spy plot."

"So? I don't know much about it, but I thought that was his business—for the Crown."

Davidson hesitated. Was it wise to be so frank with Malcolm's wife? They apparently led separate lives, but still . . . Then again, who better? Perhaps she could help him clear up the nagging, painful mystery.

"Yes, Victoria, but I'm afraid this spying is not for Britain. It's for a renegade band of Russians and their friends—the Red Chinese."

Victoria pushed aside the bed covers. She jolted up,

pressing her back against the headboard.

"No! John, you must be wrong. We've had our differences, but Malcolm is a patriot of the first order. Sure, he had a little flirtation with the left as a young man. So did I. So did most of our circle, but that's all finished." She paused, exhausted. "Do you have any evidence?"

Davidson felt foolish. He was in bed with a woman of great charm, and he had fallen into the trap of serious conversation. Slowly, he explained the five murders connected with the X-30, then the planned sting and the strangling of the two Agency men sent to protect the plane. Finally, he told her of the computer file from the Russian Embassy that had thrown suspicion on Sir Malcolm—that the famed MI5 agent might actually be "Mary," the mastermind who had planned the horrid conspiracy.

"John, that's just hearsay. Is that all you have?"

"No, there's Cavendish, Malcolm's gardener."

"Come now, what could that harmless man have to do with murder?"

"Everything."

Davidson described the thwarted attack on his life at the garden fair by a gaunt-faced man who resembled Cavendish, then of the attempt to kill his aide, young Tony Alcott, after he had tracked down Cavendish. He was convinced, Davidson said, that the Gardener was the hit man for "Mary."

He also explained the significance of the *halesia*, that a sprig of silver bells was left near the body of each murder victim.

"Then there's the appearance of silver bells—as in the nursery rhyme—at both Cavendish's nursery and here in Sir Malcolm's garden at Hollow Oaks," Davidson continued. "The tree is not a common one in England."

Victoria stared at him, first with a serious mien, then with a warm smile. Suddenly, she broke out into a hearty laugh, her nude bosom shaking in concert.

"John, you are *so* smart, but really what you're saying sounds like poppycock. Especially about Malcolm being a spy for the other side. Now, can you forget your famous paranoia for a moment and try to please a girl who finds you enchanting? Is it a deal?"

Without waiting for an answer, Victoria's hands found Davidson, stroking softly to restore his potency. Then her mouth found him as well, gently, liquidly, moving up and down as he sighed.

My God, Davidson thought, waiting for a polite moment, then removing himself.

"Victoria, I'm ready if you are. Never have I felt such emotion," he whispered as he began perhaps the greatest test of his retirement.

"NOW YOU GO up ahead and do your thing," the Gardener ordered a shaken Wing Commander Beame. "I'll stay back here in the instrument area. Just before takeoff, I'll see you up front. Remember, not a word to Colonel Dressler. Do your job as if all is well. I needn't remind you of the consequences."

Beame grimaced in response, but did as he was told, moving up to the pilot section, where he put on his pressure suit and strapped himself into the copilot's seat.

"Good to see you, Beame," Dressler said without looking up. "Ready to make history?"

"Absolutely, Colonel. I'm all checked out and ready to go."

Both men were about to put on their helmets when the Gardener, still wearing a squadron leader's uniform, moved cautiously forward until he stood just behind the pilot, motionless. He coughed to break the silence.

Dressler turned his head at the sound, and was face-to-face with the Gardener.

"What in the hell? Who are you?"

The Gardener didn't respond, at least not verbally. He slowly removed a long-bladed knife from his tunic and turned it toward the confused Colonel Dressler.

"Come on, put that thing away, Squadron Leader," the American colonel said in his strongest military tone. "It's bad enough you're aboard a classified vehicle without permission. Now give me the knife."

The Gardener stared ahead, his eyes betraying no emotion. It was as if Dressler hadn't yet spoken. He raised the knife from his waist and slashed with precision at the pilot's throat—once, twice, then again and again. Each cut tore away at the vital carotid artery, the blood splattering throughout the tight compartment.

Dressler slouched over the pilot's console, his head dangling close to Wing Commander Beame's side, his eyes vacant.

"Push him away, Beame," the Gardener ordered with a flourish of his knife. "Take over the plane and follow my directions."

"What?" Beame seemed unable to assimilate the rapid chain of events.

"Take off and set a course for Tajikistan in Central Asia—what used to be Soviet territory. There'll be a surprise waiting for you."

47

IT COULDN'T HAVE been more than thirty seconds after the lovemaking, or at least it seemed so. Davidson was jolted awake from a sweet sleep by the jangling of the telephone. Annoyed at the interruption, Victoria lifted the phone and placed her palm over the speaker.

"John, I must apologize," she said. "I should have shut off the ring before we began."

"Can I help you?" she finally said into the phone.

"Sorry to bother you." The voice at the other end was young. "This is Tony Alcott, Lady Asprey. John told me he was going to your place. I'm afraid it's an emergency. Could I please talk with him?"

Victoria grimaced. "John, it's your office. Must be the advent of World War III."

Davidson grabbed the phone and listened intently.

"Yes, Tony, I'll come right away. I'll meet you at the Northolt Air Base. Damn lousy news."

As the Baptist was dressing, he leaned over and kissed Victoria on the cheek. "Sorry to leave you, lovely woman, but duty calls."

"What's the big emergency?" Her face was slightly twisted in annoyance. "And just when we were enjoying ourselves."

"I told you about the X-30. Did you know that the plane is here at Northolt for joint flights with you Brits?"

"Vaguely. I think it was in the papers. Why?"

"Well, the multibillion dollar space plane is missing."

"Missing?"

"Well, actually more than that. It seems someone has stolen it, and it's on its way to Central Asia. Perhaps even to Red China."

Lady Asprey let out a small giggle. "China? What would that poor country want with a complicated piece of American machinery?"

As Davidson dressed, Victoria led him to the door.

"Thanks for giving an old man a thrill I'd almost forgotten existed," the Baptist said. "Now, if you don't mind, I'll wait outside on your lawn. They're sending a helicopter to pick me up."

"John, the pleasure was all mine. Or at least most of it. You were wonderful—and I don't mean in spite of your age, or mine."

Victoria kissed him long and lovingly, then started to laugh, girlishly.

"China and silver bells. Why, that's almost funny, John. Do all the spying you want, but please take care of yourself. I don't want to lose you now."

As Victoria waved good-bye, she was still muttering. "Red China? Can you imagine that?"

48

"BAPTIST! GLAD YOU got here so quickly."

Sir Malcolm shook Davidson's hand in the control room at Northolt, where a dozen American and British officials had gathered.

"It's just horrible," he explained. "The X-30 is now passing over southern Russia, near the Caucasus. The

Russkie's are tracking it for us on radar, and we have our spy satellite hooked in as well. But it's no use. The Russians have sent up some fighters, but they can't reach the X-30's altitude or match its speed. All we can do is wait and see where it lands."

Davidson had arrived at an impromptu three-nation parley. Representing the Americans was Ambassador Sy Belkin, Air Force General Malloy, Tony Alcott, and now Davidson. The Brits had Sir Malcolm, Defense Minister Nigel Gordon, and Air Marshal Sir John Twining. The Russian Republic representative, Sergei Makrov of the embassy, had been invited for his input not as his cover, "cultural secretary," but in his true capacity as Russian intelligence chief for the embassy.

"Where do you think the plane will land?" Davidson asked General Malloy.

"We'll know in a few minutes, John. They don't respond to radio calls, but our satellite shows it's now over Uzbekistan, headed for the edge of Central Asia in the old U.S.S.R., close to the Chinese border." He paused, pensively. "Or perhaps even to China itself. Hold on, Captain Scott tells me another report is coming in."

The general moved across the control room to where a U.S. Air Force captain sat at a triple radar display—signals for which were being fed from several sources, including a listening post outside Moscow and a U.S. spy-in-the-sky satellite tracking the flight.

"Sir, the plane has landed."

"Where, goddamn it, where?" Malloy barked at the captain.

"At a former Soviet air base in Tajikistan, not far from the Chinese border. The X-30 is on the ground, and it seems in good shape."

Malloy raced back to the assembled group. "The X-30 is in Tajikistan. What's going on in that country, Mr. Davidson? Can we trust those people?"

Davidson cogitated for only a moment.

"No, I'm afraid not. Despite their recent civil war, Tajikistan is mostly run by the old totalitarian leaders. Moreover, its relations with Moscow are not good. I'd say the people in Dushanbe—that's the capital—are getting closer to Iran, and yes to Beijing, than they are to the West. They could even be part of the plot against the X-30."

"Baptist." Makrov had spoken up quickly. "You don't mean that backward little country has masterminded this scheme?"

"No, it's just a pawn. There's only one real possibility. The Russian *falshivi* and Dr. Li are behind it. The Beijing government may be involved as well—by being afraid to throttle Dr. Li. I understand he's slated to move into Red China's number two slot at the next party confab."

"So what do we do now, Baptist?"

This question came from Sir Malcolm. Davidson felt uneasy, his mind seeking to settle conflicting waves of emotion. He had just slept with Asprey's wife, and the MI5 man—if the evidence held up—might prove to be the true mastermind of the conspiracy. God, never before had he felt so inadequate, so vulnerable to self-criticism and worse.

"I have no choice but to bring it to my President. This X-30 flight, gentlemen, has ascended far above all our heads."

49

THE HONORABLE ANTONY Riddle, Member of Parliament, stared into the gilded mirror of his Savoy Court apartment overlooking the Thames and the blackened stone Houses of Parliament, and had to laugh.

Once-little Anatole Resmenev, star English pupil of the Moscow Arts High School, was now a Tory MP and even mentioned as a possible deputy minister in Her Majesty's government.

Surely, he looked the part. Riddle adjusted the gray dotted silk tie, flipped the edge of his long-pointed shirt collar, and tugged at the double flaps of his Savile Row sharkskin suit. He turned and exited the fourteenth-floor apartment, heading toward his garage, where a well-tended 1982 Jaguar XJ-6 waited.

The trip to Portland Place took less than fifteen minutes on this quiet weekend morning. He was on his way to visit Dr. Li Chen, the enigmatic Chinese diplomat who was in effect *the* Red Chinese power in the Western world. Riddle was aware that Li was subservient to no one, especially his country's ambassadors, who happily housed him, whether in London, Bonn, Paris, or New York.

Riddle was now on direct assignment from John Davidson, who, with Sir Malcolm Asprey, had made their silence about his "illegal" status conditional on his using his contacts to help track down "Mary."

Riddle parked the Jaguar in an empty spot on Portland

Place. Moments later, he was admitted into the Embassy of the People's Republic of China, then escorted to Dr. Li's combined penthouse office and apartment.

"Welcome to my humble abode," Li chanted as Riddle entered. "Please have a seat."

Li waved the MP toward a red silk pillow placed so that one could sit cross-legged on the floor and still be able to eat or drink off the etched silver table in front of the pillow. Li's use of the word "humble" was partially, but not exactly, accurate. The room was sparse, decorated only with a minimum of Chinese artifacts. But each was exquisite in character and worth a Mandarin's ransom.

One wall was covered by a screen of painted wallpaper, obviously hundreds of years old, done in ageless gouache. It showed a deserted landscape of winter trees, with various birds, drawn in infinite detail, perched on their forlorn branches. Scattered through the room were pieces of blue-and-white porcelain. A large jade pendant—too large for any woman's bosom—hung from the wall, and the room was dotted with enormous celadon pots that had once held incense and diluted perfumes.

Dressed in his usual at-home green silk robe, the philosopher-spy sat opposite Riddle, working on his calligraphy. Swiftly, Li brought his hands together, but so softly that Riddle could barely hear the sound.

"Yes, Dr. Li? What can I do?" His attendant, the bespectacled Chui, who was always subtly hidden, suddenly appeared.

"Remove the calligraphy material. I have a distinguished guest, Antony Riddle, a member of Parliament."

Riddle smiled and braced himself.

"And to what do I owe this visit?" Li asked. Riddle knew of Li's reputation. He'd be given no more than five minutes, if that.

"I'm here on a mission for the British Foreign Office, Dr. Li."

"Yes?"

"As you may have heard, the American X-30 has been stolen and is apparently headed for China, or thereabouts. Simply, Her Majesty's government would like to know if you have any information about your government's possible involvement?"

Li's serious expression, which had broken the will of many subordinates, suddenly cracked. His face creased into a smile, and his body twisted in a unique posture. He bent over his silver stool and laughed, first facing downward, then jerking his head back so forcefully that the green silk skullcap fell off. He leaned over and retrieved the covering, placing it quickly back on, much like an embarrassed rabbi without his yarmulke.

"Forgive me, Mr. Riddle, but coming from you, I find that veiled accusation very funny."

Riddle looked at Li quizzically. "Why is that, sir? I come to you with the very best of intentions."

Li laughed again. "I must contain myself, little Anatole Resmenev. You, a Soviet illegal for a full generation, have the nerve to represent Her Majesty. Come now!"

Riddle shuddered with embarrassment, even fear. How had he been uncovered so easily by Chinese intelligence?

"How in the hell did you know?" Riddle asked. He was now standing and shouting, mainly in frustration. "My provenance was supposed to be secret, even from most of the KGB—let alone a foreign national like yourself!"

Li smiled, his expression one of pure condescension.

"Calm down, fancy spy. I've known all about you for years, ever since the KGB was dismantled. As the old Kremlin fell, they turned over the records of their illegals—four hundred strong—to me. You would be surprised who's on that list. Men of authority in Britain, some higher than you. Do you know Sir Malcolm Asprey . . . ?"

The breath involuntarily left Riddle's chest.

"Do you mean . . . that Sir Malcolm is a natural-born Russian, living a pose?"

Li was obviously enjoying the confrontation. He permitted himself a small titter.

"No, silly man. His people were on the expeditionary forces of William the Conqueror when they landed in Hastings in 1066."

"So . . . what about him?"

"Only that he's one of us, a traitor to the British cause. Just as were his predecessors, all Cambridge-educated. Your friend Sir Malcolm Asprey is the lead contact for the *falshivi* . . . and ourselves. Does that surprise you?"

Li was now standing. His stern visage, so animated at first, was now wreathed in disdain. He stood facing a gray-complected Riddle and stretched his fingers out of the green silk robe. He pointed them menacingly at Riddle, like an angered, vain fourteenth-century Mandarin.

"And tell your Svengali, Mr. John Davidson, late of his own country's Agency, that he had best keep out of my way. He—and you—are disposable obstacles on my mission to bring the Mandate of Heaven back to this earth. Do you understand? Do you understand?" Li screeched, then motioned toward the door.

"Chui, show this double traitor out into the street. He defiles the honor of the Middle Kingdom!"

50

ALISON MASON SET her square chin farther into the air and huffily addressed her partner-in-intelligence, Guy Lauder.

"Well, Mr. Big Shot Theater Director, what are *you* going to do about the rumors I hear from the American Embassy?"

"What rumors? Anything important?"

"Judge for yourself. It's just that someone in our MI5 group is a traitor working for the *falshivi* Russians and the Red Chinese."

Lauder, who had just come back through the Irving Theater rehearsal hall and into the MI5 office, stared at Alison as if she were mad.

"Where did you ever hear such nonsense?"

"A birdie who works with Davidson, a handsome young thing named Tony Alcott. He let it slip during a social engagement."

"Social engagement? You're dating an Agency man without letting Sir Malcolm or me know about it?"

Mason laughed. "My private life has to be my own, even if I know it isn't. Anyway, Tony said—in a private moment—that during the raid on the Russian Embassy they found a computer notebook with two notations on Mary's contacts."

Lauder seemed surprised. "And who were they?"

"Dr. Li, naturally, and . . ."

"Yes?" By this time Lauder's voice betrayed anxiety.

"Sir Malcolm himself."

Alison grasped Lauder's hand, as if to comfort him. His face was covered with disbelief.

Lauder pulled back. "Don't you go flirting with me after you've slept with the loyal opposition."

"Who says I slept with Alcott?"

Lauder placed his arm, like a loving noose, around Alison's neck, then moved his hand down and massaged the top of her breast.

"Darling, sleeping—yet not sleeping—is one of your favored exercises. Ask the man who has benefited greatly from that flaw."

Quickly, she pulled away.

"Snake! But aside from that, what are your thoughts about Malcolm? I can hardly believe what I've heard."

Lauder's expression turned sober. "Neither can I. I've known the man most of my life, and if ever there was a loyal subject, it's Malcolm." His expression was now contemplative. "But then again, can we trust anyone in our business? Even you seem suspect to me sometimes, Alison, what with your derring-do—like something out of a Bond film. I prefer the simpler, steady, sneaky type, like myself. But as to Malcolm, I think I'd bet on his loyalty. But then again, look at Kim Philby. He was apparently the most loyal, most dedicated of Her Majesty's subjects."

Alison was confused by Lauder's ruminations.

"Whatever that means, I don't think it'll wash as evidence, or as even solid speculation," she countered. "But I do have a method of checking. A bit dangerous, but I'm tempted to call in some chips. I did some old favors for someone at the Beijing Embassy on Portland Place."

"Really? How good a source is he?"

Mason smiled. "He's Dr. Li's assistant. He's never fed us any information. I tried several times to recruit him and failed. But he knows everything that goes on at

Portland Place. Maybe now I can get him to help out."

"What kind of blackmail do you have in mind? Pictures of homosexual encounters?"

"No, nothing so theatrical, Guy. I did him a big favor by getting him out of Hong Kong and into the U.K. Pulled a few strings and now I'm going to cash in—if I can."

Lauder placed his arm around Mason's waist, holding her gingerly, careful not to offend.

"Forgive my acerbic manner, Alison. I admire you enormously—in addition to loving you. So please, be careful. Anything connected with Dr. Li could be dangerous."

Slowly, she unwrapped Lauder's arm.

"Don't worry, darling, I'm a big girl now. I can take care of myself."

Lauder pecked at her cheek. "I know, Alison. That's what worries me."

"GET MALINOVSKY ON the phone! Right now!"

A furious President Briggs shuffled his large, inexact frame across the Oval Office, halting for a moment, by habit, over the federal eagle woven into the rug.

"Goddamn him," he shouted to the scalloped niche alongside the fireplace. "If he's pulling a fast one, that'll be the end of our financial help. Let them all starve!"

Les Fanning rushed into the room and surveyed her boss, who had obviously lost his temper.

"I have the Russian president on the phone, Mr. President. He probably heard that last expletive, so maybe you should calm down before you get on. He told me he wants no interpreter. He'll struggle through with his English."

Briggs stared at his aide. At first, he scowled, then he smiled at her pleasant countenance. It was hard to stay angry at Les, or even to rage in her presence.

"OK, Les. Sorry about the outburst. Put him through."

"Malinovsky," the President began in a firm tone, "I know that you have to continue your little espionage games to appease the old-guard KGB. But this is too much!"

"What's too much, Mr. President?" The Russian seemed stunned. "What have my adventuresome spies done now?"

"What's too much?" Briggs repeated. "I'll tell you what. Only that some foreign nation—and I believe some of your hard-liners are involved—has just stolen the X-30!"

Malinovsky's initial response was silence. "What—stolen the X-30? I can't believe it!" he finally blurted. "Mr. President, please trust me. I know nothing about it, and I'll do everything possible to find out if any of my people are involved."

If the Russian were acting, he was a master.

"What you can do, right away, is to bring in some of those bastard *falshivi* who are trying to undermine your democracy. It'll help us both."

Malinovsky's second silence lasted only an instant.

"Easier said then done, Mr. President. They are everywhere, spreading their poisons. They and *Pamyat*— 'Memory' in English—and *Soyuz*—'Union'—and the old party people, and 'Motherland.' They're all part of a conspiracy to bring back the days of dictatorship and glory. You know my dilemma."

"What dilemma? You're President of Russia and commander in chief of the armed forces, just as I am. No?"

"Yes, but our situations are quite different. You have the allegiance of your people. I'm still on thin ice, even in the Russian winter. President Briggs, you don't make a democratic omelette like ours without scrambling other people's eggs. So I must be very careful. If I hurt them too much, poof, that could mean a *successful* coup—the end of democracy in Russia and the return to the Cold War. You don't want that, do you?"

Briggs was caught up sharply.

"So, is there anything you can do?" he asked the Russian, now more gingerly. "My people tell me that the X-30 plot is being engineered by your *falshivi* working hand-in-glove with the Red Chinese."

"The Chinese? In Beijing?"

"Well, we're not sure if it's a direct government operation or a covert one engineered by the old Mandarin Dr. Li Chen of the TEWU secret police. But either way, the X-30 has been stolen and has landed in Tajikistan not far from the Chinese border." Briggs paused for effect. "What can you do to help?"

Malinovsky wasted no time. "I'll do all I can. First, I'll locate the plane exactly. Then, I'll call in my Air Force and ground commanders and see what they can do. Give me a couple of days, and we'll talk again. Please—some patience, Mr. President."

Briggs sighed. "Patience is not one of my virtues. I'll give you twelve hours to get back to me with your intentions. If you can't get that plane back, I may have to go in and do it myself. Do you read me?"

The President hung up, then strode over to the glass door overlooking the Rose Garden.

"Damn him, the Russians, and their Chinese cousins," he muttered to no one. "They'd better not lose that plane."

52

"COME ON, TONY, let's get a cab. The train leaves Victoria Station just before midnight. We've got to be in Hastings by 2:30 A.M."

Urgency was obvious in Davidson's voice. But on the way to the station, the Baptist was quiet, intent in thought, straining to unravel the perplexing complications of the last twenty-four hours.

"We'll talk on the train, Tony. OK?"

Moments before, at the American Embassy at Grosvenor Square—marked by its oversize stone eagle and the statue of FDR—Davidson had received a scrambler phone call directly from the Oval Office. After the X-30 had landed in a former Soviet air base in Tajikistan, the American ambassador in Dushanbe, capital of the isolated Central Asian republic, had rushed to the airfield.

As Davidson expected, the ambassador's entry was blocked. He could only report that the X-30 was seemingly unscathed and sitting like a forlorn bird on the tarmac, surrounded by scores of Tajik troops outfitted in old KGB uniforms with telltale blue stripes down the sides of their trousers.

As to the condition of the American pilot, Colonel Dressler, and the Brit, Wing Commander Beame, the President had received no word. The local military had refused to say. Beame was obviously under pressure to cooperate with those who had kidnapped his wife and child. Otherwise, the plane would never have left its original course. There were no other pilots, aside from an American standby crew still at Northolt, who had been prepped to handle the sophisticated machine.

The news in Britain was equally disheartening. Malcolm Asprey had assigned Guy Lauder and Alison Mason to lead the search—along with nearly a hundred personnel from New Scotland Yard and Royal Air Force Intelligence—for the kidnapped mother and child. But so far they hadn't found even a stray hair. Until the victims were located and freed, Davidson was convinced, the decorated wing commander was an unwilling captive— and collaborator—of the X-30 plotters.

President Briggs had also informed Davidson that added pressure was being put on the Kremlin leader, Malinovsky. The Russian had already been in touch with the Tajikistan President—Ahmed Sajoban—warning him of the consequences if the space plane was not returned immediately to American authorities. But the threats had thus far wafted uselessly into the balmy California-like air of Dushanbe. What, Davidson wondered, could Malinovsky do to control one of his former colonies, anyway?

And what of the Chinese?

Davidson had asked the same question in a static-ridden phone conversation with Preston Sommerstall, the American CIA chief of station in Dushanbe.

"The town has a lot of Chinese diplomats, and their TEWU intelligence people are always hovering around," Sommerstall had told him. "I saw a few of them— including one military attaché—at the airfield. But no, I have no information on whether the Chinese government is involved in this X-30 gambit. I've got two men on it, and I'll let you know as soon as I get more info."

Suddenly, the Baptist's logical thinking was interrupted. The black Rover taxi had pulled to a stop in front of Victoria Station. He motioned to Alcott.

"Let's go, son. They're waiting for us at Hastings on the Sea—you know, the place where William the Conqueror landed in 1066. Now it's home to some failed conquerors as well. The Russkies have a beautiful mansion—a recreation place for their tired diplomats—there. Hurry. We've got to make the 11:58."

In the first-class compartment of the late London-Hastings train, Davidson lifted his feet onto the seat and smiled at his young colleague.

"All right, Tony. Impatience is etched on your face. What do you want to know?"

"What? Just everything. And why the hell, in the middle of an international crisis—and in the middle of the night—are we chasing off to some damn spa, even if it is owned by the Russians?"

Carefully, so that Alcott wouldn't miss a nuance, Davidson related the strange phone call he had received from Harston near Cambridge at 10 P.M., only minutes after his return to the embassy from the X-30 watch at Northolt.

"SO NOW YOU know everything I do, Tony. But I hope we'll both learn a hell of a lot more when we get to Hastings."

Davidson had related the cryptic phone call he had received from a phone booth in Hastings.

"All he said was that his name was Dazindov, and that he was the second secretary of the Russian Embassy in

Kensington Palace Gardens," the Baptist told Alcott. "I should remember him, he said, because the night we broke into the embassy, it was in his office that we found the computer file that implicated Sir Malcolm. Those are good bona fides. If he's not Dazindov, he knows a lot about what's going on, so it was worth keeping him talking."

"Then what did he say?" Alcott was displaying his obsessive curiosity, a trait he had picked up, like some biogenetic virus, from Davidson.

"He said if we ever wanted to see Mrs. Beame and her child alive, we'd better take the night train to Hastings, where the Russians have their summer estate. The train gets in at 2 A.M., and we're supposed to meet him outside the station. He'll be parked in a green Ford Escort and be with two other Russians."

"Why not at the Russian summer place?"

"I have no idea, Tony. But I do know that this could be a trap—a good way for the *falshivi* to grab us, just like they've probably grabbed the Beames. Makrov warned me about Dazindov. Says he's a leader of the Red-Brown conspiracy to take over democratic Russia. But we don't have much choice, do we? If we don't meet Dazindov, maybe the *falshivi* will really kill the Beames."

Alcott nodded reluctant agreement. Davidson could see fear cross the young man's face. After all, Tony had volunteered for a business that was eons away from his ivory tower of Newtonian speculations. He was a physicist, not a spy, but he had done a yeoman's job so far.

"John, I'm going to take a nap, if you don't mind."

In a moment, Alcott was stretched out across the seats and asleep in the six-passenger train compartment, in which they were the only voyagers. Davidson walked into the corridor to exercise and, by habit, swiveled his neck in a quick half circle to establish security. Was anyone on the train interested in him? As he searched, he realized how much he enjoyed trains, especially the old

English variety. They had provided the ambience for so many Edwardian novels and the spy genre of World War II. The corridor conjured up images of Agatha Christie and antique British films of intrigue.

But this was 1993. Things were obviously quite different.

Davidson walked toward the snack car to get some coffee. Halfway down the aisle, he felt pressure at his back. He turned to see a short, burly man rudely force his way past him. Just as he recovered his balance, he felt a similar presence. He pushed himself against the corridor wall just as another man, this one tall and also heavy, pressed through, seemingly oblivious of the Baptist.

Davidson continued toward the snack car. Already seated at a table, the two men seemed to avoid his eyes. What was it about them that he found disturbing? For one, their haircuts were particularly non-Western—shorn by a mechanical clipper into a crude crew cut.

He sat at the next table and concentrated on his coffee for a few minutes, then rose and returned to the compartment. Alcott stirred from his nap as Davidson entered. "Where'd you disappear to?"

"I went into the snack car. Saw two uncharming men. Better keep alert before we get to Hastings."

Tony returned to his prone position on the long couchlike seats. Within a minute, Davidson looked up curiously—but without surprise—as the two men entered.

"Move aside, boy," the short one barked, pushing at Alcott's leg. "We're going to sit down here. Join your friend on the other side. This is a public compartment—am I right?"

Davidson smiled insincerely. "Surely, but please try to be quiet. My friend here is tired. Am I right, Tony?"

Alcott nodded and moved to Davidson's side of the compartment.

"John, I'll just resume my nap, sitting up." He also

smiled insincerely at the intruders.

The room was soon filled with a strained silence. Davidson stirred, musing, then looked out the window. In the immediate distance, he could see lights outlining a tunnel. He had never taken the London-Hastings train, so he had no idea of the route or the adjoining landscape. As the train moved into the tunnel, a strange echo of sound came through an open window. The air was pressed first against the tunnel walls, then pushed back onto the speeding train.

Davidson had been staring out when, from the other side of the compartment, suddenly came a sound that shook the small space. What was it? Surely the retort of a gun. The compartment was thrust into complete darkness. The bullet had obviously found its mark in the overhead light.

Suddenly, a second, then a third shot sparked tracers in the dark. The chaos was followed by first a scream, then a low moan. Davidson's reflexes were rapid. He grabbed the Beretta out of his shoulder holster, then jumped flat onto the brown carpet that covered the floor. He aimed toward the opposite seat, but feared to fire in the extreme darkness.

"Tony! Tony! Are you OK?" the Baptist shouted. Anxiety filled the room.

The compartment door swung open, followed by a blistering flash of light from the hall, which illuminated the compartment.

Davidson could see Alcott on his knees, bending over one of the duo. The man's eyes were glazed. The rug was spotted with the rust-wine stain of blood.

"What happened, Tony?" Davidson called out.

"No time, now, John. The other guy just ran out the door. Let's go after him."

The younger man sprinted from his crouch, followed by the Baptist, who was suddenly winded trying to keep pace with the athlete.

"Down the corridor, John!" Tony called over his shoulder. "He's headed for the snack car."

Guns drawn, Davidson and Alcott raced down the train aisle. The frightened passengers hunched into their chairs as the fleeing assailant was followed by the two Agency men.

"Stop or we'll shoot!" Alcott shouted. The handful of passengers dove for the floor.

"Hold off, Tony!" the Baptist shouted back. "It could be dangerous."

By this time, Alcott had sprinted ahead of the old spy. Davidson heard two loud retorts from the end of the train, coming from the entrance to the caboose-like car.

My God! What's happened? he asked himself as he trailed Alcott by a dozen yards, his heart sending out painful signals of age.

When Davidson arrived, the scene in the compartment was duplicated. Alcott was bent over, seeming to minister to a wounded man on the floor. A bullet had pierced the man's chest, and the blood was oozing slowly out.

"Who are you, and what do you want with us?" Davidson, who had arrived somewhat breathless, asked.

The man stared up at the Baptist. His voice, tinged with a Russian accent, was strong, even arrogant.

"Baptist. Do yourself and the Beames a favor and mind your own business. Otherwise everyone will get hurt."

His words suddenly came slower.

"Who are you working for?" Davidson asked. "Who's trying to stop the X-30?"

He leaned over to catch the response, but the bulky agent—surely a *falshivi*—was silent.

Alcott reached for the man's wrist. "He's unconscious, John, but I think he'll make it."

Davidson rose quickly and grabbed Alcott's arm. "Quick. We've got to get out of here." He paused.

"And by the way, boy soldier, how in the hell did you know to shoot it out in the compartment? And thanks for saving me."

Tony blushed. "I was pretending to sleep. I noticed the bulge in the short man's jacket, so I put my hands on the Beretta in my pocket and aimed it through my pants. See the bullet hole?" He pointed to his damaged flannels. "As soon as the light went out, I shot. Caught him before he could turn on us."

Davidson's laugh was without condescension. "You're doing fine, Alcott. But we can't afford a police inquest right now. When the train slows down for the Hastings station, jump off. Watch your ankles. We'll walk into town and meet the Russians somehow. When they find out what's happened on the train, I'm sure they'll look for us."

54

ALISON TRUDGED THROUGH the London rain, the droplets filling the air with a wall of humidity that clung to her body. She had been born in London, and had never lived anywhere else—or wanted to—but the humidity, which did so much for her pink complexion, had invaded her skeletal system with a gnawing low-level arthritic pain. But like Samuel Johnson, she never tired of the city, and her discomfort had become almost a friend.

Chui was waiting for her at Lum's, a small Chinese restaurant near the Elephant & Castle tube station, a section that had seen better days. He hadn't hesitated to meet her, though it was already 10 P.M. He had been working all day at the Chinese Embassy, obediently catering to the demanding needs of his employer, the eccentric Dr. Li Chen, master of calligraphy, philosophy, and less beneficent arts.

Alison entered the small restaurant, which was noted for the absence of any outside signs. Strangers were not welcome, and the chef cooked only for those who understood the difference between tourist fare and the subtleties of the Cantonese cuisine.

"Welcome, Ms. Mason. Always a pleasure to see you." The proprietor, the short barrel-like Mr. Weng, bowed. "The people of the Strand are always welcome in my humble place." Wearing traditional Chinese clothes, he wobbled slowly toward the rear. "Mr. Chui is waiting."

She followed Weng to a private room no more than eight feet square with a lacquered black table in the center. Four carved ebony chairs reminiscent of English Chippendale surrounded it. After Weng closed the door, Chui rose and enthusiastically approached Alison.

She sensed that his outstretched arms sought a warm embrace, but at the last moment, he judiciously pulled back. They were friends, but there was a divide.

"Ms. Mason, I came here as soon as you called. Can I help in any way?"

Alison motioned for him to sit. Weng arrived and, without seeking their order, offered a cornucopia of Cantonese food, one dish following another—dumplings, sharkfin soup, stuffed pigeon.

"Weng, enough for now." Alison tightened the leather Ralph Lauren belt that held a cable sweater against her waist, accentuating her breasts. Both men seemed diverted by the sensuous move, but she pretended innocence.

Once Weng had left, Alison leaned forward.

"Chui, I desperately need your help." Her voice was

muted as she glanced about for any hint of an eavesdropper. "You must know that MI5 has been searching for a lead to the insider who's helping Dr. Li. I've never tried to involve you in my work, but things are coming to a head. I need to know who the traitor is, and—if you know—the identity of Mary."

The Chinese aide leaned back against the stool, his tawny face turned a pale porcelain.

"Ms. Alison. These are dangerous thoughts. I trust you, but I cannot trust myself, or my superiors. I could find myself on a London wharf, and then in the river with my feet bound. A sorry way to end a young life. Surely you understand."

Alison nodded agreement, but her mind was marshaling arguments to convince Chui to play the informer role. She knew it fit his democratic instincts, if not his desire to live beyond his thirty-one years.

"Of course I understand, Chui. But then again—and forget that I helped you come to England—you are in a key position to hurt the Communists and boost the chances for a democratic China. If China stays totalitarian, its power could someday menace the West. You know that, don't you?"

Chui fell silent, picking at his pickled mushrooms, holding them in his chopsticks, and softly placing them in his mouth one at a time.

Alison stared, waiting.

"And what of my security?" he asked. "Could you arrange to protect me if I cooperated? I'd have to leave the embassy and live elsewhere."

Alison brightened. "Of course. We have a witness protection program much like the FBI's in America. We'd provide you with a new name, ID, a job, and a home far from London—perhaps in Scotland or Wales—where you could start again."

Chui took up his chopsticks. Again, he picked at the mushrooms.

"I could think about it. Or . . ."

"Or what?"

"Or I could tell you right now. At first, I had only suspicions, but I have finally plotted the full organization. It took risk and time, but I found the Chinese contact in MI5, and the efficient hit man, the head of the *falshivi* . . ."

"And the identity of Mary?" Alison's voice was shaky.

"Yes, Mary, too."

Chui looked up from his mushrooms. Alison turned toward the door and concentrated as the knob turned. She had felt no need to lock it. The door parted a few inches, then swung in as a man entered through the darkened portal. She narrowed her eyes, but couldn't make out who it was in the dim light. He was wearing Western clothes. It was not Weng, the proprietor. Across the lower half of the man's face was a tightly wrapped paisley ascot.

"Who is it? Who are you—and what do you want?" Alison's voice announced her trepidation.

The intruder walked within two paces of the ebony table and suddenly stripped off the ascot. It was Guy Lauder.

"Why, it's you! What in the hell are you doing here?"

"I told you I was worried about your bravado. Sometimes you frighten me, Alison. So I decided to trail you. When I saw you get into the tube and come to this neck of town, I was sure you needed protection."

Lauder stared at her dining partner. "And who is this?"

Alison explained, then added: "And you came in just at the right time. Chui was about to tell me everything— the double agent in MI5, even the identity of Mary." She turned to the young Chinese aide. "Now, please tell us everything."

"In someone else's presence?" Chui asked anxiously.

"Yes, it's OK. He works with me in MI5. Let's start with the double agent."

Chui looked down and speared a pickled mushroom.

"Ms. Alison, I don't personally know the British double agent working for Li, but I do know his identity. He is—"

The sentence was half out of Chui's mouth when Alison heard the unmistakable ping of a gun with a silencer. Instinctively, she thought it was a Beretta. She turned toward the sound, and there was Lauder, the 9-mm weapon in hand, the smoke still wafting into the tight room. She whirled back to Chui, who had toppled off the stool. An almost bloodless hole in his forehead was centered neatly between his eyes. The only other sound was a futile grunt.

"Guy!" Alison screamed "Have you gone mad? He was one of us!"

Lauder said nothing. He moved the gun in a small arc, away from the fallen Chui, until it faced Alison.

"Darling, you must know I love you" was all he said. The second bullet was equally true, cutting Alison's perfect nose bridge in two.

Lauder replaced the scarf over his mouth and turned. He walked out of Lum's, waving his gun menacingly as he exited.

55

"WE CAN'T GET too close to the train station, Tony," Davidson advised. "I'm sure the local police are there, handling the wounded men and out looking for us. Just keep walking. We're headed in the direction of the Russian country place." The Baptist paused. "Dazindov will probably head in this direction to find us. He's driving a Ford Escort."

They walked for over a mile on a narrow country road, watching cautiously behind them, fearful they would be run down by the very people seeking them out.

"How much farther, John?" Alcott asked, almost like a child in the backseat of a car.

"It's still a few miles to the estate, but maybe we won't have to cover the full distance. Just keep a tight eye out behind us. These roads are picturesque, but treacherous."

The night was clear and the moon almost full. The light cast an eerie glow over the silent landscape.

"Quick, John, pull over onto the grass," Tony suddenly called out. "A car's coming."

The two men jumped in time as a speeding car passed them. They watched it move ahead, then grind to a sudden halt about a hundred yards beyond. Nothing moved until someone—they could make out a small wiry man with spectacles and a full head of hair—got out and ran toward them.

"Baptist! It's me, Dazindov!" he shouted in only

slightly accented English, catching up with them at the side of the road. "It took me a while to figure out which way you'd head. Get in the car. We've got a small safe house down the road."

"Aren't we going to the Russian estate?" Davidson asked, surprised.

Dazindov eyed him quizzically. "No, that's not wise under the circumstances, Mr. Davidson. Just follow me and I'll explain all."

The safe house was a quaint cottage, the type once occupied by Miss Marple of Agatha Christie fame. The beams within were uncovered, the living room tight but high.

"Now, tell me, why aren't we discussing this at the estate?" Davidson asked politely.

Dazindov lowered his steel-rimmed glasses, which gave him the look of a professor's young assistant. "Because *they* have seized the place and have Mrs. Beame and the child there as prisoners. They're hostages to guarantee that Wing Commander Beame will comply with their plot to fly the X-30 out to Asia, where it is now. They'd kill us all on sight if we walked through the front door."

Davidson strained not to reveal his surprise.

"And what about Colonel Dressler, the American pilot?"

"He's dead. His throat was slashed on the plane by their operative. He's the same killer who's taken out six people connected with the project. A professional hit man. And I understand he's an Englishman."

"Who's that?" Davidson asked, looking for confirmation that the Gardener—Cavendish—was the one.

Dazindov shook his head. "I haven't the slightest idea, Baptist. Nor do I know who 'Mary' is—the mastermind of the whole scheme."

Some of the puzzle was becoming clear, but Davidson was still confused.

"But who's 'they'? I thought that you were the head of the Russian *falshivi* in London, the real plotters."

"I'm sorry, Baptist, but who told you that?"

"Why, Makrov, of course. He's been after you people for some time."

Dazindov's laugh filled the rafters of the high room.

"Makrov? Oh, no. Baptist, that's funny."

"In what way funny? I presume this is serious business."

"Davidson, for such a world-renowned personage, you've gone astray on this one. It's Makrov! He's the top man of the *falshivi*!"

Davidson was stunned, unbelieving.

"Oh, no." The Baptist's cry was almost a wail. "He's been working with me on this for weeks, using the embassy as the headquarters to find Mary and break open the Red Chinese–*falshivi* conspiracy." Davidson paused. "And, yes, he's been my friend—and my country's— throughout. You don't know what you're talking about. Why have you brought us here on a wild-goose chase?"

"No, my friend. I assure you that it is I, Dazindov, who is your friend. I am head of the *nastoyashchi*— loyal to democratic Russia and to our President. In fact, Malinovsky has just called me today, authorizing me to cooperate with the British authorities. We're to use any force necessary to retake the summer embassy—from Makrov—and free the hostages."

"Makrov's in there now with the hostages?" Davidson's voice now betrayed more sadness than disbelief.

"Yes, Baptist. And he's not about to release them."

Somehow he believed Dazindov. Otherwise why would the Russian want to retake his own summer estate? But Makrov on the other side? My God, the end of the Cold War had upset the most comfortable of alliances.

"And what about Sir Malcolm Asprey?" the Baptist asked, his mind still whirling. "The item in the computer file we found in your office said that either he's 'Mary' or closely tied to the conspiracy. Is that true?"

Dazindov rolled his lip and shrugged, Russian style. "I haven't the slightest idea, Baptist. Perhaps it's true, or maybe it was meant to throw you off the track. In any case, we've got to get ready for the assault on the summer estate. Are you with me?"

Davidson thought for only a moment, then relied on his instinct. He gave his head a melancholy nod.

"I wish it were otherwise, but yes, I'm with you, Dazindov. If the Beames are being held captive there, that's our passport to regaining the X-30. At least it gives a chance that the wing commander will rebel against his captors."

The old spy turned. "Tony, what about you?"

"Wouldn't miss it for the world, Baptist."

"BEAME, THIS IS Flight Officer Tang of the People's Republic of China Air Force. You will train him to fly the X-30, no matter how long it takes. Do you understand?"

The officer in charge of the X-30 detention was a tall, ascetic Russian named Colonel Leonidov, who was apparently attached—officially or otherwise—to the former Central Asian Soviet Republic of Tajikistan. The small, independent nation, situated directly on the Red

Chinese border, with a population of 5 million, had gone through a civil war and had somewhat strained ties with Moscow. But it had retained a working relationship with both the *falshivi* within the KGB and MVD, and with the hard-liners in the Russian military.

Colonel Leonidov was one of them. He was seated, arms akimbo, with his polished black boots up on the desk of the local commander. Seated across from him, expressionless, was Red Chinese Flight Officer Tang. Beame had been "called" in to meet him and now stood flanked by two Tajik MPs wearing old U.S.S.R. uniforms.

Beame looked skeptically at his captor and the Chinese flyer.

"Help you train Flight Officer Tang on the X-30?"

"Yes, and simultaneously, you'll be training a young Russian officer, Captain Malik—a former cosmonaut— who's now on extended duty to Tajikistan, reporting to me. He'll arrive here later today from a Siberian air base. How does that strike you?"

Beame smiled. "Not very well. I'm an officer in Her Majesty's Air Force, and I'll take orders only from her, or her appointed servants. If this is war—and I suppose it is, of a sort—I'll just rely on my rights under the Geneva Convention and sit it out. Officers, you must know, are not required to work when taken prisoner. And training your people to fly the X-30 would be, I assure you, work. And a distasteful job at that."

"Quiet!" a Tajik guard shouted in English. As the word left his mouth, he raised his AK-47 to eye height. With a twist of his wrist, he pushed the wooden gun butt into Beame's stomach. The wing commander fell to the floor, gasping.

Leonidov approached Beame, then stretched out his arms and pulled the Englishman to his feet. Placing a hand on the wing commander's shoulder, he laughed. At first the sound was soft, but it soon swelled to a more typical Russian howl.

"Beame, you English are magnificent. You conquered the world with your arrogance and legalities, and now look at you. We Soviets were the next great empire, and our inefficiency and corruption destroyed us. But we have one last chance for Communist empire—the Red Chinese. Once we retake Moscow from the democratic fools, as we shall, we'll make a bond of socialist unity with Beijing and recapture our power. And you, Wing Commander, will play a part in that—this very week. If not, of course, your wife and child will be killed. And you as well."

Leonidov walked over to a table at the other side of the sparsely furnished room and lifted a Panasonic tape recorder. He removed a cassette from his long tunic pocket and placed it into the slot. "Here, listen to this."

Beame winced at the sound of his wife's voice.

"Terrence," she said on the tape. "I'm here, somewhere in the English countryside—I don't know where—with our boy, as captives of a group of Russians. They are not hurting us, but every day they threaten to slash our throats if you don't do exactly as they say. First they say they will kill little Ian while I watch him bleed to death. Then they will kill me the same way. Darling, I believe they are serious. But I don't care. I'm perfectly willing to die, so—"

Abruptly, the tape ended.

"Your wife is very courageous, Wing Commander." These were the first words uttered by the Chinese pilot, Tang. "But I believe you are more sensible than she. Perhaps both of you are willing to die—for what, I don't know—but surely you wouldn't take the life of your only child."

Beame's composure shattered. He shut his eyes and, with head bent, staggered toward a chair. The Tajik MP was about to block him with a rifle, but Leonidov waved him off.

"Yes, Wing Commander. Please sit down and think about it—for a few seconds anyway."

Beame bowed his head again, then rose smartly to his feet. "I'll do what you say, you bastards. But I want assurances my family—and I—will all be freed when the training is over. Do I have your word, Colonel, as a military man, that you agree and will force your Tajik friends to obey your orders?"

Leonidov jumped to his feet. As if addressing a senior officer, he clicked his heels.

"You have my word, on my sacred military honor, Wing Commander. Now, let us go to the amazing flying object and learn its secrets."

"THERE ARE NOW six of us," Dazindov explained to Davidson, using the tailgate of his Escort wagon as a strategy table. On a large pad, he had drawn a schematic of the Russian mansion at Hastings, and the extensive grounds surrounding it. "We'll have to make a coordinated attack without outside help if we're going to free the hostages—alive."

"Why not call in the local authorities?" Tony asked.

"No, Dazindov is right. We have no real evidence that they're in there," Davidson answered. "The local police would never move against sovereign diplomatic property without absolute proof. No, I'm afraid we're going to have to trust our *nashi* friend here, and go it alone."

Now, it was Dazindov's turn to question.

"But, Baptist, why aren't you calling in MI5, and your old friend Asprey? He's been suspicious of the embassy for some time, and he's right. His people could lend a real hand."

Davidson had no desire to field that inquiry. There were now two strikes against the loyalty of Sir Malcolm: the original computer file, which perhaps seemed less authentic in light of Dazindov's claim. But there was also Antony Riddle's revelation, delivered directly from the lips of Dr. Li—that Asprey was their key player in the British bureaucracy. Davidson couldn't rule out the real possibility that Li's charge was disinformation. But neither could he disregard it. No, tipping his hand to a disloyal Asprey could unravel the whole plan.

"Dazindov, any extension of the operation could be suicidal," he answered cryptically. "Let's go with what we have."

That wasn't very much. The attack began before dawn, at exactly 4:30 A.M. Dazindov had distributed flak jackets to everyone, which included himself, three other *nashi* Russians from the Kensington embassy, Davidson, and Alcott. The strategy was based on a two-pronged attack.

The first stage began on time. Two of his men gathered a handful of rocks and threw them into the electrified fence circling the Hastings property. As they hit, the alarm went off. A series of floodlights, placed strategically around the perimeter, came on automatically. Davidson could hear noises from the house. The alarm and the brights had awakened everyone.

"All right, Tony, it's your turn. Show us those Princeton rifle-team smarts."

Alcott had placed a blanket on the dew-soaked grass outside the fence. He lay down, prone, his Connecticut-made .22-caliber Ruger sharpshooter rifle extended. His elbows were taut, serving as a supporting base. One at a time, he found the floodlights in his telescopic sight and shattered each with a sensitive squeeze of his trigger. After seven successful shots, the grounds were again shrouded in a blackness that wouldn't be relieved until sunrise, more than sixty minutes later.

Dazindov impatiently waved a hand. Two of his men advanced toward the fence carrying a set of electrical cables like those used to jump start a battery. The cables were attached to the Ford engine. Wearing rubber gloves, the two men attached the cables to the fence, then moved back. Dazindov came forward with a pencil flashlight and examined the voltage meter. They had successfully grounded the fence's electric charge.

"OK," Dazindov called. Waving his arms in a broad circle, he signaled the advance of the six men. Tony Alcott was the first to arrive at the fence. Quickly, he threw a weighted nylon ladder over the top of the cyclone barrier, then mounted the defused fence, climbing hand-over-hand until he reached the top, nine feet in the air. At the pinnacle, he grasped the pointed edge with his gloved hand, then dropped onto the ground below, tumbling expertly as he hit the tightly woven English lawn.

The others followed in the same fashion, all imitating the young athlete. At Davidson's order, they spread out like an alert infantry squad and advanced across the ground carrying their UZI semi-automatics. Darkness hid them at first, but they soon became partially exposed as the moonlight broke through the tree cover of the cultivated landscape.

They kept close to the ground, moving ahead stealthily. In unison, they fell prone after each advance, then rose and moved forward again, until they were fifty feet from the house.

Suddenly, the landscape changed. The six men hit the ground with an anxious thud. A second set of floodlights came on, this time from the parapets of the mansion, illuminating the area like a baseball diamond. A rattle of hostile fire followed from the roof of the embassy retreat. Instantly, two of Dazindov's men were struck.

"Hit the lights, Tony!" Davidson shouted.

Alcott had already positioned himself and the Ruger. He aimed, pressed, and aimed again, repeating the operation six times in less than four seconds. His aim was true. Within moments, the landscape returned to its dark, pristine state.

Davidson now waved the second prearranged signal. Dazindov and the remaining Russian were to take the rear door, which had been marked out before the attack. The Baptist and Alcott were to charge the elaborate front entry. The move began, first slowly and with extreme caution. Then, as Davidson flourished his hand a second time, they advanced with the urgency of a cavalry charge.

The foursome moved forward energetically, but were almost immediately halted. Another barrage of fire came from the Russian summer mansion.

"They must have infrared scopes," Alcott called out. "Everyone take cover!"

Within seconds, the surviving four had dispersed. Each man raced for cover, constantly moving sideways to outwit the sharpshooters. Davidson found shelter behind a stout tree that had seen a hundred summers.

He waited, pensive, frustrated, then decided to test the accuracy of his opponents' fire. Slowly, he moved the barrel of his Uzi into clear territory. It immediately drew a flash of tracers, which lit the night sky and missed the protective tree trunk by only inches. There was no doubt. He and the others were pinned down, perhaps hopelessly.

Dazindov's last aide, a tall former KGB man named Vladimir Abramovich, suddenly darted from behind a tall boxwood hedge and dashed toward the back door. The former Olympic athlete maneuvered magnificently.

He hopped, skipped, then rolled over as he ran, evading one barrage of fire after another.

When only ten feet from the small balcony protecting the back door, he stopped. But not voluntarily. His body was filled with a dozen bullets fired by a second-story guard who had flashed a light onto the rear entrance. Vladimir rolled over once more, for the last time.

"Stay where you are, everyone!" Davidson called to his surviving colleagues—Alcott and Dazindov. "We'll have to retreat—somehow."

The moment he had issued the command, Davidson reflected. In his mind, he rapidly sketched out a route that would take him only a few feet at a time, dashing from bush to tree to bush, and finally to safety. He sensed that Dazindov and Alcott were about to do the same. He started his first dash, then halted in his tracks and pulled back, all in the same instant.

The sound, loud and raucous, froze him. It filled the night air, followed by two bright spotlights, dancing over the green ground like grasshoppers. Both the noise and the light came from above. Davidson stared up into the sky. Alongside the half-moon, he could make out a helicopter, painted black, with no markings on its side.

"All right. This is MI5 and the local police. Come out of the house with your hands up!"

The country silence had been broken again, this time by a loudspeaker atop the hovering helicopter.

"We have the house surrounded," the voice on the helicopter blared. "We have another copter landing on your south lawn. Send out the hostages first, then everyone inside walk out onto the lawn—hands up. Any attempt to escape will be fatal."

As if to make the point, the helicopter's machine gun fired a volley over the roof of the mansion.

A bullhorn from the house echoed back. Davidson was curious. Was Makrov really inside? Could the suave Russian really be the mastermind of the X-30 gambit?

"This is sovereign Russian soil," the bullhorn voice responded. "You are violating our diplomatic immunity."

Yes, it was Makrov all right. No one else boasted that curious mixture of Cambridge and Moscow diction.

"President Malinovsky has personally authorized this attack to free the hostages! Now, comply!"

The diplomatic argument was over. The silence was unbroken for two minutes. Then a small procession of six Russians, headed by Makrov, still carrying arms, walked out the front door. In front of them were Mrs. Beame and her son.

"Drop your arms. Our sharpshooters have you in their sights."

First Makrov, then the others, discarded their guns. Mrs. Beame scooped up her son and ran to the waiting helicopter.

Davidson watched the scene in happy admiration. He motioned to Alcott and Dazindov, who followed him to the waiting copter. He stood in the wash, waiting to see who would emerge. The first man down the stairs was Sir Malcolm Asprey, moving toward Davidson with a broad smile and outstretched hand.

The Baptist swallowed hard, almost painfully. He should have known. He was suffering the pangs of personal chastisement for his false suspicions about Asprey. His paranoia, usually his best compass, had failed him.

"Wonderful job, Asprey," Davidson congratulated the MI5 chief. "Not even the U.S. Cavalry could have topped it. I never suspected Makrov. Did you have a clue?"

Malcolm smiled the Cheshire grin of a colleague, and friend, who had just pulled off a master stroke of one-upmanship.

"John, ever since you found that planted sting about me in Dazindov's computer, I suspected Makrov. But I didn't want to say anything until I knew more. So sorry!"

Davidson was tasting humble pie, and he sensed Asprey knew it.

"Don't worry, John. The best of us are carried away occasionally. And I'll put your professional nose up against anyone—including my own."

Davidson placed his hand against Asprey's shoulder. "I have something else to confess, Malcolm. Makrov almost had me convinced you were 'Mary.' "

"No such luck, Baptist. Makrov was running the *falshivi* in London, and in most of the West. But no, I'm not Mary, nor is he. We still have that to learn— as well as to retrieve the X-30."

Davidson brightened a touch. "Now that the hostages are free, I expect that President Briggs will be able to exert real pressure. I'll be speaking with him as soon as I get back to the scrambler at the embassy. And again, thanks."

AS THE TWO helicopters carrying Davidson, Asprey, Alcott, Dazindov, the hostages, and the *falshivi* prisoners lifted off the lawn of the Russian estate on their way back to London, a team of three MI5 men set up shop in the large study of the mansion—the start of a thorough search of the building.

Dawn had not yet invaded the Hastings countryside. With the floodlights having been extinguished during the sweep, darkness had once more overtaken the grounds.

At the rear of the building, one person, unaccounted for, used the cover of night effectively. As the agents settled into the house, the shadow moved out the back door and raced across the lawn toward the fence. A remote radio device was aimed at the gate of the cyclone fence. It opened, then automatically closed only seconds after the person had passed through.

Within a clump of trees less than one hundred feet past the fence, a red Jaguar stood waiting. The door was opened, and with the engine purring softly in first gear, the car creeped down the hardpan dirt road until, an eighth of a mile later, it reached an asphalt intersection.

The Jaguar peeked its bonnet onto the main road, then made a half right and raced toward London.

The operation had been crippled, "Mary" thought, but there were still alternatives to be called on. Several, in fact.

59

"I WARN YOU, Malinovsky," President Briggs barked into the red scrambler phone. "I've ordered a squadron of F-22 fighters and B-2 Stealth bombers to our bases in Turkey, within range of Dushanbe. If we don't have our X-30 back, in working order, within thirty-six hours, I'll order an attack on your former airfield. We have a second prototype coming off the line, so if necessary, I'll even destroy my X-30. By no means can we let the ship fall into Red Chinese hands. Do you understand?"

President Briggs's threat landed on responsive ears. Through the scrambler phone, Briggs could hear the Russian President answer through heavy breathing.

"President Briggs. Didn't we show our goodwill with the seizure of Makrov and the *falshivi* traitors at Hastings? They're being returned to Moscow and will be tried for treason. Meanwhile, I'm doing all I can to convince the Tajiks—and the Chinese—to return the plane. Be assured of that."

Briggs didn't answer. Instead, he placed the phone down on the desk and strode around the Oval Office, the jerky motion of his body evidence of his frustration. For a moment, he stopped over the federal eagle woven into the rug and stared down into the bird's sharp eyes, as if seeking counsel. Quickly, he returned to his desk and picked up the red phone.

"Are you still there, Malinovsky? Am I getting through to you? Whatever you're going to do, man, do it quick. Get back to me within a half hour. I don't want to have to go to war with a stinking little republic in Asia, or for that matter with the Chinese. But if you force my hand, you can kiss your grain credits good-bye. Do you understand?"

The breathing became heavier on the other end.

"I'll get back to you within the half hour," Malinovsky said. "I promise."

Briggs was about to issue an angry "You better," but he reconsidered. The poor Russian was obviously beside himself.

In Moscow, Malinovsky leaned back into the buttery white couch in his inner chamber, the same one used by Brezhnev, then Gorbachev, then Yeltsin. The room had seen tumultuous days of victory and defeat, and now there was a gnawing kind of unfeeling, or not knowing where Russia stood in the world—or how. His government had become a kind of ad hoc operation in which everything was both normal and politically psychotic at the same time.

The economy of the new Russia was supposed to be capitalist, especially in the new stock and commodity exchanges. In the massive speculation and wheeling and dealing, it was raw capitalism—at its best and worst. But in the state ownership of almost all large industries, there was a deadening hangover of Communism. Food was more available, but prices were astronomical. No one had any idea what was legal and what was not. Often, not even the government.

Now into this madhouse called Russia, Malinovsky mused, had come the problem of an international caper, with himself at the center. What in the hell could he do with a group of renegade Tajiks? Or for that matter, with the mad Dr. Li, whose vision of Red China in the twenty-first century was the superpower spot once held by the U.S.S.R.?

And if he, Malinovsky, didn't move into action, there was that threat from President Briggs. There'd be an American military attack on the Tajik airfield, and/or the end of American financial assistance. Why, he asked himself, had he ever yearned for the thankless job of President of the bankrupt Russian Republic?

He sat immobile, troubled for almost five minutes, staring through the Kremlin's tall French windows. Suddenly he leapt out of his chair, startled by the conclusion he had reached.

Malinovsky picked up the red phone. As commander in chief of the Russian armed forces, theoretically still the largest in the world, he barked an order:

"Get me Marshal Levtovich, right away."

He had found the deputy chief of staff a reliable can-do man who never created obstacles, no matter how challenging the project. But in this case, even the bold general might balk.

"Levtovich, come up to my office, right away."

"Yes, sir. Do you have a special assignment for me?" the marshal asked.

"Do I? Arkady, perhaps one even more difficult than you can handle."

There was a momentary pause, then an excited voice.

"Mr. President. That sounds like my glass of tea. I've been thirsty since the end of the Cold War. I can taste it already."

Malinovsky laughed and hung up. Yes, he could already appreciate the possibilities of what he had in mind.

DAVIDSON AND TONY Alcott walked along the bank of the Thames, the Baptist's favorite avenue of escape in London.

The air was misty, the slight chill invigorating to the Virginian, whose racial unconscious was stirred by the sights and sounds of England. The Potomac could be romantic, especially near the Washington plantation at Mount Vernon, but the Thames, with its city tumult and its contrasting upstream country ambience, never failed to move him.

"Tony, I asked you to come along so you could help me sort out what's been going on. I fear we've gotten in over our heads, without fully understanding it. Plus the complications of who is—and who is not—on our side. I was wrong on Makrov and Sir Malcolm, and I can't afford another mistake."

Alcott hurried his pace to keep up with Davidson,

whose walk was a quick military stride. "And what about Alison's murder? Who do you think did it?"

"She was a victim of either the *falshivi*, or the true double in MI5. I have my suspicions, and this time I think I'm right. I passed my thoughts on to Asprey, and I'm afraid I shocked him."

"Who do you think it is?"

"Guy Lauder."

Alcott stopped and stared at Davidson's back. "Lauder, the theater director?"

"Yes, Lauder. The proprietor of Lum's couldn't identify the killer because his face was covered and then he raced out. But from his description of his build and hair color, it sounds like Lauder."

"Is that all you have on him?"

Davidson laughed. "No. Hardly. I've had his house phone tapped—with Malcolm's reluctant cooperation—and . . ."

"And what?" Alcott's curiosity was peaking.

"For some time, he said nothing that would implicate him. But then he slipped. He was having a long conversation with someone, supposedly his stockbroker. But he was on long enough for us to trace the call."

"Where did it come from?"

"Portland Place, the Chinese Embassy."

"The Red Chinese?"

"Exactly."

Davidson and Alcott continued their walk along the Strand.

"So what happens now? Have they brought Lauder in for questioning?"

The Baptist shook his head.

"No, now that Asprey has the wiretap, he's decided to give Lauder all the rope he wants, then see where it leads. Who knows, it might take us to the killer, or even to Mary."

"You're pretty sure of the hit man?" Alcott asked.

"Yes, I'm almost positive it's Cavendish, the horti-culturist who tried to kill me at the garden show and almost ran you down outside Cambridge. If we're real lucky, he and Lauder will connect, and then lead us to Mary. Or that might be too much to ask. Lauder is under surveillance, but we haven't been able to spot Cavendish."

They continued their walk, then turned and retraced their steps, which led to the Savoy Hotel, where they sat for tea at 3:30 P.M.

At a table filled with finger sandwiches and Earl Gray, Alcott brought up the subject that worried Davidson the most: the status of the X-30.

"What do you think, John? Are we going to get the ship back?"

Davidson was silent for a moment. "Right now, the X-30 is in the middle of a geopolitical tug-of-war in Tajikistan, which is ostensibly an independent nation. The Moscow government has some pull, but the Russian hard-liners and the Chinese have even more. The Iranians are trying to move in, and the Chinese—who are right on their border—are providing technical help and money. It's a whole new world in Central Asia, and the Tajik president, Sajoban, is playing all sides against the middle."

"Will he buck the U.S. and actually turn the plane over to the Chinese?"

The Baptist sipped at his tea.

"Yes, Tony, if the U.S. or Russia doesn't intervene, I think he will. My guess is that there are hundreds of millions of dollars involved."

"Will we intervene?" Alcott asked, obviously excited at being so close to the storm of world affairs.

"I've recommended to President Briggs that we do it if the Russians won't. In any case, it'll be played out soon."

PRESIDENT MALINOVSKY STOOD in front of the tall
French window, stared out at the Church of the Twelve
Apostles in the rear of the Kremlin, and thought of
the improbable weakness of his country. No longer a
political superpower, it still had large, even massive,
armed forces, with little to do, and no hope of world
conquest—the drive that had dominated the U.S.S.R. for
seventy-plus years.

Now he was being asked—really ordered—by an
American president to use that force to invade a
neighboring republic, one which had been part of the
Russian empire for over a hundred years. The neighbor
was Tajikistan, which made up the southeastern corner
of the former Soviet land mass.

He walked across the large birch-paneled room to
a bare wall. At the press of a button, a large map
dropped from the ceiling, displaying every military air
and land base in the once-potent U.S.S.R. With a pointer
in hand, he followed the length of the map. In southern
Siberia was a combined Russian air and paratroop base.
With IL-76s loaded with troops—some one hundred to a
plane—he could easily send a thousand soldiers into the
Tajik airfield where the X-30 was being held by former
KGB troops under Central Asian command.

Could he? Should he dispatch his men, either to land
at the field without invitation, or by parachute, and
seize the X-30 as President Briggs wanted? Or should

he leave it to the brazen Americans, to do their own dirty work?

The answer was obvious. It was bad enough to have lost control of Russia's "little brother" allies. But to allow Americans, some eight thousand miles away, to challenge the newly granted sovereignty of a former U.S.S.R. republic would bring dishonor. Not even he— a dedicated anti-Communist—could permit that. In truth, he might be swept out of office because of it. No, he had no choice.

President Sajoban of Tajikistan had already failed to return three of his phone calls. The Tajik leader probably felt safe, protected by international law—and by the Chinese. But by permitting the Chinese and the KGB *falshivi* to hold the X-30, the Tajik president was breaking international law.

Malinovsky walked slowly back to his desk.

"Vladimir, has Marshal Levtovich arrived yet?"

"Yes, sir, he's waiting outside. Shall I show him in?"

Moments later, the tall gray-haired soldier, a decorated veteran of World War II, and still ramrod straight at the age of seventy two, came into the room. He saluted smartly in front of Malinovsky's desk.

"Arkady Sergeyevich, I have a good job for you. One I think you'll like."

The old marshal, some six-foot-four, with the lines of experience etched on his face, brightened.

"Yes, sir, what is it?"

"I want you to attack and seize our former air base in Tajikistan, near the Chinese border. How? No, not overland from Siberia. That would tip our hand. Do it before dawn, as soon as you are ready, by paratroop assault. Seize the X-30 and kill anyone who tries to stop you—including our own disloyal KGB troops and any of the Tajiks. The Americans *must* get the plane back. Do you understand?"

"*Da, da!*" was all Levtovich said, then he saluted again and marched out.

Malinovsky could see that the old soldier was pleased. After withdrawing from Afghanistan (the conflict that had created Gorbachev, he was sure), then from Eastern Europe, the Baltics, and the other republics, the Red Army could return to action. No matter that it was minor, it was still a chance to regain honor. The Americans had done wonders to lift their patriotic morale with equally minor incursions in Libya and Grenada after their Vietnam debacle.

To be sure, it was somewhat risky. The Tajik troops might resist, but he had faith in Levtovich, no matter how rusty his troops might be.

And his ally, President Briggs, would be jubilant. Now he looked forward to that call to Washington.

"JOHN, THIS IS Tony. I'm following Lauder as you asked, and he's been in a town house in Belgravia for the last thirty minutes. After he went upstairs, I checked the mailboxes. Guess who lives there?"

Alcott was calling the embassy from his car phone. His voice was filled with excitement.

"Don't play games with an old man, Tony. Who in the hell is it?"

"He's gone to visit no one less than Antony Riddle, our MP illegal. What do you make of that?"

Davidson pondered. "God knows. Maybe he suspects

we suspect him, and he's going to Riddle for help. Li probably told Lauder who the MP really was. Maybe Guy figures he can do business with Riddle—even get help from him to leave the country before we close in. Or go underground. In any case, stay where you are. I'm on my way over."

Within fifteen minutes, Davidson arrived by cab. Almost instantly, they headed for the Eaton Place house, but were quickly stopped by the bobbie on duty—assigned to protect the prestigious block, which housed several members of Parliament and the aristocracy.

"Can I help you gentlemen?" the policeman asked, a polite way—Davidson surmised—of asking what the hell they were doing there.

"We're staffers at the American Embassy," Davidson said, flashing his diplomatic credentials. "Antony Riddle, a member of Parliament, lives here, and he's asked us to drop over."

The constable studied Davidson's passport, then saluted informally.

"All right, sir. If you have any problem, just call me."

The cramped elevator, fitted into the Victorian town house, took them to the fourth floor, where Riddle's duplex was directly to the left off the landing.

"Look here, Tony," Davidson counseled in a soft voice. There was another flat on the floor, and he felt no need to disturb or alert them. "Check that doorjamb. It's been jimmied. There are the crowbar marks. Let's see if it gives."

Alcott pushed against the door, but it failed to yield. Several presses on the buzzer roused no one.

"Lets go find the bobbie. Maybe he can get us in. It looks like trouble."

Back on the street, they waved to the policeman, who had advanced halfway down the block. When he arrived, Davidson explained the suspicious marks on the door.

Stretching the truth, he said that Riddle had been expecting them. Why then wouldn't he answer the door?

The constable was skeptical until Davidson flatly said, "I'm working with Sir Malcolm Asprey on a project. You may know him—MI5?"

The policeman's eyebrows arched. "Asprey, is it? All right, come with me."

At the fourth-floor landing, he examined the jimmied door. "No doubt about it, sir. Something's not proper."

"This is the police. Open up!" the constable yelled several times. When there was no response, he stepped back and kicked hard at the door. Reluctantly, it gave way. As the trio entered Riddle's spacious apartment, Davidson felt for the Beretta in his jacket pocket. They moved from the black-and-white marble foyer into the drawing room, but the flat seemed silent and empty. They split at the hallway, each man taking a different bedroom off the corridor.

"Mr. Davidson!" shouted the constable. "Come here, quick!"

With Alcott on his heels, Davidson chased down the corridor and into what looked like the master bedroom.

In the center of the room, two men were seated on facing chairs. Their mouths were bound and their bodies tied to the chairs. Davidson stared, incredulous. Their faces were covered with a mass of blood and brain. He circled the chairs and bent low to examine the gunshot wounds. The bullets had entered at the temple, creating havoc with their exit.

"Do you recognize them?" the constable asked. His calm British exterior had eroded.

"Yes. One of them is Antony Riddle, a Tory member of Parliament."

"And the other?" the policeman asked.

"It's not easy to make the ID, but yes, I'm sure it's Guy Lauder, a theater director on the Strand, and a friend of Sir Malcolm's."

The policeman nodded and circled first the victims, then the rest of the room.

"Look here, Mr. Davidson. There's a note on the bed."

"What does it say?" Davidson asked, almost shouting.

"Simple little thing. Just says 'Love, Mary.' "

Davidson grabbed the note out of the policeman's hand and read it over and over. "Find anything else, Constable?" he called.

"Nothing much. Just a little sprig of flowers. Nice little white ones. Somebody's quite sentimental in the midst of all this mayhem. Don't you think, sir?"

Davidson stared again at the gory sight of the two men, once at their prime and now quite dead at the hands of the elusive hit man.

"You might say that, Constable. You might just say that."

"PRESIDENT MALINOVSKY," MARSHAL Levtovich said to open his scrambled phone conversation with the Kremlin, "our troops are in the air—twelve planes fully loaded with paratroopers. Within minutes, they will be dropping on the perimeter of the Tajik airfield. They have orders to secure the X-30 as the first order of business."

"Do you expect any armed opposition?"

The old soldier mused. "Yes, but nothing we can't deal with."

"Good luck on Russia's first military venture since Afghanistan," the Russian president answered. "I hope we do better this time." He laughed self-consciously and hung up.

At his command headquarters in southern Siberia, Levtovich waited anxiously for word from his commander, Brigadier Karkov, in the lead IL-76. Radio silence was being enforced for security, but the general would call in, via satellite, the moment the airfield was attacked.

It was 4:57 A.M., just moments before the ETA, when the marshal padded anxiously across the command headquarters that had prepared for war for seventy years, but was finally seeing its first moments of battle. In fact, this was the new Russia's first military move, and he confessed that he welcomed—no, loved—it.

Levtovich had done everything possible to prepare. The base had been built by the U.S.S.R. Air Force, and plans of the field had been converted into a three-dimensional model. Calling on some methods from the Israeli attack on Entebbe in the 1970s, the battle strategy was developed in exquisite detail. The move against the X-30 site would be three-pronged and had to be completed before the Tajik KGB or the Chinese (he had heard they had fifty armed men on the field) could destroy the superplane. Now all he could do, like any commander, was wait.

At 5:13 A.M., at the first hint of dawn, the word came.

"Marshal Levtovich," the brigadier reported eagerly, "all is secure. They defended the field for less than ten minutes, but our mortar attack destroyed their will. They took some eighty casualties, and we lost only one man, with two wounded. We killed six of the Chinese defenders, but I don't think the Kremlin will get a complaint from Beijing. They weren't supposed to be there, you know."

"Brigadier, what about the X-30?" Levtovich shouted.

"Oh, sorry, sir. A group of KGB *falshivi* sappers were ready to blow it up, but one of my best men, Major Rekchev, took all eight of them out seconds after he landed at the perimeter. He deserves an award." He paused. "Do we still have military medals in the new Russia? In any case, the plane is secure and safe, as is Wing Commander Beame. He's preparing to fly it back to Northolt in England."

The marshal was quiet for a moment, savoring the victory. It was no great military expedition, but it had come off like silk. Not only a feather in his cap, but a small indication that giant Russia need no longer shrink from its responsibility as a great power. The suffering, humiliated nation would be pleased.

A sudden thought struck the marshal. "What about the American pilot, Colonel Dressler?" he asked. "Is he OK?"

The short silence was punishing. "No, sir. He's been murdered. The Tajiks have his body—his throat was cut by the British traitor, the man who posed as Squadron Leader Haversham."

"What about Haversham? Do you have him in custody?"

Again a sharp silence. "No, sir," the brigadier answered, now more sheepishly. "He seems to have escaped. The Chinese leader says all he knows is that Haversham left in a plane just minutes before we hit the field. No one has any idea where he went."

Levtovich pondered that last incomplete touch, then brushed it away. That was a problem for the Americans and British. He had done his job by rescuing the X-30. He smiled inwardly.

"Brigadier, great work. I will praise you to the American president."

64

"WING COMMANDER BEAME, please look at the photo and concentrate. Can you identify this man as the Squadron Leader Haversham, who killed Colonel Dressler and stole the X-30?"

In Davidson's cubbyhole at the embassy, Beame, who had just returned from his Tajikistan odyssey, and had been reunited with his family, picked up the eight-by-ten photo of Michael Cavendish—the Gardener, as Davidson called him—and squinted, hard.

"It looks somewhat like him, but I really couldn't swear to it. That fake squadron leader had a prominent hook in his nose that this man doesn't have. And Haversham had a mustache, and his cheeks were a lot fuller. No, I can't make a positive ID—at least not one that would hold up in court."

"Alcott, it's obvious that the wing commander is not convinced. We're on our own." Davidson turned to the X-30 copilot. "Glad you're reunited with your family, Terrence. Hope we've been of some help. And don't worry. Now that the X-30's back, I think you're quite safe."

Beame extended his hand. "Thanks again, and if you need me, call."

Minutes later, Davidson and Alcott went for a walk through Grosvenor Square, one of the few settings for a secure dialogue in bug-ridden London.

"Tony, we're going to have to get more ID on Haversham for the wing commander to study."

"More? What could be better than his photo?"

"His voice. While the Tajikistan fiasco was going on, I checked Cavendish's shop and neighbors. They said he was away touring the West Country. Of course, that's nonsense. My guess is that the Chinese flew him out of Tajikistan, to Beijing, then to London on a diplomatic plane, just before the Russian troops arrived. Now he's happily back in Cambridge country—where we have to unmask him."

Alcott stared. "How?"

"I'm not sure, Tony, but I have an idea."

Tony drove by the Victorian cottage that served as home and shop to "Michael Cavendish, Horticulturist." My God, he thought, how unlikely a setting for a hired killer, one whose current toll was up to seven. Surely, any feelings the man had were reserved for plants, especially silver bells, his trademark.

Alcott parked a quarter of a mile from the cottage, half-hiding the Rover behind a stout oak. In the car, he stripped off his suit. Beneath it was a green coverall, the uniform of the East Anglian Electricity Board. From the backseat, he took out a large case, a duplicate of those carried by lighting repair men. Tony left the car and, swinging the case with aplomb, strode up the narrow lane toward the Cavendish establishment.

He came within one hundred feet of the house. Swiftly, he climbed the thin metal steps attached to the combination lighting-phone pole. Rung over rung, he climbed to the top, then removed a secure belt from the case. He clasped it first to his waist, then to a clip on the pole. Now he could work with two hands on the task at hand: placing a wiretap on the Gardener's phone.

From the same case, Tony removed a wiring diagram, graciously provided to Sir Malcolm by British Telecom. The wiring for the Cavendish place was marked out in red ink. All he had to do—based on in-house instruction by Telecom—was to place his tap onto the right wire. From then on, a miniature recorder with a small wireless modem would pump the conversation from the pole to a recorder he'd soon be planting in the woods directly across the way. A courier from the embassy would pick up the tapes at regular intervals and bring them back to Davidson.

Within twenty minutes, as Alcott listened through earphones, the system proved out, when Cavendish came on the phone. The conversation was trivial—an order for climbing wisteria—but he had what he had come for: a sample of the Gardener's voice.

"Wing Commander Beame, please listen to this tape recording. Does it sound familiar in any way?"

Davidson had journeyed to the cottage of the Beames, not far from the Northolt air base, which had become world famous for the X-30 escapade. The space plane had since been returned to Edwards AFB in the Mohave Desert, but Northolt had been the scene of its loss and return.

Beame listened to the tape of Cavendish enthusiastically describing the wonders of wisteria. The wing commander slammed his fist down on the table.

"That's him—the fake Squadron Leader Haversham, the son of a bitch who kidnapped my family, murdered Dressler, and forced me to fly him to Tajikistan. Who is he, Mr. Davidson? Tell me, and I swear I'll kill him."

"That's what I'm afraid of. His ID will have to remain secret until we apprehend him. But tell me—what convinced you it was Haversham?"

Beame thought a moment. "First, he has an obvious upper-class accent. Cambridge, I'd guess. I've heard enough of them in the RAF. And most important, even though Haversham tried to keep his voice a pitch higher, sometimes he'd drop it without thinking. That sounded just like this recording. He also makes a funny kind of soft whistle in his speech whenever he says an *S*. You can't miss it."

Beame paused. "I hope I've been of some help, Mr. Davidson. I'd sure love to get my hands on that bastard."

65

"TRY THE LEMONADE," Lady Victoria Asprey said to the three men. "It was freshly squeezed this morning."

Davidson, Sir Malcolm, and Tony Alcott, the trio of survivors in the deadly tale, were gathered in the sun room of Hollow Oaks, trying to complete the puzzle of the X-30. Lady Asprey served her guests, then softly exited. Davidson's admiring eyes followed her every move.

"It's obvious from the murder toll that no one's really safe until we get the hit man, and especially Mary, who's put the whole thing together," Davidson said to open the conversation. "So far, they've killed four of our scientists, plus Steiner, Mason, Lauder, Riddle, a MI5 operative, Dr. Li's assistant, Colonel Dressler, and several Russians on both sides."

"That's a good summation," Sir Malcolm offered, "but how does it help us find out who Mary is? So far, he's been a master at elusive behavior."

"That's what I was coming to. I've seen Makrov at New Scotland Yard, but he refuses to talk—says he has no idea who Mary is. His contact was always through the hit man, and he will not confirm that it's Cavendish, though he seemed to go out of his way not to deny it. The Crown has offered him a deal, but so far he hasn't budged. Still dreams of another coup in Russia, a new Cold War, and his eventual release by making a deal with the Allies."

"John, one thing has puzzled me," Tony interrupted. "Someone tried to run Makrov down at Hyde Park Corner—which only made us trust him more. What was that all about?"

"Dazindov's filled me in. Seems one of his trusted men decided that Makrov was the villain—before they had conclusive evidence. On his own he tried to have him killed."

"And what about Makrov turning in one of his own spies? Who was it, that fellow Kendrick out in Silicon Valley?" This time Sir Malcolm had spoken up.

"I checked that with the FBI," Davidson responded. "It seems that Makrov had the same information on the X-30 from another source, and decided to make Kendrick a sacrificial lamb to strengthen his own bona fides with us and appease President Malinovsky at the same time. It was a clever ploy—as were most of Makrov's. His mistake was kidnapping Mrs. Beame and her child. But I suppose he needed them to intimidate the wing commander.

"And Lauder and Riddle were part of the same picture," Davidson continued. "When Guy went to see Riddle, Mary obviously thought it best to get rid of both of them at the same time."

Asprey rose from the large white wicker chair and paced the bright rug. "So where does that leave us, John? How do we track down Mary?"

Davidson stretched for an instant before resuming his comfortable seat. Increasingly, he was finding the security of a chair under him comforting.

"It leaves us with Cavendish. We have enough evidence to pick him up for questioning, but I don't think

New Scotland Yard should move against him just yet. Now that Lauder is dead, Cavendish is our only remaining route to Mary. We have to use him to smoke out the leader."

At this second mention of Guy Lauder, Davidson could see Asprey wince. The two had been inseparable in MI5. The revelation that Lauder had been a double all those years, and had murdered Alison Mason to keep her from learning the identity of Mary, had wounded the aristocrat.

"But how do we use Cavendish?" Tony asked.

"Simple. We have to set up a situation in which Mary wants to silence the hit man because he's become too dangerous to the cause. We need to get gossip going—in the press, the intelligence community, and through the foreign embassies—that the Crown has new evidence. Supposedly we know the identity of the X-30 killer and kidnapper, and he'll soon be taken in. We might even hint that the suspect lives in the Cambridge area and that the arrest will take place within a fortnight. That should scare the bejesus out of Mary. If I were him, I'd find a way to eliminate Cavendish before he was brought into custody and spilled his guts in exchange for a deal."

Sir Malcolm halted his pacing. "John, I think you're right. That's our last lead, and we have to use it. If I were Mary, I'd make damn sure Cavendish didn't live another fortnight."

66

THE RAIN HAD been continuous for four days, and Tony
Alcott was beginning to feel the humid British blues. Even
when the downpour stopped for an hour at a time, the air
felt wet. His young bones—once seemingly immune to
arthritis—ached. He was sure that pneumonia, not the
identity of Mary, would be his reward.

Tony's subterfuge changed from day to day. A small
van with a "Warren Plumbing Contractor" sign and a bed
in the back had worked for a while. He then switched to
a silver tourist van. Today, he was installed in a small
horse trailer and parked almost a hundred yards from the
house. He was close enough to see with high-powered
binoculars but far enough to escape detection. At least
he hoped so.

The trailer was also home to an elaborate parabolic
listening system, a backup to the telephone tap. It was
aimed at Cavendish's office window with the help of an
antenna inside the trailer. The system worked much like
the receiver of a telephone. The vibrations of speech set
up a special frequency as they hit the window, where
they were picked up by the parabola and converted back
into speech. The tone was not always perfect, but when
there was no interference, the words were clear.

So far, Alcott had been on the scene for eight days.
Today, he had been up since 6 A.M., and it was now
5 P.M. The overcast sky made the horizon seem not
only bleak, but near-black. As he sat, he thought of

the vagaries of history. Like Davidson, his people had come from this area in England. Not in the 1600s, as Davidson sometimes boasted, but just before the Civil War, lured by free land in the New World. Now he was back, but instead of elated, he was bored, studying only the rain, doing endless crossword puzzles, inventing new palindromes, and waiting for something to happen. If it ever would. What kept him from madness was faith in Davidson's intellect—that his plan *had* to work.

Suddenly, he heard a knock on the trailer door, and jumped.

"Who is it?" By instinct, he drew out his 9-mm Beretta.

"Easy, Tony. It's only me, Davidson."

Tony felt relieved. Davidson would be company in his battle against ennui. Now he realized how much the mind controlled the energy level in humans. As Davidson came through the door, the sight itself revived him.

"Good to see you, John. I was on the verge of going bananas."

"Anything significant happen over at Cavendish's place?"

"Not really. I'm monitoring him both with the phone tap I put in last week, and with the parabolic listening device. So far, he's been ultra careful. It's all talk about plants and flowers, and not even a mention of silver bells. I hope this is not a wild-goose chase."

Davidson touched Alcott's forearm, a sign that he understood the young agent's wear and tear.

"The only thing I've learned in my years, Tony, is patience. All things come to him who waits—and of course, also plans and schemes and connives at the same time. We're doing it all."

Alcott laughed. "So what now?"

Davidson suddenly whirled about at the sound of a car sloshing through the water-laden road.

"Down!" the Baptist shouted.

Tony crouched, but peeked out at the passing vehicle. It looked like a forest-green 1950s Triumph, a collector's jewel. It was impossible to see the driver's face. All he could tell was that the figure was wearing a tweed cap and jacket.

"Look, John. The Triumph is going into Cavendish's driveway. Unless he coded it on the phone, I don't think he was expecting anyone. What should we do?"

"Wait till the driver gets out. Then we'll make a dash for the wooded plot opposite Cavendish's place. From there, we can see better what's going on. Do you have the key for his front door—the one Malcolm made while Cavendish was away?"

Tony nodded, then tapped his jacket pocket. "And I have my Beretta as well. You too?"

"Yes. Now, let's make a dash. Try to avoid the raindrops."

The two men chased across the road, resting for a moment under a spreading branch. Once the driver had entered the front door, they raced to the covered entrance of Cavendish's cottage. Davidson drew his gun.

"Wait one minute, then open the door. Do you remember the layout of the house?"

"As clearly as my room as a kid. The stairway branches off to the left. Just ten feet down the hall is Cavendish's office. The last phone call I heard placed him there only fifteen minutes ago."

Virtually on tiptoe, they opened the door and advanced to the stairs, then dropped to their knees and moved upward in a child's crawl to minimize the pressure. All they needed was a stair squeak to advertise their presence. Back on their feet, they walked slowly to the office door, which was shut. From inside, they could hear the voices. Both were tinged with anger. The heavy door muffled the voices and made any ID impossible, but the words were relatively clear.

"I haven't been paid in full yet," they could make out Cavendish saying. "You're 200,000 pounds in arrears, Mary, and I'm not happy. Not happy at all."

"There's no need to worry. You'll get your money. It's coming from numbered accounts in Berne, Switzerland, and it takes a little doing. The British and Swiss governments have new currency regulations that are slowing it up. But I assure you it'll be here in a week or so."

"That's not fast enough," Cavendish answered. "And tell me, Mary, whose money is it? Beijing's or Moscow's, or both?"

"That's none of your business. Since when have you gotten curious about politics? Is this a sign that you're becoming involved—maybe even talkative?"

Cavendish seemed cowed by the comment. "No, not at all. What you do is your business."

The wary comment was followed by a silence. It lasted no longer than twenty seconds, but Alcott could see Davidson's eyes focus expectantly. His Beretta moved to the ready.

The silence was suddenly shattered by a gunshot.

"Now!" Davidson shouted, turning the knob and pressing against the door. As it opened, his pulse seemed to stop.

Standing inside, dressed in a man's tweed suit and cap, was a woman. Davidson stared, incredulous, his eyes widening in horror.

On the floor was Cavendish, a hole piercing his shirt at the heart level. His eyes were glazed in death. Standing over him was the killer. Davidson aimed his gun and spoke in a whisper, the sight tightening his larynx.

"Victoria! God, it's you!" He paused, hoping the palpitations would slow. "Now, slowly lower your gun. It's all over, and you'd might as well make your peace."

She stood there, no less beautiful than ever, Davidson thought. Such a contradiction. The master planner of murder and international mayhem, and the soft soul of loveliness.

"John, my love, I'd like to. But I'm sure you realize it's impossible."

"But why, Victoria? Why did you do it? You had everything a woman could want in a free country. Why betray it?"

"No, John, I had nothing except a dream. It began in the 1960s. I watched others forgetting their vision. But not me. I was in a position—close to Malcolm—to bring order to the chaos of revolution. If only things had gone differently, I could have . . ."

As the sentence was almost finished, Davidson could see Victoria's trigger finger start its pressure. He reacted quickly, but before his bullet could be fired, his finger froze. His will to kill had vanished. His mind was dizzied by remorse, even anger that love had conspired against him.

The gunshot seemed louder than it should have. Davidson stared at Victoria. Nothing seemed to have changed. Then his eye caught a red spot on her vest starting to enlarge, forming an opening out of which poured more blood. Slowly, she sank to the floor, her legs just clearing the fallen Cavendish.

"What happened, Tony? I tried, but I couldn't fire."

"I guessed that, John. It was either you or her, so my hand made the choice. I did right, didn't I?"

Davidson knew he'd never be able to answer that question.

67

THE FUNERAL SERVICE was solemn and attended by only a handful of people. Accumulating friends had not been one of Victoria's hobbies.

"She was an extraordinary woman, Malcolm," Davidson said in consolation as they prepared to leave the cemetery. "And I think it was wise to leave the truth buried forever. She died, as I said in my deposition, from a gunshot wound delivered by Cavendish—who she had uncovered as the notorious 'Mary.'"

Asprey's eyes, red from tears, were now clouded.

"John, thanks for that. I loved her so, and the whole thing is still incomprehensible to me. Sure, Victoria was a flower child of the 1960s, and into every radical movement, even the Maoists. For a while she walked around clutching his little red book. But as the years went on, she said she hated politics. I just assumed she had become a country Tory, as I had. She'd have nothing to do with my business either. Said it was ugly. And now she ends up . . . God, nothing is predictable. But who can expect an intelligence man to know anything about intrigue in his own family?"

As they got into Asprey's car, shielded from the chauffeur by a soundproof glass plate, Sir Malcolm turned to Davidson.

"John, I could see that Victoria was mad about you. Tell me, what did she say to explain her behavior—you know, in matters of sex?"

Davidson wished he could sink into the car's plush velour.

"She said that you were hopelessly promiscuous outside of marriage, and that she was forced to go her own way. Any truth to it?"

Asprey quieted, seeming to form his answer carefully.

"No, John, not a word. I was totally faithful throughout. But I knew I couldn't expect that from her. She was highly individualistic, and eccentric, I suppose you could say. She had her own ideas about everything, and sex was one of them. The story about me was just an invention so she could do what she wanted. I knew about many of her affairs, but I had no choice except to forgive her. I couldn't imagine life without Victoria. And I still can't."

Davidson said nothing, just muttered under his breath. "A most extraordinary woman."

THE WHITE HOUSE, and especially the Oval Office, still seemed magical in Davidson's imagination.

No matter how often he met with presidents—and eight had received him since Eisenhower—he was awed by the place and the power it represented.

He held President Briggs in the same awe even though he had known the man for over twenty years. Davidson had completed many missions for him, the latest being the X-30 escapade. He was particularly thankful that he had come here this morning in honor and not failure. Over the years, he had learned that little was excused in his profession. A failed intelligence man was not easily welcomed back into the corridors of power.

"John." The President greeted him heartily at the door to the Oval Office. "You see, I scheduled you before 7 A.M. because you're the only one I know—besides myself—who thinks eleven in the morning is the middle of the day. So take a seat by the fire and tell me how you think the project went."

Davidson settled in, then set his mind on the events of the last month. Slowly, he related the story of what had happened, concluding with the unmasking of "Mary."

"What a tragic ending for such an exceptional person," the President said after the Baptist finished. "And what a tragedy that in Red China she saw a future that would benefit the world. Nothing could be further from the truth."

Davidson nodded agreement. "The X-30 is safe, but I also think we learned something about our new foe, a wilier Communist nation than the former U.S.S.R.," he told Briggs. "The Red Chinese bear close watching and manipulation, Mr. President. If we're not shrewd, in ten years we'll be faced with a Communist China more affluent, more sophisticated, and as well armed as the U.S.S.R. was under Brezhnev. That's something for all of us to think about."

The President rose and started to pace, halting, as was his habit, directly over the federal eagle in the rug.

"John, nothing preoccupies and disturbs me more than our relations with Red China. North Korea is a thorn, but China has 20 percent of all the people on this planet, and they're clever and adaptable. My problem is fear of isolating them and stimulating their xenophobia—which is age-old. So far, we've chosen not only to do business with them, but to tolerate their repressions. God knows if it's the best course."

He turned to his intelligence seer of many years' acquaintance. "So what do you think I should do, John?"

Davidson knew that with the attempt on the X-30, this was the best time to press home the danger presented by Red China. He was in a unique position, and he didn't want to waste a second of it.

"Mr. President, it's really an intellectual problem—how not to isolate them, yet keep them from growing too fast and too skillfully at our expense. And simultaneously to try to get them on the path to democracy. Solomon wouldn't have the right answer, but I'll give it a shot."

"Please, John, I need help on this. I may be smart, but I'm no Mandarin."

Davidson tried not to comment on that, but he knew that was America's vulnerability—the absence of trained, patriotic minds with enough intellect to play the game of GO against a newly sophisticated Red China.

"The first step is to recognize the reality," the Baptist began. "The Chinese have no intention of building a democracy or a free-market economy. They're just toying with us on that for their advantage. Knowing this, we have to trump each of their moves with our own, never for a moment forgetting that this is a Communist superpower in the making. In ten years, we could be back with another Cold War, perhaps more frightening than the last one."

"Do you think we should stop doing business with them at all?" the President asked.

"No, we can't force their hand totally. But having said that, the business we do with China has to be more on our terms. First, they have too high a trade balance with us. We have to import less from them, or force them to take more of our exports. If not, we'll soon be facing another Japan-like dilemma. Nippon outfoxed us. We can't let China—a Communist power—get away with the same."

"And secondly?" asked Briggs, obviously tied to Davidson's every word.

"Secondly, we should restrict our high tech and student exchanges with them. They gain and we mostly lose. But the most important point is the last."

The President leaned forward, expectantly. "And what's that, John?"

"Simply that we bargain for democracy."

"In what way?"

"Tell them they can't have anything unless they make a crack in their totalitarian system—even if it's just verbal dissent. That has a way of growing when it's given the slightest leeway. In the U.S.S.R. Solzhenitsyn led to Sakharov, who led to Gorbachev—who led to Yeltsin. We've got to start that chain going in Red China. We need more "Voice of America," more propaganda, more intelligence, and yes, more spying. We have to cultivate and support dissidents who are now in China, and even sneak some in. We have to penetrate their inner circle and find a potential Gorbachev. This is the beginning of the new Cold War, and if we don't start to fight it, we'll lose it. And remember, the Chinese are a lot smarter than the Russians ever were."

"And what's our leverage in this intellectual battle? How do we get them to open the door even a little?"

"Simple, Mr. President. Money. If they want to keep up their brisk trade with the United States, they'll have to pay by permitting some dissent. If not, we have to cut back a little at a time, until we close them out entirely. If they want our money, they'll have to buy some of our democracy. Meanwhile, we have to increase our intelligence and propaganda tools, as I said. If not, we'll be sorry."

Briggs took up his pacing again. "John, dammit, I think you've hit it right on the head. I've got to get up the courage and face them down. Otherwise, as you say, someone else who takes over this office—maybe after the turn of the century—will have a bigger headache than we can handle. Thanks for the advice."

"By the way, Mr. President, have you heard from President Malinovsky? Anything significant happening in the Kremlin?"

"Oh, yes, John, I forgot. He's put in new heads of the KGB and the MVD with the assignment of purging the *falshivi* from every aspect of the Russian government. Not only will that please us, but it might help head off another coup in Russia. You know, he's living on the edge all the time. And yes, I have a question for you. What happened to your new sidekick—what's his name—Tony Alcott?"

"He's back in the physics business, but I'm afraid I corrupted him with a taste of adventure. Don't be surprised if someday I ask you to assign him to my makeshift operation."

Briggs rose, indicating the meeting was over. He grasped Davidson by the forearm and walked him to the door.

"It may be makeshift, John, but it'll do until someone finds out how to clone your ingenuity."

"Thank you, Mr. President, but I am getting older—as you are."

Briggs laughed. "Now, John, that's disrespectful of the office of the President. I thought we were immortal—at least until the next election.

"John," the President added in parting, "should I listen to all that talk about the New World Order? If it's real, I won't have to call on you again, will I? How does that strike you?"

Davidson could see Briggs's eyes gleam.

"I'd like nothing better, Mr. President, but for the foreseeable future I'm afraid you're stuck with a world in conflict. And like a bad penny, I turn up every time."

The two men laughed again and shook hands, two veteran warriors annealed in the cold and hot battles of modern man.

Tom Clancy's
#1 <u>New York Times</u> Bestsellers

__THE SUM OF ALL FEARS 0-425-13354-0/$6.99
  "Vivid...engrossing...a whiz-bang page-turner!"
                                –*The New York Times Book Review*
__CLEAR AND PRESENT DANGER 0-425-12212-3/$6.99
  "Clancy's best work since *The Hunt For Red October*."
                                      –*Publishers Weekly*
__THE CARDINAL OF THE KREMLIN 0-425-11684-0/$6.99
  "The best of the Jack Ryan series!"–*The New York Times*
__PATRIOT GAMES 0-425-13435-0/$5.99
  "Marvelously tense . . . He is a master of the genre he seems
  to have created."–*Publishers Weekly*
__RED STORM RISING 0-425-10107-X/$6.99
  "Brilliant . . . Staccato suspense."–*Newsweek*
__THE HUNT FOR RED OCTOBER 0-425-13351-6/$6.99
  "Flawless authenticity, frighteningly genuine."
                                    –*The Wall Street Journal*